Rachel st[...] to her thighs. Lake M[...] a dark void. Forty-eig[...] mounting desire were about to culminate, and she was as wet as the body of water before her.

"Do you want me?" she whispered.

She slowly sank to her knees. For two days she'd been twitching like a downed power line, every nerve ending on overload. Now, as her knees settled into the soft mud, something small scurried out of her way, but it didn't bother her. Nothing in the lake would harm her, and everything was secondary to the water surging over her thighs. She slid her knees apart to let it reach her intimately. It lapped at her and she sighed, imagining the waves were fluttering fingers expertly teasing her, coaxing her open.

The water grew more solid and, with no further preliminaries, slowly penetrated her. It was torturous the way tingles built under its ministrations. The pressure built within her, and her muscles trembled in anticipation. Her whole body seemed to clench in on itself and she heard her heart thundering in her skull.

Then she suddenly seemed to leap from the lake to the sky. Before her was the face of a beautiful sad-eyed girl. The instant impression was of warmth, kindness, and affection. The girl was smiling, bathed in golden light.

Save her, the lake spirits said. *Save her....*

NIGHT TIDES

A NOVEL

Alex Prentiss

BANTAM BOOKS
NEW YORK

Night Tides is a work of fiction. Names, characters, places, and incidents either are the product of the author's imagination or are used fictitiously. Any resemblance to actual persons, living or dead, events, or locales is entirely coincidental.

A Bantam Books Mass Market Original

Copyright © 2009 by Alex Prentiss

Published in the United States by Bantam Books, an imprint of The Random House Publishing Group, a division of Random House, Inc., New York.

BANTAM BOOKS and the rooster colophon are registered trademarks of Random House, Inc.

ISBN 978-0-553-59297-9

Cover design: Jamie S. Warren
Cover photo: Getty / Photographer's Choice Collection / © Ian Anderson
Retouching: Steven Youll
Lettering: Carol Russo

Printed in the United States of America

www.bantamdell.com

2 4 6 8 9 7 5 3 1

NIGHT TIDES

CHAPTER ONE

THE TERROR BEGAN, prosaically enough, with casual rudeness spurred by a misunderstanding.

Twenty-year-old Ling Hu opened the cooler door, took a bottle of flavored water from the bottom shelf, and walked sideways down the narrow aisle to the checkout counter. The place had all the accoutrements of a standard convenience store crammed into roughly two-thirds the usual space. It was a neighborhood institution, though, and the owner had never considered remodeling.

As the college student paid for the water, a voice behind her said, "Love your ink. The design is gorgeous. Who did it?"

She turned. A man with long gray hair, balding on top, and a pasty complexion stood behind her with a six-pack in his hand. He had to be referring to the elaborate dragon's foot design across the small of her back—the only one of her tattoos her clothes didn't completely cover. And *that* tat showed only when she squatted and her jeans rode down, which meant he'd been staring at her ass while she got her drink.

"Fuck you, creep," she said, scowling. And he *was* creepy. Not only was he at least forty years old, but his skin was unhealthily pale and gleamed with sweat. She rushed out the door and into the twilight after paying, glad to get away from him. Then she put in her earbuds and cranked up the music as she headed off down Willie Street.

"Girls," the clerk said disdainfully as he rang up the sweaty man's beer. The open books and laptop behind the counter marked him as another student in the man's eyes. "They dress to say, 'Stare at me,' and when you do they say, 'What're you looking at, asshole?' You wouldn't believe some of the shit I see in here. And the ones that stay for summer classes are the worst. Must be the heat."

The man took his beer outside and gazed down the street. He spotted Ling Hu several blocks away, flouncing along to her music, the moment in the store no doubt already forgotten.

Two contradictory emotions battled for supremacy in him. One was outrage at her cavalier arrogance, while the other was wonder at the certainty that she had not recognized him.

Then an idea formed. It was a terrible idea, and a wonderful one. For the first time in weeks, his despair began to lift. After all, what did he have to lose?

He quickly went to his truck.

———

AN HOUR LATER, Ling Hu stood naked in the bathtub with her latest boyfriend, Ken, making out as the shower sprayed down around them. They'd just had sex on the rickety balcony of his apartment, despite the summer mosquitoes drawn to their sweat. After, she'd immediately hopped into the shower. He had followed. She might be late for her study session, though, since her soapy writhing against him had brought Ken—or, at least, parts of him—back to life.

"No, I have to go, seriously," she said, and pushed him lightly away.

"Are you seeing that other guy, the football player?" he said, cupping her behind.

She *was* seeing Tyler after her study session, but she didn't feel it was any of Ken's business. "No, I have to *study.* I can't afford to blow that test tomorrow."

"Can you afford to blow anything else?" Ken said with a wicked grin. He was more than a foot taller than her, skinny and pale, with a nipple-piercing and a Celtic rope design around one biceps.

She giggled and playfully slapped him. "You've got to be kidding."

He put her hand on his hardness. "Do I feel like I'm kidding?"

She felt a rush of response and looked up into the spray. "Okay, but if you're not done by the time the hot water runs out, it's you and your hand tonight."

"Fair enough," he said. He braced his arms against the damp wall as she slid sinuously to her knees.

Twenty minutes later, her black hair still wet, Ling Hu emerged into the humid Wisconsin night. Madison was the state capital and a city of 200,000, but, because of an odd quirk of geography, its downtown area was confined to a four-mile-long isthmus between Lakes Monona and Mendota. With the state capitol as its center and the University of Wisconsin at the far west end, the isthmus was the city's hub, especially for the thousands of students who inhabited its packed, iconoclastic residential neighborhoods.

Ling Hu rushed down the sidewalk of one of these neighborhoods, backpack across her shoulders, mentally trying to shift into study mode and not anticipate her tryst with Tyler. It was not yet ten o'clock, and most of the houses were lit up with activity. She was completely unafraid for her safety.

So she did not see the old truck parked beneath the shadow of a large tree.

She was yanked into the pickup so fast that she had no chance to scream, and duct tape was immediately slapped over her mouth. Her assailant muscled her facefirst into the passenger floorboard and put one foot on her backpack to hold her down. "Sit still or I'll fucking kill you," he rasped breathlessly as the truck pulled away from the curb.

She did as ordered, curling into a terrified ball. She smelled oil, gas, and some sort of mold. *Oh, my God,* she thought, *I've been kidnapped!* Surely someone had seen what happened and would call the police. Surely.

Her chest began to ache as her asthma threatened to kick in. Her inhaler was in the outer pocket of her book bag, but it might as well have been on Mars. She closed her eyes and concentrated on slow, even breathing through her nose.

They drove for what felt like an eternity. Finally the truck stopped, and her abductor yanked her up by the hair. He pushed her out the passenger door ahead of him. When she tried to look back at him, he slapped her over one ear.

She saw no lights from houses or other cars, only the dark shapes of trees. After an awkward march downhill, she heard water lapping against rocks. The hand released her and a flashlight blazed in her face, blinding her.

"Try to run, try to hurt me, try to do *anything* other than exactly what I tell you, and I'll kill you," her captor said, his own voice wheezy with exertion. "Understand me?"

She nodded.

Then she heard the command that she was certain meant her death was near.

"Now, undress. Or I'll undress you."

DETECTIVE MARTIN WALKER stood inside the big rectangle of yellow police tape. Behind him stretched 1,200 acres of untouched wilderness known as the Arboretum, located on Madison's west side. Although he saw no sign of life in any direction, the soft hum of traffic reminded him he was still inside the city.

He looked down the hill at the swampy, overgrown shore of Lake Wingra before him. It was the smallest of the three lakes within the city limits and the only one not connected to the Yahara River. The waterlogged trees and weeds stretched out from the bank for fifty feet, blurring the actual edge of the lake. From this spot on shore, though, the effluent from a natural spring cut through the marshy obstructions and made a shallow clear channel out to the open water. He could just make out the surface of Wingra at the far end, rippling in the summer breeze as the sunrise twinkled off the waves.

Of the three lakes, Wingra was the one that always made the hackles rise on his neck. Strange stories clung to it. It once housed a lake monster that wildlife officials debunked as a large sturgeon. Divers supposedly found a submerged stone pyramid that experts insisted was just a pile of rocks left behind by retreating glaciers. And although people died in all the lakes, usually from alcohol-related foolishness, only the bodies pulled from Wingra consistently gave him the willies.

Two officers stood guard while technicians from the crime lab took photos and samples. A few people out for their morning hikes had paused on the trail at the top of the hill, then gone back the way they'd come. Otherwise, the police had the area to themselves.

Marty was descended from the Hmong—the indigenous people of Laos—which meant he was a smallish, dark-skinned Asian. He'd been adopted as an infant by a white family, though, so his behavior bore no trace of his racial ancestry. But he hoped being slant-eyed wasn't the reason he'd been assigned to this particular case—though he wouldn't have bet against it. To some of his superiors, all Asians were the same and functioned almost as a different species.

Once more he looked over the pile of clothes: tank top, brassiere, jeans, socks, shoes, and a book bag. Conspicuously missing were panties, which, if they matched the bra, were black and lacy.

"Good morning, Detective Walker," a woman's voice called. "Hell of a way to start the week, isn't it?"

He turned to see a tall, professionally dressed blonde descending the hill toward him. She ignored the marked trail and cut straight through the trees, her white running shoes a sharp contrast to her business attire.

"Hey, Julie," Marty said. "Watch out for that—"

She slipped on a patch of wet leaves but caught herself on her hands before she hit the ground.

"—slick spot," he finished.

She wiped her hands against the trunk of the nearest tree and finished her descent. She held up a digital camera. "Want to be in the picture?"

"Not really."

She nodded and obligingly took a photo of the crime scene that left Marty out of the frame. "So, any sign of foul play?"

"Any information will be given out by the press liaison officer whenever there's something to actually say," Marty said. "How'd you find out about this?"

"I have my sources."

"The Lady of the Lakes?"

He watched a simmering annoyance replace her casual professionalism. "I only use that stupid fucking blog as a last resort. Unlike you cops."

"A tip is a tip. The source isn't important."

"Is that who tipped *you* off?"

"I can't discuss an ongoing investigation, you know that. All statements come through the liaison officer."

Julie smiled sarcastically. She was a rising reporter for the *Wisconsin Capital Journal*, just as Marty was an up-and-comer in the police department; they both knew the rules. She put away her camera and reporter's notebook and said, "Yeah, I know that. But can you give me a sneak preview? I did come all the way down here in my best slacks."

Marty arched an eyebrow. "Those are your best?"

"You're mocking *my* fashion sense?" She shook her head. "Marty, you may *be* gay, but I don't think you'll ever be able to *act* gay."

"All right, but this is all off the record." He gestured at the clothes on the ground. "A jogger reported finding these just before sunrise. Just a book bag and a suit of clothes belonging to a UW student named Ling Hu. Two sets of tracks leading down here from the road, and only one leading up. I figure boyfriend and girlfriend. They might have gone down the channel to skinny-dip in the open water. Probably drunk. Either way, it looks like only one of them came back."

"And you're assuming the worst."

"I always do."

"I guess you'll have to drag the lake to look for her body?"

"Nah, some fisherman will probably find her floating by the time we check with all her family and friends to make sure she's not just sleeping off a binge. Unless *The Lady of the Lakes* tells us where she is, of course."

Again Julie's eyes blazed with fury. "I wouldn't spend my time worrying about what those amateur gossipmongers have to say about anything."

"Whoever runs it may be an amateur, but they get the scoop on you guys a lot."

"Marty, are you *trying* to piss me off? I've only had one cup of coffee and half a bagel, so it wouldn't be difficult."

He sighed. "I'm sorry. I just have a bad feeling about this one."

"How so?"

"Well . . . I don't think it's personal."

"What does that mean?"

"It means that if anything bad *did* happen to the girl, it's not due to a boyfriend, a husband, or an unrequited crush. It's a stranger who either picked Ling Hu at random or used some criteria we don't know about. And if I'm right . . ." He trailed off and looked back out at the lake.

She finished for him. "She won't be the last one."

THE DISAPPEARANCE of Ling Hu was duly noted in Tuesday's paper, then almost immediately forgotten by the predominantly white, entirely Midwestern Madison.

After all, she was foreign, and foreign people were always getting themselves into trouble.

That was not the case with Faith Lucas.

From the *WISCONSIN CAPITAL JOURNAL:*

UW HONOR STUDENT DISAPPEARS
By Julie Schutes, staff reporter

MADISON, Wis.——Madison police detectives are investigating the disappearance late Wednesday or early Thursday of a University of Wisconsin–Madison student whose discarded clothes were found near the zoo Thursday morning.

The woman has been identified as Faith Evangeline Lucas, 21, of Green Bay. The family allowed police to release her name and picture in hopes that it will prompt people to come forward with more information about her disappearance.

According to police, it is too early in the investigation to tell if Lucas's disappearance is connected to that of fellow UW student Ling Hu.

Posted by The Lady
to The Lady of the Lakes *blog:*

According to the official police party line, there might be no connection between the recent disappearances of two UW students. As if we're supposed to believe that their clothes jumped off by themselves.

A sexual predator is on the loose, people. The street cops who work on the isthmus know this, but their bosses don't listen. So, until they do, don't go out alone, don't go into strange places at night, and don't trust anyone you don't know.

CHAPTER TWO

Carrie Kimmell's bare feet slipped on the erosion-blocking stones lining this section of Lake Monona's shoreline. She stumbled, off balance because of the duct tape that bound her wrists behind her back. The same tape covered her mouth, muffling her cries.

Her foot slid into the water and sank ankle-deep into the mud. No doubt due to her panic, it felt as if something in the water grabbed her, encircling her ankle in a gentle but unbreakable grip. As it began to pull her into the water, she managed to wrench free, then fell facefirst onto the rocks. Since she was nude except for her panties, the impact was especially painful. She knew that this late at night she would find no help, even in the middle of downtown Madison, and that certainty only terrified her more.

Whimpering, she tried to rise. If she could reach the street or one of the big dark houses silhouetted against the night sky—

A flashlight blinded her. She squinted into the light,

praying it was a policeman or even a stranger who might have come to her rescue. But the distinctive labored breathing coming from the darkness dashed her hopes at once.

"Nice try," the voice said softly. "Now get up. And don't try anything else, because I'm really tired of messing with you tonight. You're right on the edge of becoming more trouble than you're worth."

Carrie clumsily got to her feet and climbed from the rocks onto the soft park grass. In a few hours this place would be alive with people sunbathing, children playing, and dogs chasing Frisbees. But now it was abandoned, and in the moonlight the huge cottonwood trees cast immense shadows that hid her, and her assailant, from view. She might as well have been standing naked deep in the Wisconsin woods.

Her attacker grabbed her by the hair and pulled her close. "Understand me well, bitch. Go along quietly like a good little girl, and you eventually might see your friends again. Give me any more shit, and all *they'll* see is your corpse. Clear?"

Choking on sobs, Carrie nodded.

The abduction had happened so fast she'd had no time to react. One moment she was walking alone down Gorham Street toward her apartment, minding her own business. It was near midnight, but in the student district the porches were filled with people drinking beer, smoking pot, and making out.

She'd passed under a maple tree so tall it blocked all light from the streetlamps, and in that brief darkness she'd been tackled and pushed into a truck's cab. She slid across to the passenger door, where the top of her head slammed painfully into the armrest. It had taken all of three seconds for her assailant to slap tape across her mouth and jam a gun behind one ear. "Make a sound," he warned, "and I'll blow your whole freshman year out the top of your skull."

The truck's vinyl bench seat smelled of sweat, paint, and rubbing alcohol, and the engine rattled as if exhausted from overwork. He drove her to the deserted park and marched her into the shadows. Then he'd blinded her with the flashlight and uttered the words she knew were a prelude to her own rape and murder:

"All right, strip. *Now!*"

What choice did she have? She fumbled with the bottom of the tank top and pulled it over her head. She slid her bra straps off her shoulders and blushed with humiliation as that garment joined her shirt on the ground. Then she unsnapped the khaki shorts and slid them down her legs.

Carrie could hardly breathe through the tape. She was a nineteen-year-old sophomore, and every awful thing her mother had feared about college in the big city was about to happen to her.

When she was down to her white cotton panties with little red hearts, tears welled in her eyes. Then, as she'd hooked her thumbs in the elastic, the voice said, "Stop. That's enough. Turn around."

It's the same man, she suddenly realized. She'd heard about the other girls but had never thought it could happen to her. Now it had, and she did as instructed, facing the dark surface of Lake Monona. The man yanked her wrists back and crossed them at the small of her back, her knuckles brushing the elastic band of her panties.

When she felt the tape zip into place around her wrists, it sent her over the edge. She made a wild dash for the street, not caring if she was seen in this state of undress. Unfortunately, she had gotten turned around and, instead of finding safety, had run straight into the lake, where *something* had tried to grab her.

Now she felt the obscene touch of her abductor's fingers on her exposed body. Tears trickled past her jaw and down her neck. What would her boyfriend, Nathan, think of her disappearance? Her parents? Would they even know she was the latest girl to be kidnapped, or would they believe she'd just run away again, like she'd done as a teenager? How long would it take their anger to turn to worry? And what would happen to her by the time her clothes were found and they realized the truth?

Her abductor scooped up her discarded clothes and muttered, "Wouldn't want to be litterbugs, would we?" Then his hand lightly caressed her sweaty, bare shoulders. With a sigh of satisfaction, he added, "There you are."

RACHEL MATRE surfaced with a gasp.

Lake Monona was warm and, as always, smelled of mud, moss, and fish, but its effect on Rachel had nothing to do with its odor. She stood on the bottom and felt the soft silt ooze between her toes, settling delicately on the tops of her feet. The waves patted her chin, and she wiped wet hair from her face. She wished she had something to lean on; even with the water supporting her, her knees were so weak she feared she'd fall. But, as always, the lake protected her and kept her from harm. As a lover, it was unfailingly considerate.

She looked around, unsure if she'd still been underwater when she let out her last climactic cry. If not, its intensity might have attracted unwanted attention, even at two in the morning. The water sparkled in the night; a small boat in the distance, some late-night fisherman out after walleyes, left a trail of rippling quicksilver. The stars were visible around the few clouds drifting across the sky. Tiny Hudson Park, where she'd entered the water, was a blank dark space between the stately lakeshore houses.

A flashlight momentarily stroked the water's surface in a wide arc. Reflexively, she ducked down until, froglike, only her eyes and the top of her head showed. The beam came from the nearby, and much larger, Martyn Park. She watched the light shine along the big gray rocks dumped there to prevent erosion. Then it winked out. Probably some bored cop checking for teenage lovers.

She swam quietly for the edge of Hudson Park, where she'd left all her clothes. She *had* to be naked; the lake allowed no barrier between her body and its touch. She luxuriated in the way the water stroked her as she moved through it. No human hands could ever mimic that liquid combination of caress and embrace—not that too many had tried lately.

Suddenly something grabbed her and pulled her

firmly underwater. She was startled but knew better than to struggle. She recognized the touch at once. Although it was unusual for the lake spirits to take her twice in one night, she was not afraid. Quite the opposite, in fact.

As she slid deeper beneath the surface, the liquid sensation against her skin changed to something more solid. Hands made of water, but somehow firmer, touched her everywhere at once, gently squeezing and stroking. She was parted to allow the entrance of something warm and phallic, which filled her expertly and unerringly found her most sensitive spot.

We love you, the voices sighed in her head. *We want you to know it.*

Oh, God, I know it, she thought back. *Take me, use me, I'm yours.*

We need you, the voices said. Often she'd tried to remember if they were male or female, or even if they spoke English, but the effects on her body kept any such in-the-moment analysis at bay. She understood them, and they, her; that was all that mattered.

She was pushed gently down to the bottom and felt the soft silt against her back and shoulders. Her arms were pulled out to the side and held there, while her breasts were encircled and caressed. She undulated against the pressure, driving it deeper inside and moaning silently into the enveloping darkness. She clenched and opened her fists, straining against the gentle pressure holding her down, knowing she was both entirely helpless and completely safe.

Since she was still afire from their earlier session, her

orgasm came easily and quickly and left her with a tingling rush deep in her belly. Her body opened wantonly, without shame or hesitation, ready for the next one.

You have me, she cried in her mind. *You have me completely. Always.*

We need your help, the voices said. She was turned, her hips were raised, and she was taken from behind, with the same gentle insistence and inevitable result. Her hands and knees sank into the silt. She knew she should be drowning but had no trouble breathing. And yet it wasn't precisely breathing—more a stasis where no air was necessary.

Hands reached beneath her and found her nipples. Fingers tangled in her hair. *Oh, God, yes, I'll help, I'll do anything.*

Help her. *She needs you now.*

Rachel's mind filled with the tableau of a terrified young woman, nude except for her panties. Every detail was vivid and intense, like those adrenaline-fueled slow-motion moments before a car crash. The girl had soft brown hair and a Celtic knot tattooed on one shoulder blade. Her pale skin gleamed with sweat. Gray tape covered her mouth and bound her wrists behind her back. Her eyes were wide, teary, and held the blank stare of shock. She sprawled facedown across the big gray boulders that lined the lakeshore, with one foot in the water—which explained her sudden connection to the spirits. Above her, a figure shone a blinding flashlight down into her face.

Even in her disembodied state, Rachel could not see

past the glare. But she felt a chill, as if the shape behind the light somehow clearly and malevolently saw *her*.

Then the vision dissolved in the rush of another orgasm, as the sensations around her became too strong to resist. *Who was she?* Rachel cried, the question mingling with the release. *When did that happen?*

Help her, the voices repeated again. And then it was over.

The spirits, or beings, or demons, or whatever the hell lived in the lakes around the Madison isthmus, guided her back to the surface. She emerged floating on her back, limbs splayed, the stars shining down on her. Waves—natural ones, without carnal intent—lapped at her ears and made the city sounds cut in and out. She took a moment to catch her breath, to let her body tremble out the last shudders of pleasure. Then, limbs heavy and relaxed, she turned onto her stomach and swam wearily for shore, to her clothes and her mundane life.

The vision stayed with her, though. Bereft of clothes, exposed to the unwanted gaze of her captor, the girl looked soft and vulnerable. Her body was not fat, but neither was it toned or tanned the way modern girls with all the money and time at their disposal strove to achieve. No, this was a real person who spent her time outside herself, not a narcissist putting every spare minute into self-improvement. Her body wasn't displayed publicly as an accomplishment or possession, like a new car or fashionable jewelry. It was meant to be shown in private, to someone who'd earned the right to admire and touch it. Damn the world for abusing someone like that.

Rachel climbed from the lake. The little rivulets running down her skin recalled the spirits' caresses and sent a distracting tremor through her. She crouched and listened to make sure no one was nearby. Madison used to be one of the safest cities around, but with the growing presence of gangs and binge drinking, that was no longer true.

Her record wasn't bad, though. Twice in twenty years she'd been caught emerging nude from the lake; the first time she'd startled two lovers hiding on the shore, and they'd run away as fast as she had. The other time, though, a pair of Hispanic teen boys had confronted her, and she'd been forced to jump back in the water and swim away, waiting offshore while they drunkenly, and bilingually, described what they wanted to do to her. It had been dawn before they wandered away, and at least one jogger had spotted her dressing frantically.

She waved her hands to disperse the mosquitoes drawn to her naked flesh. The humid night made drying off pointless. Nearby, her running shorts, shoes, and T-shirt lay folded in the shadow of the trees.

The out-of-body experience had left her shakier than usual. It was odd enough being a sexual partner for the disembodied entities that lived in the lakes. Now they could apparently disembody *her* at will. Despite her intimacy with them, she really had no idea who or what they truly were or what they wanted with her. Well, beyond the obvious, of course. Were they ghosts? Elemental beings? Aliens, even?

Help her, the voices had said—not the usual *Tell people*

about her. And Rachel wanted to help, but there was no way to determine when the events in the vision had occurred. The spirits plucked images anywhere from distant prehistory up through the recent past but never, alas, from the future. All the images were connected, usually directly, with the water itself. This one had been as well, with the poor victim's bare foot slipping beneath the surface. Rachel knew about the two girls kidnapped recently, of course, but this one did not resemble the photographs she'd seen in the newspapers and on TV. Had Rachel been shown an old crime related to the new ones? Or one from the recent past that simply hadn't been discovered yet?

There would be time to worry about that later, when she wasn't quite so vulnerable herself. She tied her wet hair back with a ponytail holder and was about to dress when light raked across the water's edge before her.

She jumped back into the darkness, too far from her clothes to reach them, and her hands reflexively flew up to protect her modesty. Soft, steady steps approached on the dew-damp grass, accompanied by the jingle of keys. She hunched down, annoyed, and then froze. Her involuntary gasp of fright sounded like a scream in her head as something obvious occurred to her.

It was true that she'd never been shown the future, but what if the vision was absolutely contemporary, happening in real time as she watched? *She needs you now,* they had said. Had the flashlight that momentarily shone her way earlier been held by the girl's abductor? Was he only now taking her away, where she would be abused and discarded? Or was the girl stashed in the trunk of his car while he trolled other parks, *this* park, for additional victims? Was he standing near her now, keys jingling with every step?

Momentarily she could not even breathe. Like the girl in the vision, she, too, was naked, unable to run or escape. She could be stared at and mocked and fondled, her body no longer her own, belonging to some man who—

No, she shouted at her panic. *I don't think that way anymore. Now I'm in charge. No one will do anything to me.* Only the lake spirits had the right to take her, and then only when she allowed it. She would die before she submitted to someone unwillingly.

The distinctive radio crackle brought a flood of relief. The policeman walked slowly along the hill just above her, his flashlight moving across the water's edge. She'd left one clear footprint in a patch of mud, and if he swung the light to the left he'd spot her easily. But he turned off the flashlight and spoke into his microphone. "Unit 512 here," he said. "Just checking Hudson Park. Continuing on to Elmside. Jiminez out." Then she heard the unmistakable trickling sound as he relieved himself against a tree. She bit her lip to keep from laughing, especially when he let out a long, contented sigh.

When he returned to his car and drove away, she emerged from the bushes, trembling and fighting the giggles. Then she dressed.

Hudson Park was located in a lakeside neighborhood whose residents had the kind of clout to ensure regular police patrols. Less than a block in size, it existed to protect the remains of an effigy mound built by the long-departed Native Americans. It was the earthen silhouette of a four-legged animal with a straight tail that extended as far as the curb. Before the street, and the huge houses that lined it, were built, the tail had continued another hundred feet or so, according to the people who studied such things. Constructed centuries before Europeans arrived in the New World by a tribe that no longer existed, its origin and purpose could only be conjectured. Even the animal it depicted was disputed. Some called it a lizard, others a panther. Most used the generic term *water spirit*.

Rachel knew *her* water spirits did not dwell within the mound, like ghosts haunting a mansion. But they considered the spot sacred, along with all the other areas around town, some now lost, where the mounds once existed. Often, the visions they shared with her depicted native tribes gathered around these special places, in solemn rituals whose purpose she could never fathom. And so, to honor her lovers, she always paused by the irregular outline of the effigy's head, its shape worn away and distorted by time and disrespect, and bequeathed it a moment of solemnity.

She reached beneath the waistband of her shorts and touched the spot below her navel where she had a small, simple tattoo of the mound silhouette. It was invisible beneath her clothes, unless she wore particularly low-slung pants, but it was always there, a sign of her commitment to her lover—or lovers, or whatever they might be. And sometimes, like now, she swore it tingled along its edges.

RACHEL JOGGED DOWN the empty streets toward home. Her tennis shoes slapped the pavement, sharp in the post-midnight quiet. All the big houses were dark, except for those whose motion-triggered security lights blinked on as she passed. These mini-mansions were far too expensive for someone like her, and it always seemed ironic that the people who could afford them had little or no respect for the lake they so desperately wanted to overlook. They thought nothing of tearing out great sections of the shore for their docks and boathouses or cutting down ancient trees that dared obstruct their view. Then they wondered why the unspoiled lake they'd admired seemed to turn all brown and choked, once the plants that anchored the soil had been removed.

She turned a corner and skidded to a stop.

A car was parked at the curb, and two young men leaned down to talk to the driver. All appeared to be in their twenties, with that air of privilege and narcissism distinctive to economic security. As she turned to leave, the car's headlights bloomed, pinning her the way the flashlight had done the girl in her vision. She froze.

"Hey, honey," one of the men slurred, "why you in such a hurry?"

"Yeah, we having a party," another one said, using a ghetto accent that made him sound even more white. "Why don't you swing around and hang with us, yo?"

Don't show fear, she told herself. Maybe it was a coincidence and unrelated to her vision. Still, the warning echoed vividly: *Help her.* Was this what the spirits meant? Was the poor girl waiting in the car, hoping Rachel would save her?

No, she decided. There had been only one consciousness, one malignant entity behind that flashlight. These were just aimless boys looking for someone to scare.

She turned to face them. The car's stereo exploded into the quiet night, the bass making her chest vibrate. She raised one hand to block the light. "Hey," she began, "I don't think—"

Suddenly one of the men was right in front of her, his hand on her wrist, pulling it away from her face. "Hey, yourself. You're kinda hot, you know that?" He reeked of beer, sweat, and body wash. "You must run all the time to keep those abs so tight." He lightly patted her exposed belly.

"Man, she a MILF for sure, yo," said ghetto boy.

"Bring her over," the car's driver called. "We'll all go for a ride. Want to get high, honey?"

Rachel said nothing. This was a situation she could handle. She gave the boy a friendly smile, then drove her right foot down onto his instep. As he hollered and bent double, she slammed the heel of her hand into his nose. His head snapped back and he fell to the pavement.

"Hey, what the fuck?" one of the other boys exclaimed. But by then she was already running, flat out, in the other direction.

She was not panicked, but she knew that if it came down to a physical confrontation, she was outnumbered and overpowered. And if they got her into their car, it would be over. So when she heard the vehicle's tires squeal as it pulled away from the curb, she left the sidewalk and cut across the silent, dark backyards.

She left a trail of security lights and startled family dogs behind her. Glancing back, she saw the car's headlights sweep around as it turned the corner and tried to anticipate where she would emerge. She stopped, pivoted, and ran back the way she'd come. They'd have to loop the block to catch her, if they even realized what she'd done—if their Halo-shortened attention spans could even *care* for that long. By then she'd be long gone.

And as she was feeling proud of herself for her strategy, she ran straight into the path of an old pickup truck driving without headlights.

Its tires bit the pavement and she slammed her hands onto the hood, as if she had the strength to stop it. It halted inches from her, engine wheezing as it fought not to stall.

For a long moment, neither she nor the truck moved. The metal was warm beneath her palms, and she felt the engine's rough trembling. It was an uncharacteristic vehicle for this neighborhood, and doubly so for riding with its lights out.

Then the headlights came on. The driver leaned out and said, "Sorry about that. Forgot to turn on the lights. You okay?"

Something about the voice seemed familiar, and it chilled her far more than the rowdy would-be fraternity rapists following her. But she couldn't see past the light.

"Yeah," she said, and moved aside. "I should've been paying more attention too. No harm, no foul."

The truck rattled off into the night. She tried to see into the cab as it passed, but the driver remained a faceless silhouette.

Porch lights were coming on around her. She took off again, indirectly toward home. She'd had more than enough excitement, in every sense, for one night.

AT LAST SHE emerged onto Williams Street, the demarcation line between the quiet upper-class neighborhoods and the rest of eclectic downtown Madison. Minutes later, she unlocked the back door of the diner she owned. She looked behind her to make sure she hadn't been followed, but all the streets were empty and silent.

In her apartment above the diner, she methodically locked the doors and ensured that all the blinds were down. Then she undressed again, showered, and pulled on a clean, oversize T-shirt. She wrapped her wet hair in a towel, then checked the blinds again. Satisfied that no one could see, she went to her bedroom closet.

On the top shelf, in the back, inside a Kohl's department-store box and wrapped in a silk scarf, lay her weapon of choice. She carefully removed the laptop computer from its hiding place and carried it into the living room. She cultivated a reputation as a technological Luddite; none of her friends knew she even owned a computer, let alone that she used it for a single—and singular—purpose.

As she reached for the touch pad, she noticed that her fingers were shaking. She smiled; at one time, a night like this would've left her huddled, sobbing, in the back of her closet. Now it barely made her hand tremble.

She got online and clicked on her lone bookmark: the blog for *The Lady of the Lakes*. This was her secret identity, something no one else knew about. It was also the only practical way to pass on the things the lake spirits showed her.

The spirits had first requested her help five years previously. It had been a particularly maddening encounter, as they repeatedly teased her almost to orgasm and then pulled back, leaving her hovering on the edge. When she was finally allowed to climax, the sensation had overwhelmed her, allowing the spirits to communicate with her in an entirely new way.

She'd been given her first vision—so vivid she could recall even the most minor details. She saw a white police officer gleefully beating a skinny black teenager at one of the isolated boat ramps located along the isthmus. The wet crunch of each blow stayed with her, as well as the muffled "Oomph!" from a boy too battered to cry out. The cop occasionally dunked the boy's head in the lake, to revive him when he passed out from the pain. When the scene faded, the spirits told her in no uncertain terms: *The truth must be known.*

The next day she cautiously went to the police to report it as an incident she'd personally witnessed. They insisted there was no officer matching her description, and no similar crime had been reported. She got the same response from the newspaper. Embarrassed, she'd tried to avoid the lakes after that, but the spirits' hold on her body was too much to resist.

Months later, on a visit to the state historical museum, she'd stumbled across the officer's face again, in a photograph from 1975. With his name as a starting point, she found that he'd been acquitted of beating a black teen in 1970. Yet, if the vision was true, he'd actually been guilty.

Rachel found an e-mail address online for the victim, now a middle-aged bus driver living in Mount Horeb. The spirits insisted *the truth must be known,* but, after her experience with the police and newspapers, she was afraid of more humiliation if she wrote him directly.

Then it occurred to her that an anonymous blog, where she could post these visions, would be ideal. And so *The Lady of the Lakes* was born. And with the judicious addition of local gossip and legitimate news, plus a few tricks to make sure she remained untraceable, she managed to hide the lake spirits' messages in plain sight.

The response had been immediate and overwhelming. Posters jumped to add opinions and other bits of gossip, making the "Comments" section as full of information as any of her entries. And one of the first replies had been a heartfelt thanks from the bus driver's daughter, who said it was the first time she'd seen her father cry with joy.

She paused for a moment, wondering again if this time they meant something different by *Help* her. *She needs you.* But what? The lake spirits had said nothing about the first two girls; Rachel had picked up the details from the idle talk of the police who frequented her diner.

They never glanced twice at her when she refilled their coffee, and it never occurred to them that their gossip might be overheard. She was careful to paraphrase and re-word, though, so that nothing could be traced back to the officers involved, and from them to her.

Finally she began to type, transcribing what she'd been shown by the spirits. It did not take long. Then she posted it, verified it was up, and shut down the computer. She returned the laptop to its hiding place, turned out the lights, and crawled beneath the cool sheets, only then disturbing the cat sleeping obliviously at the foot of the bed.

She was asleep within minutes, although her dreams were filled with terrified girls pleading from the lakeshore and menacing silhouettes behind bright, blinding lights.

CHAPTER THREE

POSTED BY *The Lady* to *The Lady of the Lakes* blog:

The police won't tell you about it yet, but another young woman was accosted on the isthmus last night. She has dark hair and a Celtic knot tattooed on her shoulder. The Lady hopes that she's not in the same predicament as Ling Hu and Faith Lucas, but I'm afraid she might be. Maybe if the police spent more time patrolling and less time worrying about making their ticket quota on the Beltline, this would be a safer town.

From the *Wisconsin Capital Journal,* published four hours after the above posting appeared on *The Lady of the Lakes:*

THIRD UW STUDENT DISAPPEARS
By Julie Schutes, staff reporter

And another one gone, leaving only her clothes.

Madison police have classified UW sophomore

Carrie Elizabeth Kimmell as officially missing after personal belongings, including items of clothing, were found at a lakeside construction site.

According to Detective Martin Walker, Kimmell's case was filed as an endangered missing person, due to her history of depression. He would neither confirm nor deny any connection to the recent disappearances of Ling Hu and Faith Lucas, both UW students. In both prior cases, personal belongings were found at isolated locations on the isthmus.

At seven that morning, Rachel stood behind the counter of her small, eponymous breakfast-and-lunch diner, Rachel's. The sun blasted through the big front windows and off the white walls, filling the place with clean, natural light. Conversations, clinking silverware, and the soft music of Jamie Cullum provided the soundtrack. The place smelled of fresh cooking and the slightly metallic odor of air-conditioning.

There had been no diner in Rachel's future when she graduated from La Follette High School, then started college with dreams of being a veterinarian. But she had no head for memorizing arcane scientific information, and the bloody dissections sent her scurrying instead for a fallback business degree. An internship with a local catering company convinced her she could do a better job than they were doing, so she dropped out a semester from graduation, borrowed some money from a fund for women-owned businesses, and started Rachel's Soirees to

Go. A year at that showed her that what she really wanted was her own place, where the people came to *her*.

So she sold the catering business at a loss and used the money as a down payment on Trudy's, a well-established diner whose owner was ready to retire. That had been ten years ago, when she was twenty-four. It had been the one constant through the ups and downs—mostly downs— of her life since then. Well, it and the lakes.

Now she waited patiently while a white-haired professor of literature decided what to order. Oswald Dunning, expert on Chaucer and author of the thick textbook a nearby student patron was reading, had walked the five blocks from his house to breakfast every morning for twenty-two years, first for Trudy and now for Rachel. Rachel had seen his iron-gray hair go white, then thin, and finally sparse. Age spots and thick knuckles marked his once-wiry hands. In contrast, she was pretty sure the nigh-indestructible tweed jacket he wore in all weather would outlast not just Professor Dunning but them all.

Other regulars lined the counter, while a few newcomers sat at the tables. Usually the newbies were college students: trim, sexy girls in fashion-magazine casuals and boys still learning to groom themselves without their mother's insistence. Rachel never advertised and was content that word of mouth spread through the bohemian isthmus population just fast enough so that when one set of student regulars graduated, others appeared to take their place.

On a whim, Rachel had redone the walls in white

dry-erase marker board, and now elaborate customer graffiti danced alongside descriptions of the day's specials. As she watched, one of the college girls put the finishing touches on an elaborate line drawing of a unicorn standing among flowers, then signed her name and, beneath it, wrote her Web site address. She crouched so low on her heels that her jeans displayed a third of her turquoise thong and all of the tramp-stamp tattoo across the small of her back.

"I believe I shall have an omelet of ham and cheese," Professor Dunning said at last, and stood the laminated menu between the napkin holder and ketchup bottle. "I'll need the protein to reach the blank slates in my freshman class. The girls are little more than suntans and brassieres, and the boys know nothing except computer games and pornography."

"Oh, they can't be that bad," Rachel said as she wrote down the order. "After all, we were young once."

"When I was young, men had goals and women had modesty." He smiled and shook off the bitterness. "And you still *are* young, my dear."

"I'm thirty-four; that's not young. It's the point where people start planning their midlife crisis." She put the order on the carousel and spun it for the cook.

"I'm not an expert on semantics, but if you can plan it, I doubt it qualifies as a 'crisis,'" Dunning said.

"I plan all my crises," Rachel said with a wink. "And I use index cards instead of a spreadsheet. That's how I know I'm not young."

"Well, the man at the end of the counter is also young

by my standards, and he hasn't taken his eyes off you since he sat down."

She turned, then realized the man in question actually *was* watching her. She blushed and looked away quickly. That end of the counter was Helena's area, so Rachel had not taken his order. She slipped into the kitchen and peered out through the narrow serving window.

"Whassup?" Jimmy the cook asked as he glanced up from the griddle.

"Nothing," she said. "Just checking on something."

The man was about Rachel's age, with unruly brown hair that needed cutting. He wore a dark-blue button-down shirt with no tie and carried a PDA in his pocket. He was broad-shouldered, clean-shaven, and square-jawed, and he perused his newspaper with eyes that, at this distance, looked either blue or green. He radiated intelligence, strength, and total self-confidence—exactly the kind of man Rachel couldn't stand. Her ex-husband was that kind of man—or, rather, desperately wanted to be: a beta male striving futilely to become an alpha. His bitterness had been one but not all of the things that had finally driven Rachel away, and she had no patience left for men like that.

And yet the man at the end of the counter didn't give off that sense of physical danger she encountered in so many big, muscular men. He seemed to lack the simmering need to prove himself physically, and with a start she realized just how attractive that made him. Well, that and his boyish good looks. She felt a distinctive tingle in the pit of her stomach that she did her best to ignore.

The man looked up, and around, clearly wondering where she'd gone. When he glanced toward the kitchen, Rachel ducked out of sight.

Her waitress, Helena, poked her head around the corner into the kitchen. Helena had black hair, sharp features, and an easy smile; she'd known Rachel for most of their adult life. "Are you hiding?"

"No, I'm . . . looking for this," Rachel said, and held up a spatula. The head fell off and clattered into the sink.

"You're looking for a broken spatula?" Helena said doubtfully.

"Well, if I'm going to replace it, I need to know what size to—" She stopped, defeated. "*Yes*, I'm hiding, are you happy? The man at the end of the counter was staring at me."

"All the straight men stare at you the first time they come in here," Helena reminded her. "And the second and third time too. They don't stop until you bite off their heads."

"I wish you'd quit saying that," Rachel snapped. "I know better." But that wasn't entirely true. Rachel was secretly proud of her lean, athletic body; she knew men loved her wild semifrizzy hair, even though she hated it. She also tended to inadvertently dress in ways that showed off her assets, as she had this morning, in a sports-bra top and tight denim shorts.

"You don't know squat," Helena retorted. "So what if he's staring at you? You're an attractive woman, he's . . ." She stood on tiptoe to see past Rachel through the serving window.

The man lifted his coffee cup but was so busy looking around that he missed his own lips and spilled the hot liquid on the counter. He quickly put down the cup and wiped up the spill with a napkin, checking to see if anyone had noticed his clumsiness.

Helena suppressed a giggle. "Ooh, he's an ice-cream cone on a hot day, isn't he? Look at those eyes."

"Please," Rachel said with a scowl. Helena had been out as gay since junior high school. "You never licked an ice-cream cone in your life. You told me that, remember?"

"Even a vegetarian can admire a well-cooked steak," Helena said archly.

"He probably watches the Packers religiously, ice-fishes and deer-hunts, has a snowmobile, a Jet Ski, and a porn folder on his laptop. I bet he even knows Brett Favre's birthday."

"October tenth," Helena said. "And that's a lot of hostility to cook up for nothing more than a simple look. It's been a while for you, hasn't it?"

Rachel put her hands on her hips. "Helena, if and when I decide to date again, it won't be with some square-headed walking cheese log." Yet even as she protested, she knew her assertions were wrong. Something about the man told her that, whatever else, he was more than he appeared. And despite her best efforts to negate it, the need to learn what that might be was growing exponentially.

The bell over the door chimed, announcing a new customer. Helena said, "Excuse me; my public demands me," then froze in midstep. "Oh, *shit*," she hissed. "It's *Caleb*."

In the doorway stood a tall man with graying hair worn in a crew cut. His unbuttoned flannel shirt revealed an olive U.S. Marines T-shirt. He had a few days' salt-and-pepper beard and regarded the dozen patrons at the counter with utter disdain. As he walked past them, the cuffs of his unbuttoned sleeves raked across the backs of the customers' heads. "Hey!" the girl who'd drawn the unicorn said, but Caleb ignored her. He chose a stool at the far end, in Helena's section, next to the man she and Rachel had been discussing. The man glanced at Caleb, then returned to reading his paper.

Caleb grabbed the edge of the counter and, with a theatrical groan, twisted on the stool until his back popped audibly.

Rachel's stomach tightened into an apprehensive knot. After the events of the previous night, she was already on edge, and this didn't help. "What's he doing?"

"That spine-cracking thing he does," Helena said. "Maybe this time he won't—whoops, there he goes."

Caleb fished a pack of cigarettes from his shirt pocket, stuck one between his lips, and lit it. He snapped his old-fashioned metal lighter closed with a flourish. He turned to the blue-shirted man and asked, "Are you done with the sports section?"

"He's smoking again," Helena observed disdainfully.

"Christ," Rachel muttered. She scanned the other patrons to confirm what she already knew: None of her cop regulars was around. Caleb would've checked that too, before he came inside. "Hey, Jimmy?"

The cook, who had ignored both women and lingered

diligently over his grill, now shook his head without looking up. "Uh-uh, I'm not paid enough to deal with that. He's one of those crazy ex-soldiers. He might hide in the bushes and gut me like a trout when I leave."

"Oh, grow a pair, will you?" Rachel said. "Besides, I was just going to say, get ready to call 911 if I tell you to. I'm hoping it won't come to that."

"Do you want me to come with you?" Helena said quietly.

"No. It's my diner; it's my problem. Just try to keep everyone else distracted." She took a deep breath, let it out slowly, and set forth to face the dragon.

This wasn't her first clash with Caleb Johnstone. On his initial visit a year earlier, he'd come behind the counter—something *no one* did without permission—and rifled through the order tickets to add something to his sandwich. Rachel would have asked him to leave, and possibly banned him for good, but Helena got there first and handled it more gently.

Then, eight months ago, he'd picked a fight with another patron over the boy's gay pride T-shirt. He'd broken the boy's nose and threatened to show Helena how a "real man" treated a woman, saying it would "stop all that carpet-licking." Rachel had sworn out a restraining order against him that was still in effect, which meant he could be arrested immediately. Still, she hated to involve the police except as a last resort. That kind of publicity was hard to overcome.

Caleb looked up at her as she approached. "Hello, bay-bee. Still afraid of me? I bet you've already called the police to come protect you and that cute little dyke over there."

Rachel felt silence spread through the room. She crossed her arms and said evenly, "Put out the cigarette, Caleb. And leave."

He deliberately took another puff and said, "For a kiss."

Rachel knew she was turning red, as she always did in situations like this, as much with fury as embarrassment. Still, she couldn't back down. Quiet and steady, she said, "Caleb, completely aside from the fact that you could be thrown in jail just for being here, there's a no-smoking ordinance in Madison. So put out the goddamned cigarette, then go."

Caleb deliberately looked straight ahead, an infuriating little smirk on his lips. "Make me."

She laughed for the benefit of the people watching, then leaned her hands on the counter. Through a forced smile she said, "Caleb, come on. Do you *want* to go to jail?"

"Sure." Then, in a loud voice, he added, "After all, wouldn't want to offend the goddamned hippies who let people like me fight their wars while they pass all these 'poor me' laws. Pretty soon a man won't be able to fart without a license."

"Come on, Stephen," a tall, dark-skinned girl in a tree-pattern T-shirt said as she stood. "It's *my* right to eat without *his* smoking taking years off my life. I *will* be calling the city about this."

Her companion, a slight, shaggy-bearded young man,

put some money down beside their plates. "Smoking sucks," he mumbled, and slunk out behind her.

"Oh, Christ," Rachel said. "Caleb, seriously, don't make me—"

"Buddy, put out the cigarette."

Caleb and Rachel both turned to the blue-shirted man. He was looking steadily at Caleb.

"Kiss my ass," Caleb said. "In the nineties I fought Saddam Hussein for you pissants, you know that? Desert Storm, does that mean anything to you?"

"Sure," the man said. "Does Operation Iraqi Freedom mean anything to you? I fought him for every loud-mouthed asshole in America." His voice remained steady and soft, so that only Rachel and Caleb heard him. "Now, this lady's asked you in a nice, friendly way to stop doing something you already knew you shouldn't be doing. I'm *telling* you to stop doing it before you walk out of here with that cigarette burning in a real uncomfortable place."

Rachel froze. The potential for violence had appeared so suddenly that she could do nothing to defuse it. Both men were large, but Caleb was middle-aged, dissipated, and used to intimidating people who never fought back. The younger man looked quite capable of making good on his threat. Could she have been that wrong about him?

For a moment the only sound was the incongruously smooth voice of Jamie Cullum on the CD player. Then Caleb stood and said loudly, "The hell with all of you!" He tossed the cigarette into the coffee cup left behind by the outraged girl and slammed the door on the way out.

For a long moment no one spoke. Then old Mrs.

Boswell at the counter's far end began to applaud, and everyone joined in. Even Rachel, tight-lipped, did the same. But as the patrons turned to one another to discuss the showdown, Rachel glared at the victor, her attraction to him now balanced by annoyance.

"Thank you," she said. "Now I'd like you to go."

He blinked in surprise, his triumphant smile fading before it had entirely formed. He was younger than she'd initially thought, perhaps not yet thirty, and the way the veins stood out in his neck said he was in better shape than the baggy shirt implied. He seemed none the worse for the confrontation, which also told her he was used to scenes like this. "I beg your pardon?"

"I was handling the situation. I know Caleb; I would've threatened to call the police, and he would've left on his own. Now, thanks to you, his pride's hurt, and each time he sees you're not here, he'll be sure to come in and make an even bigger scene."

"So you'd rather call the police than have someone just handle the problem?"

"Handle?" she snapped in a low, urgent voice, wanting nothing more than for this whole thing to be over. She must have read him completely wrong. He was one of the boys from last night writ larger, and older, and (she still hated to admit it) far sexier, but still a mere testicle with the power of speech. She took a deep breath and closed her eyes against her own fury and unwanted attraction. "I know you think you were doing a good deed, but try to understand this. Caleb was threatening *my* authority, not yours. *You* brought the prospect of violence into this, not him. You may be used to solving problems that way, and it may even work for you, but you won't do it here. I won't stand for it." She was proud of her own eloquence; usually when she was angry she sputtered like an old outboard motor. "Now, I've asked you politely to leave. Or do I have to call the police?"

He stood and tossed a ten-dollar bill on the counter. "It's your diner. Sorry for causing so much trouble."

As the door closed after him, Helena said from behind Rachel, "That might've been an overreaction."

"Probably," Rachel said. And in the pit of her stomach, she knew it was true. Because at the last moment the emotion in his eyes had not been anger or humiliation but hurt. A man who could both back down Caleb Johnstone and still get his feelings hurt was a lot more than a walking gonad. And yet he had pride enough not to make a scene and to acquiesce to her demand that he leave. She felt the little shiver that, when she'd been a younger woman, meant she was half in love with some stranger she barely knew. She hated that feeling now.

"But I'd rather overreact on principle," Rachel continued, "than let anyone think they can start a pissing contest in here."

"You realize you chased off a man whose butt looks good in khakis even to me?" Helena said.

"He's just Caleb with better hygiene," Rachel said with a scorn she most definitely didn't feel. Then she turned to the room. "Okay, everyone, show's over. Apologies for the disturbance."

"That's how men were in *my* day," Mrs. Boswell said as she sipped her tea. "They had *spines*."

The bell over the door rang again, and Rachel looked up in time to glimpse another man leaving. She didn't recognize him and looked around to see where he'd been sitting; it wasn't that unusual for people to try to skip out on their checks. "Who was that?" she asked Helena.

Helena looked around. "Oh, it was the guy way in the back there. He paid. Don't worry."

Something about the brief view of him sent a shiver up Rachel's spine. "Who was he?"

"I don't know," Helena said. "He looked familiar, so he's probably been in before, but he wasn't a regular."

Rachel went to the window and looked out, but the man had vanished.

Helena shook her head and sighed. "Remember the good old days, when working the breakfast shift wasn't dangerous?"

"Everything's dangerous now," Rachel said distantly, but Helena had already walked away.

CHAPTER FOUR

Ethan Walker stopped in midmotion as he climbed into his truck and looked back at the diner. The two-story building occupied a triangular lot where Williams Street and East Washington met at a forty-five-degree angle. His builder's eye told him it had been erected sometime in the sixties and significantly refurbished at least three times since. The hand-painted sign over the door read simply, *Rachel's,* in black letters on white, and flyers for local bands, yard sales, and political events covered the lower half of the big front window.

He slapped the edge of the truck's door, and the impact traveled painfully up his arm to his shoulder. He closed his eyes and took a deep, slow breath. How *dare* that woman throw him out, when all he'd done was stand up for her? Where was her gratitude? Everyone else in the place appreciated his actions. Why not her?

He wanted to slam the truck's door, stomp back into the diner, get right in her smug face, and say ... well, what? What could he say? Clearly, despite the undeniable fact that she had lips he'd fantasize about for weeks and legs whose silkiness he could almost feel against his hands, she was not a woman he could get along with. In Madison, the great liberal-blue enclave in the middle of red-state Wisconsin, that wasn't a surprise. Some days it seemed like every current and former hippie from all over the Midwest had landed here the way runoff collects in low spots. Unfortunately, there was no way to drain these people away to Iowa or Illinois the way water could be sent back into the lakes.

He closed his truck door and started the engine. The annoying *ping* continued until he finally gave in and fastened his seat belt. He'd be sure to pay Marty back for this humiliation. *I know it's out of your way, but it's my favorite local place and you'll love it,* his brother had said. *I can't believe you've never tried it.* Now he fervently wished that were still true.

As he put the truck in reverse, he glanced in his rearview mirror and saw the woman standing in the window. Her hands were on her hips, which pulled the apron snug and accented her curves. It also made her resemble a parent ensuring that a troublemaking child left the playground. He couldn't make out her expression through the glass and wondered if perhaps she regretted her words and would apologize if he went back inside.

Just the sight of her made his belly tingle, and other body parts also announced themselves. Annoyed, he adjusted himself and put the truck in drive. Could his two heads *never* agree, not even once? It didn't matter anyway;

she had publicly humiliated him, and that was that. The way she looked in that apron, one strand of wavy hair falling into her eyes, was completely besides the point.

Not to mention that, in a clinch—in *the* clinch—he'd likely fail to launch. *That memory* would return, and what now stood at attention would fall resolutely, immovably at ease.

He turned on the radio as he drove down East Washington, and .38 Special's "Hold On Loosely" blared out, loud enough to cover his sing-along. And even though he knew the actual lyrics, he always sang the way he'd misheard them as a child:

> *Hold on, Lucy*
> *And don't let go*
> *If you swing too highly*
> *You're gonna lose your toe. . . .*

Within a verse and a chorus, he was smiling again.

A FEW TURNS brought him to the shore of Lake Mendota, the northernmost of the two big lakes separated by downtown Madison. Here his company, Walker Construction, was building a condominium complex in an area whose residents had exhausted all legal remedies—and the original builder—in an attempt to keep out the new development. The project was hugely behind schedule, and Ethan found out about the troubles only after he'd taken the contract. His company had almost tanked during his two years in Iraq, where he'd learned just how hard long-distance management could be even in the Internet age. And so he'd jumped at the first job that came along without doing his normal due diligence. *Lesson learned,* he told himself often and vehemently.

Ethan had spent his childhood on a working dairy farm outside the nearby town of Monroe, the polar opposite of bohemia. His father had always described Madison as the place where the liberals and freaks collected so they could best influence the state government. "Seventy-two square miles of druggies and homos surrounded by reality," he called it, modifying the famous Lee Dreyfus quote.

Certainly the presence of the university had something to do with it, and when Ethan left home to attend school in Madison, he'd briefly flirted with both the liberal student establishment and the liberal student girls. But his small-town work ethic, morals, and sense of common decency drew him back from the excesses of sex, substance abuse, and relativism. By the time he graduated, he'd grown so disgusted that he didn't even attend the ceremony. The presence of Al Franken as the commencement speaker didn't help.

Since returning from Iraq eight months earlier, he'd been even more aware of the differences between the people he knew and respected and the rest of the city's population. He hadn't been around in the sixties, but it wasn't hard to imagine that the tension was similar. Only the lack of a draft kept most of it off the streets and instead confined to the radios, newspapers, and blogs.

He slowed as he approached the construction site, and his reverie abruptly ended. Five police cars, an official-looking van, and an ambulance blocked the entrance. Yellow *Do Not Cross* tape encircled the property. A TV-station truck was parked farther down, although it appeared to be leaving. Neighbors stood outside their homes, clustered in small groups. His stomach dropped, and he felt suddenly cold. What the hell had happened?

He parked and climbed from his truck. Although it wasn't yet nine o'clock, the heat was enough to plaster his shirt to his skin within three steps. He walked quickly over to his workers gathered next to the port-a-johns. "Who's hurt?" he demanded.

The men looked blank.

Ethan clenched his fists. "There's an ambulance."

"Nobody hurt," one of the electricians said.

Ethan's mouth went a little dry. "Please tell me this isn't an immigration raid," he said.

"No, it's your brother," the welding foreman said. "The real cops."

A quick look around verified that the cars were all city patrol vehicles and most of the men were in uniform. He felt a little relief. "And why are the real cops here?"

"Some girl got attacked here last night," one of the bricklayers said.

"Attacked?" Ethan repeated.

"*Sí.* The police got here the same time we did this morning. They found her clothes but no trace of her. I think they sent the ambulance in case someone finds her body."

"And none of you bothered to call *me* when you called the cops?"

"Hey, *patrón,* we didn't call the cops," the bricklayer said. "They just showed up."

"We thought your brother would call you," the foreman said with a hint of petulance. "He said he knew where you were."

"Ethan!" Martin Walker called as he came around the end of the Bobcat parked in the driveway. Clearly the small Asian and the tall, thickly muscled Caucasian had no blood connection, but growing up under the same roof had more than compensated. "I wondered if you were going to show up."

"What the *hell,* Marty?" Ethan said. "Why didn't you call me?"

"If I'd known you were going to be this late, I would have. Did you stop at Rachel's diner?"

"Forget the *diner,* Marty. What's going on?"

Marty nodded that they should move away from the workers. When they were out of earshot, Marty asked softly, "Didn't you see the paper this morning?"

Ethan shook his head.

"Another college girl disappeared last night."

"Here?"

"Maybe. We're still working on that. Anyway, this one was just like the others. You know what Dad always says: Once is a fluke, twice a coincidence, but three times is a pattern, man, and I'm going to start feeling the heat. These are the kinds of things Nancy Grace gets her panties in a wad over."

The shift in tone from the breakfast scene to this one left Ethan a little off balance. So a third girl had vanished from the busy, overpopulated downtown isthmus. He knew about the others, from the news and from Marty. The first girl had been a Chinese exchange student and thus merited little media notice; Faith Lucas, though, was a white, blond cheerleader and swimsuit model who came from a prominent family of Green Bay Lutherans. The Sunday headline after her disappearance referred to her as the *Golden Girl Gone,* and the national media was sniffing around more than anyone liked. And now a third girl had vanished.

"Shit," Ethan muttered softly. "So what exactly did you find here?"

"A set of footsteps across the site, a cut security fence, and more tracks down to the water's edge. The missing girl's clothes in a pile. No blood on them, and they weren't ripped or torn like she struggled. Every button, zipper, and snap was undone. I don't think she was attacked here, though; in the other two, there were two sets of tracks down and one set back. I think the perp left the clothes here to throw us off. He probably called the tip line himself."

Ethan looked past his brother at the dozen officers and investigators carefully examining the ground. Beyond them lay the orange fence netting that warned equipment drivers of the soft lakeshore, and beyond that were the trees he'd been told to leave intact regardless of how their roots interfered with the plumbing. One section of the fence was cut and pushed aside, and a man powdered it for fingerprints. "I know this is a big deal, Marty," Ethan said, his teeth clamped tight against his fury at the universe, "but do you know how far behind we are on this project?"

"Yes, and I'm really sorry, Ethan. But I didn't pick the site."

Ethan nodded. "I know. How long will it be before we can get back to work?"

"At least a day."

"A whole *day*? Marty, every day *counts* on this one. It's my first job since I got back stateside. We're supposed to be roofing this thing by now, and we just started putting up the girders. That kind of delay means we won't finish before winter, and *that* means we'll have to finish next spring. Contractors don't get good references if they're a year overdue."

"I'll do what I can, but this is a crime scene, and we have to keep it pristine until we've gotten all the evidence."

"If all he did was walk across it and throw down some clothes, how much evidence can there be?"

"Not much, probably. But these days the crucial clue might be microscopic. You watch *CSI*, you know how it works. I suppose you could have your lawyer yell at the chief about it...."

Ethan snorted. "Yeah, that's the publicity I need: *Local contractor couldn't care less about missing girl.* That'd be all over *The Lady of the Lakes* by lunchtime. Hey, maybe it was that blogger who called in the tip."

"If we could track him down, I'd sure have a few questions for him. He knows way too much about a lot of things. But we've tried before. No judge in touchy-feely Madison will give us a subpoena for the ISP records, because he stays just this side of probable cause and everyone's concerned about his right to free speech."

"I thought it was a woman."

"Online you can be anything. And more than one thing."

Ethan fumed silently for a moment longer. "Okay, I'll leave you to your job; that way at least *one* of the Walkers will be working here. I've got to send the guys home, and then Dad's supposed to meet me at the office."

Marty's eyes narrowed suspiciously. "He is? Why?"

"You know why. Why does he ever come to the big city?"

"Well . . . tell him I said hi. Chuck and I will try to get out there sometime soon."

"Does he let Chuck in the house yet?"

"No, just onto the porch. I guess he's afraid of fag tracks on the carpet. But he offers him a beer now."

"I thought Chuck didn't drink."

"He pretends. He even wore a Packers T-shirt last time. Fake it 'til you make it."

"He'll never be able to fake it enough for Dad."

Marty patted him on the arm, then walked back to the crime scene. For something that needed to be kept immaculate, Ethan thought, they'd done a tremendously good job of tearing up the muddy area in their search for clues. He took a deep breath and went to tell men who got paid only when they worked that, for the next day at least, there was no work for them.

CHAPTER FIVE

IN HIS OFFICE DOWNTOWN, Ethan poured himself a drink from the whiskey bottle in his desk. He seldom drank before noon, but since the day was probably shot, he figured no harm done. Besides, he had to deal with his father.

Walker Construction had its offices on the third floor of an office tower three blocks from the state capitol. As a teenager looking for work experience, Ethan had helped install the building's light fixtures during summer vacation—for no actual pay, thanks to the unions. It had been his first taste of the utter, absolute satisfaction of seeing something *built*. Through his window, the capitol's dome—identical in design to the one in Washington, D.C., but smaller in scale—rose above the tops of all the other buildings. In a real city, it would be surrounded by modern high-rises, but in Madison an antiquated law said that nothing downtown could be taller than the capitol. Ethan contributed to a PAC determined to change it. So far, they'd had no success.

The suite of offices was clean, sparsely furnished, and barely used; Ethan was too hands-on to supervise from a desk. And once contracts were negotiated, all problems could be handled on-site. He kept a receptionist to answer the phone and handle correspondence, but otherwise the office was empty. During busy times, he'd been known to go three weeks without setting foot in it. But his dad always wanted to meet there, seeing it as a tangible sign of his older son's success. According to Marty, he never asked to visit the police station or city hall. It still amazed Ethan that a man who could adopt and unconditionally love a boy from another race had no problem making his love *entirely* conditional once Marty came out as gay.

Ethan tapped the touch pad, and his laptop screen came to life. His browser's home page, as always, was *The Lady of the Lakes* blog. No one else in Madison knew more about what occurred on the isthmus than the man, woman, or group who anonymously ran this Web site. The real journalists hated it, even though they all referenced it; his reporter ex-girlfriend, Julie, swore like a sailor whenever its name came up.

Sure enough, there was the post about the girl's disappearance, put online at 3:35 A.M. But the post was vague and didn't even mention the girl's name. He supposed the reference to the Celtic knot tattoo told the police it was the same girl, but those were now as common a fashion accessory as flannel shirts in the early nineties.

He scrolled down to the readers' comments posted at the end. As always, someone claimed a conspiracy—in this case, a drive by the religious right to punish women who dared to step outside society's preconceived roles. Others berated the police for not stopping the serial rapist or murderer clearly at work. Still others blamed the girls themselves for being *provocative* and *dressing like Tijuana whores.* When he got to the guy from Poland, Wisconsin, who blamed aliens, he smiled and switched over to his e-mail account.

Within moments, lost in the minutiae of correspondence, he'd forgotten all about the vanished girl. Not that he didn't feel sympathy, but his own world was busy enough. Except for the dumb luck of having the bad guy leave evidence at his work site, the crimes ultimately didn't affect him. Men like Marty were paid to worry about strangers. Ethan's job was to build homes for them.

Almost as soon as he'd put the whiskey away and closed the drawer, his desk phone buzzed. "Your father's here," his secretary, Ambika, said in her lilting Hindi accent, then added, "He has an appointment."

Ethan popped a breath mint, stood, and waited as the door opened. The man who entered the office was small and wiry, with a head that seemed too large for his body. The overalls and John Deere cap added to the effect. Ethan recalled how large his father had seemed when he and Marty were children, before the heart attack, before the cancer and chemotherapy. Still, the old man stood tall, and his hand didn't tremble when he extended it. "Son," he said almost formally.

"Dad," Ethan replied, shaking the frail hand. "Sit down. How was traffic?"

"They've got University Avenue all torn up to build something. And I nearly ran over a kid with some kind of radio in his ear, one of those seed-pod things."

"They're called iPods."

"They go in your *eye*?"

"It's just a name, Dad. Want me to have Ambika rustle you up a cup of coffee?"

"No, thanks." The man ran his sun-browned, age-spotted hand along the chair back as if brushing away the residue of the last person to use it. Then he sat, easing himself down with both hands on the chair's arms.

Ethan knew better than to mention his father's evident pain. Walker men didn't hurt in public. "What brings you to town, Dad?"

"Well, hadn't seen my boys in a while..." He trailed off and looked out the window. After a moment he said, "How is Marty, by the way? You see him much?"

"Saw him this morning. He looked good. Said to tell you hello."

His father looked down. "He's a good man, I suppose, for what he is. So are you, son. You both do me proud."

It took everything Ethan had not to rankle at this little tap dance of feigned interest and approval. His father's heart had closed with an echoing *bang* when Marty came out to him, and nothing seemed likely to reopen it. And whatever he truly felt for Ethan he kept just as secret these days. "Thank you, Dad. So how's the farm?"

"Not too good, not too good. Production's down, and some of the cows have been sick. Had to let the Lopez brothers go. I couldn't afford to pay 'em anymore."

Ethan knew this scene by heart. "Well, let me help you out, Dad. Things have been pretty good for me lately. How much do you need to get them back to work?" It didn't matter that his two years in Iraq had left the company in such desperate financial straits that he barely had enough money to make his next payroll without liquidating some investments. He knew his part required him to be the successful, upright, heterosexual son who made good. It was a nonnegotiable clause in their parent–child contract, and it would terminate only with the old man's death.

His father had his role down pat too. He raised one hand in weak, token protest. "Oh, son, I couldn't ask that."

"Dad, it's the least I can do." He reached for the ledger he'd put out on his desk when he saw his father's name on the day's appointment list and tore out the check he'd already made out and signed. "Family helps each other out, right?"

MARTY WALKER SAT at the counter in Rachel's diner and watched the owner as she gracefully placed a plate of pancakes in front of a black man with dreadlocks, then twirled almost like a dancer to retrieve the carafe and fill a blond girl's cup. The breakfast crowd had thinned down to half a dozen people, and the atmosphere was relaxed and casual. Light rock trilled from the CD player.

Marty shook his head. Rachel was a beauty, all right, all the more so because she had no idea of it. And, even more than that, she was a beautiful woman in a college town full of beautiful *girls*. If his idiot brother couldn't see it, then he deserved to die as the lonely, bitter old man he was on his way to becoming, just like their father.

Rachel topped off Marty's cup. "Good morning, Detective Walker."

"Hey, Rachel. Sorry for tracking up your floor."

"How'd you get so muddy?"

"Crime scene. Another girl disappeared."

"I read about that on *The Lady of the Lakes* this morning," Helena volunteered as she joined them. "Was it like the other two?"

"Yeah. I hope you and Rachel are being careful."

"Neither of us are young, sexy college girls," Rachel said with forced glibness. "We're off the killer's radar."

"Speak for yourself, straight woman," Helena said playfully.

"First, we don't know it's a 'killer,' we only know it's an abductor," Marty said. "Second, we don't know what connection the girls have, or even if there is one. The M.O. is identical, but that's all we've got. He might be choosing them in advance, or he might be going after random women who cross his path. So right now we want *everyone* to be careful." He shook his head. "And I'd dearly love to find out how that goddamn blogger knew about it so fast."

"You know, we needed you in here this morning," Rachel said. "I almost had a cockfight break out, and I don't mean the kind with roosters."

"Oh, yeah? What happened?"

"You know Caleb Johnstone, that ex-Marine who's always talking about how he 'fought for' this, 'fought for' that? He came in and insisted on smoking even though I asked him not to. I was going to throw him out, but one of the other customers decided I was a damsel in distress and tried to joust for my honor. I'm surprised you can't still smell the burning testosterone."

Marty smiled. "Did your knight wear blue button-down armor and khaki pants?"

"Yeah," Rachel said guardedly.

"That's my brother, Ethan."

She scowled in disbelief. "He wasn't Asian."

Marty, mock-offended, said, "Who are you calling Asian? Anyway, it's my fault. I've been telling him about the food here forever, so I guess he decided to finally try it. Did they really get in a fight?"

"No, just a pissing contest. Caleb left, and I asked your brother to leave too. I don't need two ex-soldiers seeing who has the biggest Rambo over something as silly as a cigarette."

Marty's eyes opened wide. "Ethan told you about Iraq?"

"Yes. Well, not exactly. He mentioned it to Caleb, and I was standing there. Why?"

"Ethan doesn't talk about it. Ever."

"Why not?"

"Something happened. He had to go to Washington and testify right after he finished his tour. He never said why. Now he doesn't even tell people he was a soldier."

"He didn't seem shy about it this morning," Rachel said.

"Huh." Marty finished his coffee. "I have to go. Paperwork calls. Listen, ladies, seriously: Watch yourselves. Tell everyone who comes in to do the same. We don't know how this guy picks his victims or what he does with them, but it's doubtful it's for a picnic. Okay?"

"Sure," Rachel said seriously. As he opened the door she called out, "Hey, Marty?"

He paused.

"Tell your brother—Ethan, right?—tell Ethan, um . . . maybe I was a little harsh. If he'd like to come back, the first cup of coffee's on the house."

Marty grinned. "I'll pass that on."

Helena took off her apron and said, "Rach, I've got to run out to my car before the lunch rush."

"If you're heading out, I'll walk you," Marty offered.

"Thanks," she said, and preceded him out the door. When they were out of sight around the corner of the building, Marty said, "So it didn't go too well this morning?"

"Ha! That's an understatement. Didn't you tell your brother that Rachel *hates* big macho types? He came on like Rambo and Schwarzenegger combined." She scratched at a spot just beneath the waistband of her pants.

"I didn't tell him anything, except that the food here was good. If he thought I was trying to fix him up with a girl, he'd run me over with one of his bulldozers." Marty pointed his key chain at the distinctive unmarked sedan, and the doors unlocked with a loud *thunk*. "What did you tell Rachel?"

"Nothing," she said with a guilty little smile. "If I had, I'd have been the new ingredient in the omelets." Wincing, she scratched again.

Marty frowned. "Do I *want* to know why you keep scratching down there?"

"It's a new tat, smart-ass. I don't think the guy used clean needles. It's been itching ever since I got it."

"Where did you go?"

"A new franchise place. I got my other ones at Korbus Inks, down by the thrift store, but he went out of business."

"Conventional wisdom says if it's itching, it's healing."

"Conventional wisdom says Rachel and Ethan would make an awesome couple too."

Marty laughed. "We're terrible matchmakers, aren't we? Maybe a fag cop and a dyke waitress shouldn't try to fix up straight people."

She slipped her arm through his and kissed his cheek. "I think we set our goals too high. We have to work up to Rachel and Ethan. Maybe we should start with something easier, like Ann Coulter and Michael Moore."

"Well, Rachel said to send him back, so I will. I may have to Taser him to get him to cooperate, but I'll do it." He climbed into the car and buzzed down the power window before closing the door. "*Your* job is to make sure she's in a good mood."

"Honey, God Himself would have a hard time guaranteeing that."

As the afternoon sun baked Madison, the basement door opened and a harsh rectangle of light shone in on the three captive girls. They huddled together in a dark corner, gagged with duct tape, their wrists bound in plastic ties in front of them. They were still clad only in their panties. All were dirty and sweaty, since the basement had no air circulation and the day was sweltering, but they were otherwise unharmed. Ling Hu moaned with fright at the silhouette in the doorway, while Faith Lucas, her athletic body gleaming with sweat, looked numb. The newest girl, Carrie Kimmell, just stared, tears in her eyes.

"You know the rules," their captor said. "If you try to escape, try to undo the handcuffs or make any sound, you'll suffer for it. Now take the tape off your mouth."

Faith pulled hers off quickly, while Carrie slowly peeled hers away. Ling Hu scratched at hers, whimpering, but was unable to get it loose. The trauma of the past few days had left her weak in every sense, and her breath came in harsh, panicky gasps. Blood smeared her bare skin. She began to wheeze until Faith reached up and pulled the tape away.

Plastic bottles rolled across the concrete floor. "You each get one bottle of water. When I come back, they better be finished. If they're not, you won't get any tomorrow at all."

The heat had made the girls ravenously thirsty, and they tore the caps from the bottles, neither noticing nor caring that the safety seals were already broken. Their captor knew the ground-up sleeping pills in the water would shortly have them all unconscious. Then he would carry Ling Hu upstairs to continue her transformation. Already he trembled with eagerness at the thought of touching her again.

Faith looked up from her bottle. Her blond hair, shiny and shimmering in all her pictures, was now matted and plastered to her skull. "Please," she croaked, her voice ragged from alternating disuse and futile screaming. "Can we have something to eat too? It's been days, and we're starving." She looked down, afraid to make eye contact.

The others, too cowed to even speak, clutched their bottles and waited for their captor's response.

He left without any answer. And through the closed door, he heard one of them begin to cry.

OUTSIDE THE BASEMENT door, their captor idly mused over the situation. Keeping them weak from hunger and dazed with sedatives made them much easier to control, but perhaps some saltines or croutons wouldn't hurt next time.

He was almost giddy with his sense of power. His plan had started as a whim, a response to an undeserved slight, but now it seemed to be almost divinely guided. The night he grabbed Ling Hu, he'd taken her to the Arboretum intending simply to kill her. Having her undress had been a spur-of-the-moment idea, but once he saw her naked he realized there was a much better form of revenge. He'd left her clothes behind accidentally, not even realizing it until he was halfway home. Then, reading the paper, he learned that the abandoned clothes were inadvertently brilliant, because the cops couldn't make heads or tails of his motives.

Once he'd secured Ling Hu in the basement, he dug through his records and made a list of eleven others he would, in a perfect world, also like to encounter. He'd done some research online and discovered that only four of them were still in Madison. Still, five vengeances were better than none, especially given his limited time.

He stalked Faith Lucas mostly as an experiment, certain another abduction could not be as simple as the first. Yet it had been. And so had the third. At that point he modified his approach, to create even more confusion. Now he snatched his victims in one spot, undressed them in another, and dumped their clothes in a third. He'd carried all three girls away so the police would find two sets of tracks going down, but only one back up. It was unwieldy, and by all rights he should've been caught long ago, but it continued to work. He'd even tipped the cops off to the clothes left at the construction site. Maybe for the last victims he'd leave their garments where he kidnapped them, just to add even more confusion.

He'd considered stopping at those three, but then by sheer luck he'd crossed paths with yet another of his marked women, at that diner where the two men almost came to blows over a cigarette. He took that as a sign, as if God Himself was encouraging him to keep going. With a growing euphoria, he realized that he might very well be able to acquire all *five* of those still in the city. And when they were all neatly arranged in the basement, all looking up with tied hands, bare bodies, and terrified eyes, then the work they'd interrupted could finally be finished.

CHAPTER SIX

A T **THREE-THIRTY** that afternoon, Rachel sagged against the inside of her apartment door. Another day down. Open at seven, close at three. Pray that Denny's wasn't running a special. The life of an independent businesswoman was never dull.

On the couch, her cat, Tainter, yawned and stretched until his claws skitched on the fabric. Then he trotted over and twined around her ankles. "Hey, you," she murmured as she bent to pet him.

She had four rooms above her diner, with hardwood floors, big windows, and a twelve-foot ceiling. Her furniture was thrift-shop eclectic, each piece having some innate quality that intrigued or amused her. Helena claimed her decor looked like somebody's dorm room, but Rachel didn't care. She had no one to impress but herself, and, from the look of her nonexistent social calendar, that wasn't likely to change. Besides, *why* would she date? The lakes gave her everything she needed from a man, and no man could give her what the lakes did.

Tainter returned to his spot on the couch. She kicked off her tennis shoes without untying them and pulled off her socks with her toes. She was greasy from work, and her lower back ached. She stripped off her tank top and bra and stepped out of her shorts. She started the water in the tub and, while it warmed up, went into the kitchen and poured a glass of wine. As she sipped her wine, she held the cold bottle first against her forehead, then her bare belly. It made goose bumps around the tattoo beneath her navel.

She returned to the bathroom, lit three big aroma-therapy candles, and sank into the bath. She worked her neck until it cracked softly. Then she put the wineglass on the floor and washed off the residue of sweat and cooking oil she always seemed to accumulate.

When she was done, she stepped onto the battered rug and toweled off. Her reflection in the mirror was hazy from the steam, and she smiled wryly, recalling the way middle-aged movie stars used soft-focus filters to hide their wrinkles.

Then she wiped the glass and saw herself clearly. Maybe too clearly. She had the sharp features of her father, with her mother's soulful eyes and ridiculously full lips. Her neck was still smooth and unlined, and her breasts remained firm enough to pass the old high school "pencil test." But there were crinkles, faint but discernible, at the corners of her eyes, and more and more her joints reminded her that she was no longer a lithe young girl.

But she could still run six miles without feeling winded, and she recalled every song, in order, from the first seven

Heart albums. And she could still draw the eye of handsome young men when she passed them on the street....

A rush of physical desire hit her, and her knees wobbled. The image of Marty Walker's brother—his dark hair falling boyishly on his forehead, his muscular arms straining the material of his blue shirt, his apparently effortless moral strength when faced with Caleb's assholeness, and, yes, dammit, the way his butt looked in his khakis—once again filled her senses and ignited her lust in a way she'd never experienced. She knew he was probably an overly macho bully, potentially as big an asshole as Caleb, but she also vividly imagined his weight atop her, her legs around his narrow waist, her hands clutching at his broad shoulders. She could almost hear herself moaning, *Ethan...oh, Ethan...* She grew wet and tingly at the thought.

She leaned on the sink and splashed cold water on her face. "Oh, for God's sake," she told her reflection. "Get a goddamn *grip*." Her neck and shoulders had flushed red, and her nipples stood out tight and hard. She took several deep breaths, then went to refill her wineglass. Before she opened the refrigerator, she scrawled words on a Post-it note and slapped it on the front of her cell phone. The warning to herself said, *Don't call anyone just because you're horny.*

THE NUMBERS ON the laptop computer screen told Ethan what he wanted to know. Now he really *was* depressed, and not even *The Lady of the Lakes* could cheer him up; the blog hadn't been updated since that morning. No juicy town gossip, no reports on local crime or university debauchery. No rants against the religious right or Republicans.

He sat back in his chair and kicked off his shoes. The late-afternoon sun streamed through the blinds, casting bright auburn bars across his living-room walls. He opened a new browser window and checked his investments but found no joy there either; nothing in his portfolio had miraculously doubled or tripled in value. He was in a bind, all right, and would be until this condominium project was finished. And with Marty's police pals swarming all over it, that might not happen this year at all.

And then there was that damn woman at the diner. Rachel of Rachel's.

He shook his head and made a frustrated sound in his throat. If the events of *any* day could keep his mind off some girl, it should be this one. But no matter what, he kept flashing back to that moment where she stood in the window, hands on her hips, her face hazy and inscrutable. It was way too easy to imagine that same expression on her face in his bedroom, with her clothes crumpled at her feet.

He paced to the patio doors and looked out at his backyard. A half acre of smooth lawn, with a dozen trees for shade, stretched to the privacy fence. The grass was slowly consuming the bare spot of earth beneath the basketball goal, as he'd been far too busy in the eight months he'd been back to shoot hoops with Marty and Chuck. If these delays kept up, though, he might actually have time to reclaim his high school jump shot.

He dropped onto the couch, turned on the TV, and surfed the channels without really seeing them. Instead, he was still thinking about the way Rachel looked in her tight shorts, her eyes crinkled with annoyance and those delectable lips twisted in a scowl. And once again he adjusted an unwanted, and uncomfortably intense, erection.

HER PHONE RANG just as Rachel attached the self-warning note to it, and she was so startled she dropped it. It hit the hardwood floor and skittered under the microwave stand. Annoyed, she dropped to her knees, retrieved it, snapped it open, and snarled, "Hello?"

There was a long pause, and Rachel was afraid she'd missed the call, but finally a familiar voice said accusingly, "Do I need to block caller ID now so you won't know it's me?"

"What? Oh. Hi, Becky. What's up?"

"Just calling to talk to my big sister, not get my head snapped off."

"Christ, Becky, I just dropped the phone, that's all." Rachel poured another glass of wine, then took an extra swig from the bottle.

"Yeah. Well, okay, let's get this over with. How are you?"

"I'm tired, and my back hurts, and I'm not sure I

can pay the electric bill for the diner this month. How are you?"

"Don't pretend you care."

"I do care, Rebecca. What do you want me to say?"

"Nothing. Your life is so much more important than mine, after all. *I'm* only trying to stop animal cruelty at the university labs; *your* omelets and hamburgers are much more—"

"Rebecca!" Rachel snapped, then took a deep breath. More calmly, she continued, "Becky, I'll be glad to talk to you about anything you want, but we've been having this discussion for ten years. I just got out of the bath and I'm dripping all over the floor, so if you're just calling to debate lifestyles—"

"Terrell and I broke up," her sister blurted.

"Oh, baby, I'm sorry," Rachel said sympathetically. She was used to sudden gear shifts when talking to her sister.

"Yeah, well, I just wanted you to know." Becky's phone snapped off.

Rachel looked down at her own phone, then across the room at the picture of the two Matre girls on her coffee table. They were twelve and fourteen then, both with frizzy hair and enormous smiles. It was taken about a month before Rachel first drowned and was the last time they'd both been completely happy at the same time.

She recalled Terrell, the latest boyfriend, no doubt chased away by Becky's mercurial temperament. He was a teaching assistant at the college, neat and well behaved, and had no doubt fallen under the spell of Becky's passionate beliefs. She certainly *talked* a good game, as her string of sensible, levelheaded boyfriends illustrated. But once they saw past the words to the chaos, they always ran. If they were smart. Terrell, evidently, was smart.

Rachel went to the small window over the kitchen sink and looked out at Williams Street. The sun flickered through the trees shading the parking lot. Becky was on her way to a life of total bitterness as she moved from one lost cause to another, both political and romantic, and no one, especially Rachel, could steer her away. That certainty always made Rachel sad.

Something drew her eye to a truck parked at the curb across the street. She could see only the bed and tailgate through the branches, but it sent a shiver up her spine nonetheless, and she reflexively covered herself and shrank from the window.

When she looked again it was still there, exhaust coming from the tailpipe. It was a burgundy Ford, rusted around the wheel wells, but she could not see if anyone sat inside. Yet she felt that someone *was* there and that this person was somehow dangerous to her. Her first thought was Caleb, but he drove an ancient Toyota hatchback; at least, he used to. She was about to call the police (*And report what?* her common sense demanded. *A mad parker on the loose?*), but the truck abruptly drove away. She felt a rush of relief far out of proportion to what she'd seen.

She scurried back to the bathroom, took her red terrycloth robe from its hook, and cinched it around herself.

There was only one thing to do now, one way to overcome this sudden panic and feel like she had some control of the world. She locked and bolted her front door, made sure all the blinds were drawn, then went to her bedroom closet for her laptop.

THE PHONE RANG. Ethan snatched it from the coffee table and snapped it open. "Hello?"

"So how much did Dad hit you up for this time?" Marty asked with no preliminaries.

Ethan, in a T-shirt and boxers, shook his head to clear it before answering. His normal after-dinner beer had become an uncharacteristic five, and he always slurred his words when he drank. "Five thousand," he said with perfect enunciation. "Same as last month."

"Damn, do you really have that kind of money to just give away?"

"Hell, no. And I sure won't if you guys don't stop tying up my work site."

"It's a crime scene, Ethan."

"Yeah. Maybe someday I'll come tear down the police station so I can interfere with *your* job."

"Oh, *that's* mature."

"I know you are, but what am I?"

"I'm rubber, you're glue."

Both men burst out laughing. When the moment passed, Marty said, "I also hear you were quite the manly-man this morning."

"Huh?"

"At Rachel's diner on Williams Street? You bravely stood up to some old guy with a cigarette."

"How the hell do you know about that?"

"It's all over *Lady of the Lakes: Local builder shows ass.*"

He looked at his closed laptop and suddenly felt very sober. "Bullshit."

Marty laughed. "No, seriously, I talked to Rachel this afternoon."

Ethan felt the kind of relief that comes only when you've had more drinks than you're used to. "Oh. Well, she's not very grateful."

"No, she's not very easily impressed. There's a difference."

"I wasn't trying to *impress* her, Marty. The guy was a jackass, and until somebody stood up to him, he was going to keep on being one."

"And that had to be you."

The amusement in Marty's voice made Ethan genuinely angry. "*Yes,* it had to be me. If I have to hear one more self-pitying soldier whine about how the world should kiss his ass because he did a job he volunteered for and was fucking *trained* to do, I'll—"

"Whoa, calm down. I wasn't questioning your patriotism, Mr. America. I just thought you'd use more charm on a girl as pretty as Rachel."

"She's not a 'girl,'" Ethan snapped, surprised at how defensive he sounded. "And what would you know about pretty girls, anyway?"

"A man who drives a truck can still admire a beautiful car, can't he?"

Ethan barked out a laugh. "My God, *that's* the best analogy you've got?"

"I'm winging it. But she *is* a beautiful woman, Ethan. And she runs her own business, and she's smart, and—"

"*Wait* a minute. You were trying to fix me up with her, weren't you?"

"Me? Hell, no."

"Yes, you were. 'Oh, you have to try the food, it's not like it was when Trudy ran the place.' I warned you about that after you set me up with that accountant. She had five ferrets, Marty. *Five.*"

"I'm just leading you to the water, Ethan. You'll have to decide if you want to drink."

"I'm not very thirsty these days. Julie did a good job of almost drowning me. I think it'll hold me for a while."

"Uh-huh. What happened with Julie was as much your fault as hers, you know."

Ethan closed his eyes and rubbed the bridge of his nose. The air suddenly rang with the echoes of Julie's final tirade. *You can't just keep everything inside, Ethan. It's eating you alive! I don't know what happened to you in Iraq, but you're home now and you've got to deal with this. You won't be yourself until you do, and you won't be worth spit to the next woman idiotic enough to date you!* "Okay, Marty, I've had enough to drink that I can tell you to fuck off with a clear conscience. So screw you."

"You wouldn't like it, I'd just lie there."

Ethan laughed as he snapped his phone shut. Marty

never cut him any slack or let him hide behind excuses. It was why they were true brothers, whatever their genetic differences.

And now, thanks to his brother, Ethan's slightly tipsy brain once again filled with images of Rachel Matre.

CHAPTER SEVEN

Females of the isthmus, the cops won't tell you this, because they probably haven't noticed, but watch out for a dark-red Ford pickup that might be lingering just a little too long in your area. I'm not saying there's any connection to the girls who have disappeared, but it's the same part of town, and it's creepy. So watch your asses, because I'm pretty sure he is.

Until next time...

In the work shed behind his house, the man thumbtacked the image of a naked woman to the plywood wall. It was a large photo, in color, and the woman was arched and positioned to display herself to the most carnal advantage. Every potential flaw had been airbrushed away, except for the page folds creased across her breasts and thighs.

The man stepped back to the opposite wall and picked up one of the short, heavy throwing knives he'd lined up on the worktable. He held it by the tip of the blade and flipped it so that the handle smacked his palm. Then he again grasped the tip and drew back his arm.

The first knife struck the unnaturally clean-shaven spot between her legs. The next two impaled her breasts, and the fourth stuck into the carefully airbrushed bridge of her nose. "Take that, you bitch," the angry man muttered as the fleeting satisfaction faded almost at once. "That's what you all deserve."

He wrenched the knives free, tore down the centerfold, and replaced it with another one.

RACHEL KICKED OFF the covers and sighed loudly. Tainter trilled in response and raised his head but did not move from his spot beside the bed. Shadows from the miniblinds drifted across the ceiling as a car passed on the street, trailing the bass thump that so many young men used to compensate for other inadequacies. She pressed her hands and heels into the mattress, stretching the muscles and tendons to dissipate some of the twitchy, persistent energy. She took several deep breaths and licked her lips, tasting salt from sweat that had nothing to do with the summer night. The clock beside her bed informed her, in huge red numbers, that it was 2:30 A.M.

Not even her usual routine had diminished the effects of her overripe imagination. Hours later, she still suffocated in a swelter of physical desire. Her nipples were tight beneath her sleep shirt, and her panties damp. She sprawled with her legs thrown apart, her toes flexing in the dark. The ceiling fan hummed above her, stirring the air but doing nothing to cool her down. She could not remember a time when she'd been so infuriatingly, inexplicably horny.

She stared at the turning blades and slid one hand inside her panties. Both fabric and flesh were moist. She could not get the image of Ethan Walker out of her mind, only now it wasn't the way he'd looked back at the diner. In her imagination he lay atop her, his muscular body as naked and sweaty as her own. His weight pressed on her, and his erection filled her. She could feel him swell with nearness, hear the ragged catch in his quickening breath. She spread herself wide for him, ankles crossing at the small of his back, as his lips closed over hers and his tongue claimed her mouth. *Yes . . . let it go, give it to me, yes . . .*

No! She sat up, wiped her hand on the sheet, and rolled onto her side, clutching her pillow. She thought of menus, limericks, grease traps, and cat food. Anything but Ethan Walker.

But her resistance lasted all of thirty seconds. Now in her mind it was earlier in the encounter, before the surrender and conquest. He was sucking her nipples, his teeth closing around them and tugging, his tongue flicking over the tips. His hands, big and rough, ran possessively over her skin, and she moaned in her fantasy as she begged for him to take her, pleaded with him, arched her back and raised her hips to allow him to reach her.

She was moaning in reality now, almost pitifully, her

fingers once again probing in place of what she so desperately wanted. Her other hand slid under her nightshirt to cup her breast, her own small palm a poor substitute for the broader hand she imagined. He wouldn't be tentative, he'd crush her soft flesh, knead it, pinch and caress it. He would own every part of her.

Whining low in her throat, she flopped onto her back and tossed her head on her pillow. There could be no release, she knew, and that infuriated her the most. Only the lakes could bring her to ecstasy. For a moment she wondered if they were somehow behind this, using their magic or mind-control powers on her to magnify her natural attraction to this unnatural level. But for what purpose? She could go down to the lake and ask, but she doubted her legs could carry her across the room right now, let alone down the street to the park.

She rolled onto her stomach, again hugged her pillow, and pressed her hips down into the mattress. She imagined Ethan on top of her this way, one hand pinning the back of her neck, the other guiding himself into her from behind. She hated that position with a man, hated the subservience of it, but now she could think only of his hardness splitting her in two. She bucked her hips helplessly as the fantasy, more real than some actual encounters she'd had, slowly drove her mad.

IN HIS BEDROOM, Ethan also lay wide awake and stared at the pink glow from the security light outside. It illuminated a rectangular section of his ceiling and cast its faint light over everything in his bedroom. He had his fingers linked behind his neck and took slow, deep breaths. Even though it was a cliché, he truly did try thinking about baseball. It didn't help.

He couldn't recall being so rock-hard since he'd been a teenage virgin. Since his return from Iraq he'd been prone to arousal at the most inopportune times, only to have his libido fail him when he needed it most. Now his erection poked from the fly of his boxers, and he could even feel the slight breeze from the air conditioner on it. For the first time he understood those warnings on TV commercials for Viagra and Cialis: Four hours of this and he'd be rushing to the emergency room too. Yet he knew that it would fade at once as the unwanted memory of what he'd seen returned, as vivid and awful as ever.

Still, at the moment his imagination worked overtime to conjure the image of Rachel astride him, her knees on either side of his chest. She would slide her hips toward his face, and he would eagerly set about licking, kissing, and nibbling her offered intimacy. *That,* at least, he could still do. He wondered if, like Julie, she'd be clean-shaven; in his fantasy she wasn't, and the gentle curls, softened by his kisses and her own juices, would press against his face, filling him with her scent and taste.

He imagined lifting her, rolling her gently onto her back, trailing musk-scented kisses down her belly until he returned to her wettest place. He would look up the length of her body as he used his tongue on her, licking her with light, slow strokes. Through the valley between her breasts he would see her face, lips swollen with desire, and he could almost hear the sounds she'd make.

He stroked himself and moaned.

RACHEL WALKED INTO the bathroom, her calf muscles shaking. Tainter, disturbed by her mood, softly yowled his concern. She envied the cat his neutered placidity.

She winced against the light, pulled off her nightshirt, and splashed cold water on her face. In the mirror the signs of her discomfort were plain. The red flush across her shoulders had spread to the tops of her breasts, and her expression was fixed in a kind of faint, perpetual desperation. She opened the shower curtain, turned on the cold water, slipped her panties down, and stepped into the spray. She shouted as the stinging droplets pounded her skin.

The icy water cleared some of the overheated fog from her brain. She was not going to give in to this and let her stupid hormones dictate to her in the middle of the night. She would *not* get dressed and go all the way down to the lake just to exorcise this man's image, even though she knew she was primed for an orgasm that would rattle her teeth. She wanted to know she could wait it out, that she was stronger than her hormones' demands. She could handle this alone.

Or not. She could always call someone. Just another physical presence, a body to rub against and explore, might ease some of the tension. Men were always giving her their numbers, often written on the bottom of their credit-card receipts. Some of them were even nice guys. Sure, it was the middle of the night, but she doubted if a man got a call from a willing woman he'd hesitate.

She took deep, calming breaths and let the icy water pummel her aching flesh. "No," she said aloud. She would endure it. It was just sex, after all. People lived without it all the time. And somehow she knew that any man other than Ethan Walker would just add to her frustration.

ETHAN'S HAND WAS a blur in the darkness. Then he stopped, gasped, and resumed stroking with slow, firm movements. A moment later he ejaculated copiously onto his bare stomach and let out a soft, deep sigh of relief.

He'd imagined Rachel astride him, accepting him into her wet, open body with her own loud cry of release. He could almost see her silhouetted against the ceiling, back arched so that her breasts jutted out.

He ran his other hand through his hair. He had no moral problem with masturbation; hell, lately it had been his only outlet. But somehow this felt different. No porn was involved, no fantasy of some untouchable young starlet *du jour*. The woman who'd inspired this voluminous release was very touchable and easily found. Of course, she also despised the sight of him, which made him feel both foolish and, oddly, sad. Would he ever be able to have normal, clean, healthy sex with a woman?

After a few moments he went to the bathroom to wash up. He smiled wryly at the red blotches across his neck and shoulders. He washed his belly, then his hands, and fell back across the bed with a loud sigh of relief. He was asleep in moments. But even though his physical need was momentarily sated, Rachel now filled his dreams. They weren't dreams about sex, though. In them, he lay in her arms and felt safe enough to release the things lurking deep behind the wall he'd built in his own heart. He dreamed of the compassion and tenderness he somehow knew, even though he'd spent less than fifteen minutes in her presence, he'd find with her.

CHAPTER EIGHT

"CARRIE KIMMEL, *age nineteen, of Belson Street in Madison, is five feet three inches tall, weighs 125 pounds, and has brown hair,*" Jimmy read aloud. The flyer showed two photos of the girl, one a high school graduation shot, the other a more recent candid taken at a party. In both she smiled, although in the latter her eyes were red and heavy-lidded and she clutched a plastic beer cup. "*She was last seen in her apartment-building laundry room around midnight on June twenty-third. If you have any information, contact the police,* etcetera." He turned to Rachel, who was also a little red-eyed. "Put 'em in the window and the bathrooms?"

Rachel nodded, stifling a yawn. She had finally drifted off at about four, and her alarm woke her at four-thirty. She was edgy, tense, and semiconscious. Now, at the tail end of the breakfast rush, she seriously contemplated going upstairs for a nap. She couldn't imagine making it through lunch this weary. "Next to the others," she said, indicating the two similar flyers already displayed along the front glass.

"Thanks for putting them up, Rachel," said Alice, a student feminist and weekend regular. She had short, mannish hair, the face of a cherub, and a bundle of identical flyers under her arm.

"Did you know her?" Rachel asked.

Alice shook her head. "No."

"My God, how many more will there be?" Mrs. Boswell said. She'd finished her breakfast an hour ago, but as always she liked to sip her tea and observe the other patrons. Her straw gardening hat rested on the empty stool beside her. Rachel had inherited her from Trudy and accepted her as part of the decor.

"Madison used to be a safe place," said Casey, a graduate student studying sculpture. He tossed his long bangs, cultivated like a fringe of ornamental grass, from his eyes. "Safest downtown in the country once. That's why I wanted to come to school here."

"It's still safe for you," Alice said, her voice tense with practiced outrage. "You're a man."

Before the usual gender conflict could develop, Professor Dunning said, "Isn't that a little odd? I mean, I'm no expert, but don't they usually go after boys and young men?"

" 'They'?" Helena repeated.

"Serial killers. Wisconsin's second-largest export after cheese. Remember Ed Gein?"

"And Jeffrey Dahmer," Jimmy called from the kitchen.

"How about David Spanbauer in Winneconne?" Casey said.

"No, he was into girls," Alice said. "I did a research paper on him."

"Well, what about that guy in La Crosse?" Casey said. "He keeps throwing drunk young men into the Mississippi."

"Drunks don't need any help falling in the river," Helena said.

"I read about that one," uniformed patrol cop Alonzo Hyland said. "The FBI says there's no connection between the deaths and they were all alcohol-related accidents."

"The FBI said John Lennon was a threat to national security too," Mrs. Boswell said.

"I think it's weird that so far no one's found any of these girls' bodies," Jimmy said from the kitchen entrance. "Do you think he's butchering them and eating them, like Dahmer?"

The patrons who still had breakfast in front of them exclaimed various forms of outrage. Professor Dunning added, "Jimmy, people are trying to *eat* here."

"Okay, okay, sorry," Jimmy said. He skulked back to the griddle and stirred the potatoes just before they began to burn. "I'm a concerned citizen, you know. I mean, I have friends who are girls."

"Has anyone seen that truck around?" Helena asked.

"What truck?" Casey said.

"The one they talked about on *The Lady of the Lakes.* A red Ford, I think."

"I see a dozen red Ford trucks every day," Hyland said. "By the time we tracked them all down, the killer would be dead of old age."

Rachel shook her head. "Really, people, you put way too much stock in that blog thing. It's the Internet. You can write anything you want, whether it's true or not."

"But she's usually right," Alonzo admitted. "I hear even the chief checks it twice a day. And I know of at least one domestic-violence conviction that came directly from a tip she wrote on it."

Rachel knew of that conviction too. It had been a simple thing to spot the black eye on the woman's face as she put the local paper into the rack, while her glowering husband waited in their newspaper-stuffed station wagon. It looked like a prescient tip because, by the time the police acted, he'd beaten her even more severely, which both she and he claimed was the first time he'd ever hit her. But it was just unobtrusive observation, something at which Rachel excelled. No lake spirits required.

"How do you even know it's a 'she'?" Rachel said. "Or even one person?"

"She writes like a woman," Helena said with certainty. "You've read it, haven't you?"

"Me? You know I don't even have a computer."

Exclamations of disbelief and amazement rang out. "No, I'm serious," Rachel insisted.

"She is," Helena agreed with exaggerated sadness.

"But you put wireless in the building," Dunning pointed out, indicating the modems on the ceiling.

"I did that for the customers," Rachel said. Would-be

poet Elton Charles looked up from his laptop at a corner table and raised his coffee cup in salute. She added, "Me, I prefer good old-fashioned newspapers. Even one like *this* rag." She gestured at the *Wisconsin Capital Journal,* left abandoned on the counter.

The bell over the door announced a new customer. A tall blond woman dressed in a skirt and light summer blouse entered. A single line of pearls circled her neck, providing an odd, matronly touch to her otherwise toned, just-touching-thirty appearance. She took in the long diner counter, the smattering of tables, and the elaborate graffiti on the walls.

"Just sit anywhere," Helena called. "I'll be right with you. The menu's beside the napkins. Would you like some coffee?"

"Yes, please," the woman said. She took a seat at the end of the counter. Carefully, she placed her shoulder bag on the floor, reached inside, and pulled out a pen and a distinctive small notebook.

"Excuse me," the newcomer said loudly. When everyone turned her way she continued, "I'm Julie Schutes, of the *Capital Journal.* I wonder if I might get some comments from you regarding the recent disappearances of young women in this area. The local, street-level response, if you will." She looked up expectantly, pen poised.

Everyone else turned as a group to see Rachel's reaction.

Speak of the devil. Rachel scrutinized Julie. The journalist had big blue eyes and dramatic blond hair that swept back from her face, emphasizing her strong Nordic features. The skirt revealed tanned, enviable legs. Rachel already hated her on these general principles, but she also recognized the name. "Julie Schutes," she repeated. "I think I've read your work. Didn't you write that series on the dangers of pornography about six months ago?"

Julie smiled the way people do when they're recognized for an accomplishment. "Why, yes, I did," she said with a polite nod. "And you are...?"

"I thought so," Rachel continued, ignoring the question. In her sleep-deprived state, her temper was far too close to the surface. "That would be the one with the huge color photo of the big-busted girl in the barely there bikini standing in the middle of State Street with the crowd of smiling frat boys around her?"

Julie's smile remained, but all the juice left it. "I didn't pick the photo or do the layout, I'm afraid."

"I remember that," Professor Dunning said. "That was crass and insulting, even for the *Cap Jo.*"

"I'd call it a lot worse," Alice said, glad for a legitimate opportunity to display her righteous indignation. "I'd call it a goddamned insult to all your female readers."

"Thank you for sharing your comments," Julie continued, still forcing the smile. "We strive to do the best we can, but with deadlines, sometimes things just—"

"You never see crap like that on *The Lady of the Lakes,*" Casey pointed out. "Maybe you guys should try to be more like it."

Julie put the pen aside. Her color had returned with a vengeance; now she blushed with both shame and anger. Her voice remained calm, though. "Yes, well, blogging has its place, but it will never replace newspapers, because we have the time and resources to report on events more accurately."

For just a moment there was dead silence except for the air conditioner's hum and the sound of something sizzling on the grill. Then everyone burst out laughing.

Julie's smile resolutely refused to diminish. She calmly put her notebook back in her bag and placed a business card on the counter. "I'm available if any of you would like to comment privately. I'm sorry for disturbing everyone's breakfast." Then she left.

Helena sighed and put down the coffee she'd poured. "That'll get us another good write-up in the restaurant guide," she said dryly.

"If I depended on the *Cap Jo*'s opinion, I'd have closed down three years ago," Rachel said. That was when the *Capital Journal*'s anonymous restaurant critic had published a scathing review of Rachel's diner, describing the fare as *cholesterol and fat shaped into vaguely food-shaped lumps.*

She reached for the business card and accidentally knocked it to the floor; when she bent to retrieve it, she banged her knee on the corner of the counter and snapped, *"Dammit!"* She went into the kitchen and stomped around the tight space until the sting went away.

Jimmy looked up from the grill. "You okay?"

"I'm fine," Rachel almost snarled.

"Whoa, just asking," Jimmy said, and returned to his cooking. "Man, this is a day when I just flat-out shouldn't talk."

The toaster, directly beside Rachel, suddenly ejected four pieces and startled her. Embarrassed and furious, she grabbed one slice of toast and threw it into the garbage.

Helena stared at her from the kitchen entrance. "The nerve of that impertinent toast."

Rachel said nothing. Jimmy reached past her to retrieve the rest of the toast as if he expected her to wrench his head off.

"I didn't know you hated the *Cap Jo* quite *that* much," Helena continued. "What's wrong?"

Rachel sighed and ran a hand through her hair. What was wrong was that she was still just as frustratingly horny as she'd been all night, and there was no way to resolve it until she could skinny-dip in the lake after dark, more than *twelve hours* away. Until then, every inch of her body was feather-sensitive, and every look from a male customer—even old Professor Dunning—convinced her that they knew about her condition. But only one man dominated her thoughts, and each time the bell over the door jingled she looked expectantly toward it, though she knew there was no way he'd ever show up again. Even with her offer relayed through Marty, she doubted he would appear. He had pride. And even if he didn't, surely *her* pride would restrain her. Wouldn't it? "Nothing," she answered, eyes down.

"Ah, this must be a definition of *nothing* with which I was previously unfamiliar," Helena said dryly before returning to her customers.

Rachel took a deep breath, then put her hand on Jimmy's shoulder. "I'm sorry for snapping at you, Jimmy."

"Hey, not a problem," Jimmy said without looking at her. He scraped madly at the pile of hash browns sizzling on the grill.

She patted his back. Jimmy wore short sleeves this morning, which meant he had no fresh needle tracks to hide. Oddly, she felt no sexual charge from him, probably because she knew how fragile his sobriety was. Jimmy's demons were far worse than hers, and his struggle to resist them infinitely more heroic. The day after he'd applied for the job a year ago, mumbling his way through the interview and then preparing a magnificent series of breakfast dishes in record time, the lake spirits had shown her Jimmy as a young man, taking his first dose of heroin. She instantly understood the circumstances that drove him to it, as well as the inner strength that enabled him to resist the devil lurking in his blood. He might still fall off the wagon as everyone else expected, but it wouldn't be because no one had given him a chance.

By the time the breakfast crowd thinned out, Rachel was ready to scream. She went outside and paced in the parking lot, wishing she still smoked. She kicked at the loose gravel.

Helena stood in the back door and regarded her oddly. "Are you all right?" she asked softly, with genuine concern. "You seem kind of edgy today."

"I'm fine," Rachel said. "I'm just a little distracted."

"Oho," Helena said, suddenly comprehending. "Who is it?"

"Nobody," Rachel said guiltily.

"It's that guy from yesterday, isn't it? Marty Walker's brother. The blue eyes and the tight ass."

"And the excess testosterone, and the assumption that I couldn't handle a disruptive customer in my own place. You think I'd be attracted to that?"

Helena grinned. "I think parts of you would be."

Rachel tried to stay annoyed, but she couldn't hold back a smile. "Yeah, well, this, too, shall pass."

"Do you want it to? I mean, hell, Rach, all he did was try to help. You assumed he was showing off, but maybe that's just you reading stuff into it. He's Marty Walker's brother, after all, and Marty's a good guy. That's got to be some kind of reference."

"He's not applying for a job, Helena."

"Are you sure?"

Rachel sighed and put her hands on her hips. She sounded far more certain than she felt. "I'm *sure* that I've been by myself for a while and that it could easily cause me to make less-than-sensible romantic decisions if I let it. Like it has in the past, as I'm sure you recall. But I'm not a little girl, and I'm not ruled by my hormones anymore."

"Don't women's sex drives increase once they pass thirty?"

"You'll find out yourself soon enough."

"No worries for me. I've got Michelle."

"Well, no worries for me either," Rachel snapped. "I can control myself just fine."

"Uh-huh. Just worries for the people who have to

work around you." And Helena went back inside, leaving Rachel to pace some more.

Rachel went to the tree that shaded the south end of the tiny lot and leaned against it. The bark, ragged and sharp against her shoulders around the straps of her tank top, felt deliciously tangible.

Then she froze. Far down the street, past the old battery-factory building and over the railroad tracks, a truck was parked in front of the row of houses. The glare off the windshield kept her from seeing if anyone was inside, but a little jolt told her that it was the same truck she'd spotted outside her building the afternoon before. Suddenly all thoughts of sex were wiped out by the primal fear of being stalked. The truck did not move, and at this distance she could not make out the license plate or tell if its engine was running.

She'd been stalked before and would not allow it to happen again. She could grab Jimmy from the kitchen and walk down the street to confront the driver; in broad daylight, with a man accompanying her, she should be safe. And that would be fine, unless it turned out that the driver lived in the neighborhood, in one of the old houses refitted as student apartments. Or worked nearby, at one of the neighborhood bars, or the big bank on the corner, or the convenience store five blocks away. Parking was always at a premium on the isthmus, and that might be the only free spot he could find. Maybe it was someone who'd just pulled over to make a phone call.

She shook her head. Maybe she *was* losing it. Perhaps the strain of running the diner, having sex with a body of water instead of a man, and passing thirty without children or family had finally overwhelmed her to the point that she now imagined every strange event represented some threat. She and Rebecca might turn out to be more alike than she ever thought—an idea that terrified her more than any pickup-driving stalker.

"Screw this," she muttered to the universe, and went back inside.

THE ANGRY MAN stared at the laminated menu. He'd stolen it months ago, on a whim and for no purpose. Yet now he focused all his rage on it and all the unrequited fury of a life of feeling unwanted and unappreciated.

The calligraphy across the top said simply, *Rachel's.* The motto beneath read, *Cooking like your mother's, without the nagging.* His brows furrowed in annoyance; did the bitch think that was *funny*? Did she and her snotty friends sit around laughing about it over their lattes and bagels? One day soon he'd show them what he thought was funny, and they definitely wouldn't laugh at that.

Beneath the logo was a bad photocopied picture of Rachel Matre. She was smiling, her hair was unnaturally coiffed, and she wore a button-down collar. The image reeked of cheap professional photography, the kind done in fifteen minutes at the mall and sold in $19.95 packages. But it was still *her*, still showed that irritating superior smile and conveyed the sense that she was somehow better than everyone else.

He clenched his fist. He wanted more than anything to slap that smile from her face, to knock her to the floor and see her on her hands and knees, begging. He wanted her to know his power and to fear it.

He struck a match, blew it out, and stuck the still-hot tip to the plastic menu cover. It melted through right over her mouth and blacked out her smile. The sharp smell tickled his nose. Then he methodically did the same twice more, putting out both her eyes so that the picture now had the vague appearance of a skull.

He checked his watch, locked the work shed, and went inside, to the door that led into the basement.

CHAPTER NINE

HELENA TURNED OFF the diner's lights and made sure the front door was locked. The afternoon sun quickly heated the room once the air conditioner shut down. As Rachel made a final, ceremonial pass with a rag down the counter, Helena said, "So what *are* you going to do about it?"

"About what?" Rachel said without looking at her.

"About the fact that you want to jump Marty Walker's brother's bones."

Rachel scowled. "That's just silly."

"So's the fact that we drive on parkways and park on driveways."

"Helena, leave straight sex to the straight people. No matter what my hormones may want, they still have to take orders from here." She tapped her temple. "And here says there's no way I'd allow some ham-handed ex-soldier to paw all over me."

"Well, speaking for your coworkers and friends, we

think you should find *someone* to paw all over you before you bite all our heads off."

Rachel tossed the rag down vehemently. "Dammit, Helena, just *stop*. I'd like to think I can count on you to be considerate, if no one else."

Helena looked startled, then hurt. "Sure, Rach," she mumbled, then untied her apron and went out the back door. In a moment her car started and spun gravel as she quickly drove away.

Rachel stood alone in her empty diner, half blinded by the sun's reflection off the tile floor. She could never tell Helena the truth: that *no* man pawing all over her could ease her desire. She'd never told anyone about the lakes, ever. Not even—*especially* not even—her ex-husband, Don, who considered her "sexually maladjusted." But if she didn't get some relief soon, she might indeed start biting off heads. She'd go mad if she didn't visit the lake tonight and only hoped she could keep it together until then.

JULIE SCHUTES DROPPED into her chair at the *Capital Journal* office and kicked off her shoes beneath her desk. She looked around at the slumped shoulders and weary heads of her fellow reporters, most of whom stared blankly at their computer screens. She recalled the dynamic Rosalind Russell in *His Girl Friday* and wondered how she'd ended up more like Jessica Lange at the end of *Frances*.

She checked her e-mail, but none required her immediate attention. Her voice mail, likewise, had nothing. She had all the material needed for her article on the effects of the recent abductions, but she couldn't focus on writing. She was still furious over the scene at the diner—not so much the criticism of her story, but the implication that the gossip found on that *goddamnedsonofabitching blog* was better than her own careful work.

Just as she was about to force herself to write something, a voice said, "Why, hello there."

She looked up. The *Cap Jo*'s editor, Sam "Garish" Garnett, stood in front of her desk. As always, he was dressed impeccably in a suit and tie, his salt-and-pepper hair immobile in its cocoon of product. In the year he'd been at the helm, the former tabloid editor had made changes that included increasing the typeface size so shorter stories took up more space and gradually shifting the editorial emphasis to what he called "infotainment." "Remember," he often said at staff meetings, "in today's world the 'tainment is as important as the info."

He sat on the edge of her desk like Paul Drake on *Perry Mason* and asked, "How did the man-on-the-street stuff go?"

"It went great," Julie said. "Until that goddamned bikini picture came up again."

Garnett sighed with elaborate patience. "Jules, you need to get past that. It might have been over the line, but it's also over and done with. Move on."

"*I* didn't bring it up," she said through her teeth. "And don't call me 'Jules,' Garish."

He blushed slightly beneath his tan. Because of his background in celebrity rags and supermarket tabloids, being taken seriously was his Achilles' heel. "Very well, Juliet," he said, deliberately using her full name. "As I've told you several times, the use of attractive young women to sell products is as old as civilization itself." He raised his voice so that others nearby could hear. "And as I will doubtless tell you again, when the opportunity presents itself, I feel strongly we should take advantage of it."

"The news shouldn't be a 'product,' Sam. What we print should fucking *matter.*"

From the cubicle behind her, Tony Russo, the sports editor, called out to Julie, "Get him to show you the picture to go with your current story."

She stared up at Garnett. "What?" she hissed.

Russo peeked over the cubicle wall. "He got a swimsuit shot from the Kimmell girl's boyfriend."

"You didn't," Julie gasped, too appalled to even be angry. "Sam, for God's sake, the girl's been kidnapped, probably raped and murdered. You can't turn her into a sex object."

"We should use her high school graduation photo, then?" Garnett said defensively. "Or the one where she's drunk at some party? People can get those for free on flyers all over town."

Julie was on her feet now, leaning across the desk, and Garnett stood so he could back away. "We should have some goddamned *dignity,* Sam. And some standards. We want people to trust us, don't we?"

Heads gophered over the other cubicle walls. Garnett,

seeing that he had an audience, straightened his tie and said loudly, "We *want* people to spend their pocket change to get our newspaper out of the machines. If the picture of a pretty girl—who, I might add, is part of a legitimate news story—makes them do that, then I say we use it. And since I sit in the room whose door says *Editor-in-Chief,* what I say goes." He met Julie's eyes. "Is that clear, Juliet?"

She wanted to hurl the stapler beside her hand at his smug face. Instead, she said, "Perfectly, Garish." Then she sat down and deliberately turned her attention back to her computer screen.

Garnett turned and strolled, carefully and calmly, back to his office. Julie knew that one of his management secrets was to always act as if he'd won every argument. It didn't make the back of his head less a target. She pointed her finger like a pistol and said softly, "*Bang,* you bastard."

ETHAN PUSHED the bar away from his chest, then pulled it back. Sweat trickled into his eyes, and his bad shoulder protested. But he kept going.

The cavernous Harvard Fitness Club was almost empty this late, as the after-work crowd returned to their families, flat-screen TVs, and Internet surfing. Through the big windows, traffic on the Beltline made trails of white and red lights in the darkness. Only one other man, much younger and slighter than Ethan, was working out nearby, and he simply ran on a treadmill, aware only of the music provided through his iPod's earbuds. That suited Ethan fine; he definitely didn't feel chatty.

He finished the last repetition and sat, gasping, head down, watching sweat drop to the rubber mat beneath the machine's bench. He'd pushed himself past the sensible point and knew his shoulder would repay him with soreness for a week, but he had to burn off the nervous energy that had kept him twitching and distracted all day. He'd paced his office, driving Ambika mad and drinking far too much coffee, until Marty finally called to say that the work site was cleared for use. Now he had to figure out a way to make up the last two days.

He wiped the sweat with a towel. He was lying to himself, he knew. What had distracted him wasn't really work. It was the image of Rachel Matre that simply wouldn't leave his mind.

Why should a woman like that, a smug pseudohippie who lacked even the courtesy to say thanks after he chased off that dickhead, have such a strong hold on him? He'd gone out of his way to flirt with a dozen women that day, from the college girl who worked at the video store to the fiftyish lady who delivered his office mail. One, a stunning redhead so engrossed in her cell phone she'd nearly trampled him on the sidewalk, had actually given him her business card along with an apology. He hadn't called her, but he *had* dialed Julie's number, except for the last digit. But none of it got Rachel out of his head. Or out of other, more insistent parts of his anatomy.

Now it was dark again, and he faced the possibility of another sleepless, solitary, repeatedly tumescent night.

He could work on his taxes, or take cold showers, or simply jerk off and get it over with. It wasn't like he had no options.

He pounded his forehead on the weight machine's handle. What was *wrong* with him? Was Marty right, and he'd closed himself off so much since returning from Iraq that he risked an unplanned, and no doubt embarrassing, explosion of repressed feelings? What he'd seen, and done, festered just below his consciousness every moment, yet he resolutely refused to discuss it. Even when it took away his sleep, his peace of mind, and sometimes his very manhood, he'd keep his word and hold his tongue. It made people like Julie believe that the army had stripped away his humanity and left him just an efficient, and violent, machine.

He went to the mats near the wall and began his cooldown stretches. He extended his right leg and bent over it, his fingers hooking over the toe of his shoe. As he did, a pair of worn white running shoes passed in front of him, and a matching set of long, pale legs knelt and then straightened. He looked up and saw the redhead he'd bumped into earlier.

For a moment her face scrunched in annoyance at his scrutiny, then she recognized him. "Well, hello. Isn't this a small world?"

"Round too," he said with a smile. "Haven't seen you here before."

"I usually go to the one on the east side, but I had a late meeting over here today."

He watched her eyes flick over him, evaluating him as

blatantly as he might a woman on the street. He didn't mind; for some reason, women had always found him attractive, and the hard, lean edge he'd acquired during his tour of duty seemed to only enhance that. He reciprocated, enjoying the way her workout clothes displayed far more pale, freckled flesh than she'd shown earlier on the street.

As she stretched, she said, "Do you even remember my name?"

He grinned and shook his head. "Don't take it personally. Some days I barely remember my own."

"It's Ethan," she said as she bent low over her knee, allowing him an unobstructed view down her sports bra cleavage. She had freckles there as well. "I'm Cindy. Cin for short; no pun intended."

He laughed. "No pun?"

"Well, maybe a little pun," she admitted. She got to her feet and looked down at him. "I'm just starting, and you've already finished. A metaphor for our relationship?"

"We have a relationship?" he said, and stood. She was shorter in her tennis shoes, but the force of her personality made up for any loss in physical stature. "I thought it was just a pedestrian fender bender."

She gave him an open and inviting smile. With no makeup and her hair pulled haphazardly back, she was still a stunner. "I'll be done in half an hour. If you don't mind me a little sweaty, we could meet for a cup of coffee before I head home."

He started to say yes—*intended* to say yes. Her physical beauty was matched by her honesty and bluntness, two qualities he found immensely attractive. And he had no history with her, so perhaps his other issues might not trouble him. Yet, before he could utter the words, the memory of Rachel standing in the window flashed vividly before him. Inexplicably, infuriatingly, he felt that making a date with anyone else would be a mistake. "I'm sorry," he blurted. "I can't."

"Married?" she asked simply, with no indication that it would alter her interest.

"No, just . . . off the market at the moment."

She nodded in acceptance. "Okay. Well, Ethan, you've got my number if you decide to relist yourself." And with that she turned and trotted off down the indoor running track that circled the machines. He made sure he was gone by the time she finished her first lap. The scruffy kid behind the greeter's desk barely looked up from his online poker as Ethan headed to the dressing room.

THE *Capital Journal*'s offices were mostly deserted, which suited Julie just fine. She'd restrained herself as long as she could, and now she had to let it out. The humiliation at the diner had weighed on her all afternoon with the vivid intensity of something from high school. Garnett's comments only added to it. Just like in eleventh grade, all she wanted to do was curl up and cry.

Tough reporters didn't cry, though, and few in Madison were as tough as Julie Schutes. A homemade desk sign given to her by the previous editor read, *She Schutes, She Scores,* and she loved being the paper's go-to reporter for breaking crime news. The abducted Chinese girl had not really moved the public, but readers latched on to Faith Lucas: beautiful, blond, young, and vanished. Just like that teenager who'd disappeared in the Bahamas, the Lucas girl cast a seductive spell over these plain Midwesterners, giving them the schadenfreude their mundane, unglamorous lives needed. Julie and Garish Garnett were alike in understanding that, and that fact made her hate him even more.

But as she'd tried to write about the thoughts of those same Midwesterners, from the ones offering prayers for safe returns to those who felt it was, ultimately, the girls' own fault, even Julie began to lose her enthusiasm. There could be no happy resolution; the forty-eight-hour window had passed for all the victims. Now it was simply a matter of reporting where, in the vast woods all over Wisconsin, their bodies would be found. After that, it would be standard crime reporting, dry and by the book, until the perp was caught. She hoped he was, at least, an interesting lunatic and not some standard, dull-eyed serial killer.

She should be glad to be involved in such an important ongoing story. But instead she sat in the back stall in the deserted women's restroom, sobbing so hard it made her cheeks hurt.

At last she blew her nose, checked herself in the mirror, and returned to the newsroom. Only the lights over her cubicle were lit, and she settled into her desk secure that no one would ever know she'd been crying. She checked *The Lady of the Lakes.* Nothing new.

She scrolled down through the blog's old posts and comments. *Here* was a story, if only she could get a handle on it. Who was this person, or group? How did they know these things? Often they reported crimes on the isthmus before even the police knew about them, whether capital ones like the kidnapping of Carrie Kimmell or misdemeanors like graffiti attacks or broken windows. It often seemed as if only the actual perpetrators could know these things so quickly, yet what criminal, or even gang, could be so clandestine?

Far more interesting were the posts about crimes of the past, pointing the authorities toward fresh clues and new suspects. A pedophile priest, a serial rapist, and the man behind a sixties' campus bombing had all been brought to justice long after their crimes because of tips found on this blog. It almost seemed as if the victims' ghosts must've risen from the grave to provide some of this stuff.

So who was behind the blog? No one had any clue. Still, Julie kept her eyes and ears open. All she needed was one stray thread, then she could follow it to the source and unmask *The Lady of the Lakes* for all to see. Maybe then people would finally forget about the girl in the bikini.

She glanced inadvertently at the empty space beside her phone, where for two and a half years a photo of her with Ethan Walker had rested. Instantly she felt the unmistakable tug that memories of Ethan always sparked. He'd been such an all-consuming passion that his absence, even after three months, still seemed overwhelming. She wanted those huge arms wrapped around her now, wanted to smell that distinctive mix of musk and industrial odors he always had at the end of the day. Even his issues with sex would be secondary now to just being in his presence.

She opened her phone and dialed his number. It couldn't hurt to just hear his voice. After four rings his voice mail said, "Hi, this is Ethan Walker of Walker Construction. Leave a message and I'll get back to you ASAP." He actually said "ASAP," a holdover from the military acronyms drilled into him by the army.

She snapped the phone shut. She couldn't leave him a message. Tough reporters didn't go crying into the arms of their old boyfriends.

As HE WALKED to his truck from the gym, Ethan retrieved his cell phone from his pocket and turned it on. The night air was so humid that the effects of his shower vanished almost at once. He examined the lighted screen and immediately recognized the last number.

He climbed into his truck, shut the door, and started the engine, trying to ignore the sudden tingling in the pit of his stomach. *Julie.* She'd called but left no voice mail. It must've been a misdial out of old habit. He doubted it was deliberate; when they broke up, they'd agreed never to call the other at night no matter how bad the loneliness got.

Yet she had.

He took a deep breath, his thumb running back and forth over the send button. Finally he pushed it twice.

It rang several times, but she never answered. When her voice mail picked up, he snapped the phone closed.

She'd know he called, of course. But then, she started it. Just like she always had.

He glanced back at the club, where Cin the redhead was probably delightfully sweaty and winded by now.

Then he put the truck in gear and drove too fast out of the parking lot.

FAITH LUCAS SOBBED as she pulled her panties up her legs. The tiny scrap of fabric no longer seemed to provide any modesty. If anything, its presence emphasized her nudity and helplessness. She felt blood trickle down her leg and could barely stand from stress and lack of food.

"What are you crying about?"

"It hurts," Faith whimpered, eyes downcast. The pain, shame, and constant terror had reduced her to primal submissiveness.

"Of course it hurts. You know better than to fight me. Next time just lie there and take it. Or do you want me to start drugging you again?"

She shook her head. The greasy ends of her hair slapped against her shoulders.

"Then stop whining. Hold out your hands."

She did, and a fresh plastic tie snapped around them. She winced and gasped; the bruises from where she'd once fought to escape were still tender. Then came the ripped-fabric sound of the duct tape before it was pressed firmly over her mouth. Her tears ran down over the silver material, and she was physically turned away from the bright light toward the dark doorway where she spent her time between sessions.

She no longer raised her arms to cover her bare breasts. It seemed pointless. A hand between her shoulder blades guided her back down the stairs and into the room where the other two waited. They watched her silently over similarly taped mouths, no doubt wondering who would be next. The Asian girl curled her own battered, pale body into the tiniest possible size, as if that would somehow hide what he had already done to her. The other girl, the newest, watched with the wide eyes of someone yet to comprehend her full helplessness. After all, she still had not truly felt his touch.

Faith felt the jagged concrete beneath her bare feet and took her place on the dirty floor. The hand pointed at Ling Hu and motioned for her to stand.

The Asian girl shook her head. But she got slowly, awkwardly to her feet and ascended the stairs.

CHAPTER TEN

THE ANGRY MAN sat at the red light, his hands tight on the steering wheel. Even at night, the summer heat made the plastic wheel cover sticky to the touch, and his vehicle had no working air conditioner. Sweat beaded on his upper lip, and he wiped it impatiently. The red light obstinately stayed red, despite the fact that the cross street was entirely empty. On the radio, a man explained why immigrants would destroy America.

Out of the darkness emerged three college-age girls. They were in animated conversation, one of them with a cell phone held tight to her ear. They displayed long, slender legs and boobs augmented by either surgery or push-up bras. None was older than twenty, he guessed, and not one of them even glanced his way.

Paying no attention to the crosswalk, they strode obliviously in front of him just as the light turned green. His headlights illuminated their lithe, supple forms. Angrily, he honked his horn, and they all jumped. The one with the phone did a little dance as she tried to catch it before it hit the pavement. Another flipped him off as he gunned his engine. "Fuck off, Grandpa!" one yelled as he roared past them.

He resisted the urge to floor it. He did not want to draw the attention of the police, not tonight. Especially not tonight. But the girls just added to the rage festering in his belly, and his only comfort was the knowledge that shortly all that fury would be unleashed.

THE MAN TURNED off the ignition and sat very still. His heart pounded, and for a moment he wondered if this was it, if after everything he would be felled by a heart attack. His rasping breath fogged the truck's windshield, and he opened the window to let in some fresh night air. It was just as humid outside.

Finally his heart rate slowed and his breathing returned to normal. Panic would not help him, any more than it had helped Ling Hu. He had watched her die slowly and painfully, eyes wide and body trembling with effort, reaching out for help that he could neither give nor summon. Now she was ninety pounds of dead meat he had to dispose of quickly, and in a way that would confuse officialdom when she was finally found.

He got out of his truck and dropped the tailgate. He had triple-bagged the girl's body in industrial-strength garbage bags and now dragged her across the wet grass to the lake. This part of the shore was near the zoo, and, during the day, families fished and picnicked beneath the trees. At this time of night, though, it was deserted. At least, it seemed to be during his three drive-bys, and he couldn't just tool around with a corpse in his truck all night. If he was meant to be caught, nothing would change it. And if not, he had nothing to fear.

When he got the bag to the water's edge, he tore it open and stretched out the girl's body. Rigor mortis had not yet set in, and he dragged her by the ankles into the lake. His booted feet squelched in the mud, and his splashing steps sounded gunshot-loud in the silence. He towed her a few yards away from shore, then shoved her toward the drop-off. He knew she would eventually float but hoped the currents might take her away from this spot before it happened.

He stood with his hands on his knees, gasping for breath. Something rubbed against his foot, probably a catfish or small sturgeon. The way it seemed to grasp at him, like a hand trying to hold him in place, must've been his imagination. Still, he returned to shore as quietly as possible and drove away toward Park Street, still unable to believe his continuing luck.

RACHEL STOOD NAKED in the darkness, in water up to her thighs. Lake Mendota stretched out before her like a dark, intermittently sparkling void, threatening to suck the big shoreline houses into oblivion.

Just ahead, the bottom dropped away into the deepest part of the lake. The moon was hidden behind the trees, so for all intents she was invisible, standing some fifteen yards from shore, rubbing her hands slowly up and down her hips. The familiar frisson of being so publicly vulnerable ran through her, raising chill bumps despite the heat. She was stark naked literally in the middle of Madison, surrounded by thousands of people. But the late hour, the darkness, and whatever lived in the lake protected her from discovery.

She took several deep breaths, enjoying the moment of delicious anticipation. Neither the swarming mosquitoes nor the sound of hip-hop from a distant lake house could distract her. Forty-eight hours' worth of frustration and mounting desire were about to culminate, and she was as wet as the body of water before her.

"Do you want me?" she whispered. "Show me you want me."

She slowly sank to her knees. The lake as always matched her mood. If she wanted to be romanced, she had to approach it in a tender way that built in intensity. If she wanted to be screwed senseless (and on extremely rare occasions, she did), she dove in and let the lake ravish her. And if she wore any clothing or jewelry, it would be nothing more than a normal swim.

This was a night to take it slow. For two days she'd been twitching like a downed power line, every nerve ending on overload. It grew so bad that even the sensation of clothes against her skin drove her crazy. Fantasies of Ethan Walker fueled the fire, but the source no longer mattered, only relief from the ever-tightening tension.

Her knees settled into the soft mud. Something small scurried out of her way, slapping the surface with its tail as it fled, but it didn't bother her. Nothing in the lake would harm her, and everything was secondary to the water surging over her thighs. She slid her knees apart to let it reach her intimately. It lapped at her and she sighed with relief and delight. She closed her eyes, imagining the waves were fluttering fingers expertly teasing her, coaxing her open.

"That's it, baby," she breathed, so softly only the lake could hear. "I've been aching for you."

She held out her arms and bent forward. The delicious moment her nipples touched the water made her gasp and pause to savor it. Was the water actually closing around them, hardening enough to deliver firm yet gentle pinches? Then she slid smoothly into the warm, dark liquid, moving beneath the surface and into the depths, where her lover's embrace awaited. The city night sounds vanished, replaced by the rumbling heartbeat of the water itself.

It was a feeling almost impossible to describe—which was one reason she'd never told anyone. First the water solidified ever so slightly, providing a silken liquid cocoon molded to her skin. It filled her nostrils and mouth, too, and there was always an instant of *OhmyGodnoairNO-AIR!* Yet she could still speak and scream, although there was no one to hear.

The water grew more solid and, with no further preliminaries, slowly penetrated her, forming itself to fit inside her so that it addressed every sensitive spot. She was free to respond in any way she wanted. She could clamp her thighs together and curl into a ball or spread wide and wantonly pump her hips. The water filled her either way.

She was its voluntary plaything, and it was her liquid paramour.

Don't make me wait, she said through the water filling her mouth. *I'm nearly insane from waiting. Please.* In response, the water within her began to move.

Anyone watching would not have noticed even the slightest ripple on the lake's dark surface. But Rachel hovered deep in the murk, her naked body squirming, hips bucking against the warm liquid presence that filled her in every way. *That's it . . . yes, oh, yes . . . harder . . . don't stop. . . .* Rationally she knew she should be drowning, and she used to wonder if perhaps she *were* already dead and this was some Owl Creek–ish fantasy of her dwindling life. But somehow she was able to get the oxygen her body needed. She couldn't literally "breathe" underwater, and when she once tried during a nonsexual swim she very nearly *did* drown. But when the lake, or lake spirits, or whatever force was behind this, took its pleasure from her body, it or they made sure she was safe. The way a lover should. *Oh, God, yes . . . more . . .*

The tension of the last two days exploded in a rush of fulfillment that, had her cry been audible, would've made bystanders call 911. It released a mass of emotions she could express in no other way, and the lake absorbed her tears and sobs with the same tenderness as it embraced her body. But this was only the beginning. Before she even realized it, the rush began again, and she built toward another orgasm.

The water caressed her intimately, not like something hard and masculine now but with the fluttery touch of a tongue. It was torturous the way tingles built under its ministrations, and she writhed and screamed in delicious torment. She felt the same flicking attention on her breasts, and she cupped them in sympathetic anguish. Finally she exploded, a wrenching inner spasm that brought tears of emotional release to her eyes. She'd never experienced anything that powerful.

And they weren't done with her yet.

As the spirits returned to a rougher, more possessive approach, she felt a thrill of fear. She was parted and penetrated, the water supporting her hips to give leverage to whatever pushed its way deep into her. Her heart pounded painfully in her chest, and her exhausted muscles tightened again under the relentless pounding. *Feather and hammer,* she thought, *alternating to drive me insane.* Could she survive much more?

It didn't matter. If she had to die, this was how she wanted to go. She rolled her hips wantonly, legs spread wide, hands massaging her breasts. *Take me... go deeper... give it all to me....* Her cries, screams, and whimpers were silenced by the delicious water in her mouth, and she felt now that all the tension, of two days spent so horny she could barely think, had somehow been worth it. *I'm yours, baby, all yours.*

In the darkness it was hard to tell direction, but she sensed she was near the lake's bottom. She rolled onto her stomach, the soft silt touching her with featherlight fingers, and raised her hips for more. She would never have been so willingly subservient, so traditionally feminine with a human lover, but no man ever made her feel this good. Her cheek sank into the mud, and the soft sediment brushed the tips of her nipples just as the surface waves had done earlier. A firm presence held the back of her neck with just enough strength, and she flashed to her fantasies of Ethan from the night before. She squeezed handfuls of the mushy silt between her fingers as she came yet again.

Please never stop, she begged. *Please, never let this end. . . .*

The pressure built within her, the tingling rush grew stronger, and her muscles trembled loosely in anticipation. When it happened, her whole body seemed to clench in on itself and she heard her heart thundering in her skull. It was an orgasm stronger, longer, and more intense than she'd thought her body could tolerate.

In the midst of it, something new and extraordinary happened: She suddenly seemed to leap from the lake to the sky, as if astrally projecting into the night. It occurred too fast to fully comprehend, and then she dove down again, toward the city, into a building she had no time to identify. Before her was the face of a beautiful, sad-eyed girl.

Rachel hovered there, seeing without eyes, the details crisp and unnaturally clear. This was no interior vision like the ones she usually got—this was reality of a new and rather terrifying kind. She had no sense of her physical self, neither the lust that had been driving her nor the fear that she should be feeling. Had she been separated from her body somehow? Would she be returned when she was done?

This stranger had curly black hair that fell to her

shoulders and pale, freckled skin. Her nose was long and vaguely Semitic. She had a small diamond stud in her left nostril and wore a turquoise and leather choker. The instant impression was of warmth, kindness, and affection. The first word that popped into Rachel's mind was *sweet*. The girl was smiling, bathed in golden light, with a familiar-looking wall behind her. The ambience was like a princess in a castle.

Then suddenly the whole view changed and the girl was somewhere else, somewhere dark and filthy, her mouth hidden behind a duct-tape gag, her sweaty face smeared with dirt. The necklace was gone, and she was naked, her hands tied above her. A shadow fell over her, and she screamed through the gag.

Both scenes could not be true, or happening simultaneously, and it seemed unlikely that the terrified girl could become the smiling, kind one. It had to be the other way around. Was she finally being shown a glimpse of the *future*?

Save her, the spirits said. *Save her.*

RACHEL SURFACED with a ragged cry, half sob and half protest, and stumbled as her wobbly legs refused to support her. She had no memory of swimming this close to shore. She was gently lifted again and this time managed to stay on her feet, gasping and crying as fresh tears ran down her face. She choked back the sounds, so no one would think she needed rescuing, and wrapped her arms protectively around herself. Suddenly she truly *felt* naked, with all the helplessness that entailed. Just like the girl, in the second part of her vision.

The night had grown overcast, with the city's glow reflected on the clouds. Without the stars, she had no idea how long she'd been under. No boats moved in the darkness, and she heard nothing but distant traffic. Most of the lakeside homes were now dark. She was immensely glad about that; the emotions roiling within her were too strong and contradictory, and she could only stand in the water crying until she'd released enough of them to think straight again.

For the first time she knew she'd been shown, if not *the* future, at least *a possible* future. Perhaps it wasn't even real, just some sort of projection of a surmise on the spirits' part. After all, she had no real knowledge of their limitations or even their motives. If they *did* know the future, then why after all this time would they start showing it to her *now*?

Save her, the spirits had said. But how? Call the police? Warn the girl? Neither would believe her.

And there was another new feeling, something Rachel had never experienced from her prior visions. Somehow Rachel knew that this girl was important in the purest, most guileless way. She brought light and joy to those who knew her. She was a rarity, a *treasure*. Not like the other victims, who were just unfortunate.

But how could she know all this with such certainty? Had the lake spirits communicated with her on a new, deeper level? Or, more chillingly, had they begun to control her mind the way they did her body? If so, could she trust their beneficence?

Rachel moved toward shore, the water now impeding her steps. The waves pushed against her thighs, then her knees, and finally her shins. Their resistance mirrored her own. She hated the feeling of having no choice, of being something's mere tool. If the lake spirits wanted the girl saved, why didn't they do it themselves? They'd once saved Rachel, after all.

The vision stayed fresh in her mind even as she exited the lake. Something in it was familiar. The wall *behind* the girl reminded Rachel of somewhere she knew. Her brain was still fuzzy, but she knew it was something she should recognize.

The lake fully released her as she stepped onto dry land. She ran quickly into the bushes where she'd left her clothes. She pulled on her cutoffs and T-shirt and slipped her sockless feet into her old tennis shoes. The night was humid and warm, and the mosquitoes accosted her almost at once. Swatting at them, she climbed the hill into the park and turned toward home but stopped when she reached the sidewalk.

There had been no chance to help the girl pinned in the flashlight beam, who she now knew was Carrie Kimmell. She'd made certain that people knew about it and left it to the professionals after that. But there *was* time before this girl started screaming. Rachel had the opportunity, if not the responsibility, to do something.

She clenched her fists. She was physically exhausted and emotionally ragged, neither of which encouraged heroic busybodying. She smelled like the lake and wore only enough clothing to be legal. Wherever the girl had been—no, wherever she *was*—it was indoors, lit with soft lamps and sporting artwork on the walls. A damp and bedraggled Rachel certainly wouldn't fit in. She wanted only to go home, bathe, and sleep.

But those eyes. And that scream. And the sense that only she, Rachel Matre, could save this sweet girl, this *treasure.*

She turned to the lake. It reflected the cloudy sky now and looked like some huge, dark bruise on the surface of the earth. "You sons of bitches," she hissed. "I do enough for you. I don't *deserve this.*" But, as always, there was no reply.

She ran a hand roughly through her wet, tangled curls as she searched her memory. Where *was* the girl now? A local art gallery? One wouldn't be open this late. What would? A bar, a restaurant, a coffeehouse—

A *coffeehouse.*

Suddenly she knew where to find the girl. And with that knowledge came the certainty that she would *have* to. If she didn't at least try, she'd never be able to live with herself.

She ran, not toward home but toward the crowded nighttime chaos of downtown Williams Street.

CHAPTER ELEVEN

FATHER THYME'S was a tiny coffeehouse, one of a half dozen within ten blocks on the isthmus. It occupied a freestanding brick building with big glass windows along the front. Early in its existence, the owners reached a truce with the graffiti artists who ransacked the neighborhood and initiated a creative, occasionally controversial solution: The flat, windowless side wall could be painted by anyone, at any time, as long as it was neither libelous nor obscene. The current mural depicted the President, seated on a throne made of human skulls, all of which had dollar signs in their eye sockets and vomited black oil from their grinning mouths. Fresh gang tags already obscured bits of it.

Inside, the walls also sported art, of the overpriced kind. The regular clientele spent most of its time reading, tapping on laptops, or murmuring along with iPods. The floor rose slightly in the corner by the front window, providing a small stage for solo musicians. No real amplification was needed, so it was a popular venue for performers just starting out, usually folkies from the college.

As Rachel reached her decision on the sidewalk by the lake, the girl from the vision sat onstage, fine-tuning her acoustic guitar. And the eyes that would soon see her scream watched with hungry determination.

THE HEART OF Williams Street, several blocks from both the diner and the lake, ran through the last true bohemian neighborhood on the isthmus, where gentrification like Ethan's condo project met with resistance at every turn. Blocks of old houses divided into apartments ran from Williams down to the lakeshore, and the establishments serving such a community—bars, restaurants, coffeehouses, and the small shops catering to more-specialized clientele—made "Willie Street" a place where people hung out twenty-four hours a day. Students, hippies, and nonconformists of all stripes called the area their own. Unfortunately, at this time of night many of those people were close to that line dividing "colorful" from "dangerous."

Because she ran regularly, Rachel made good time jogging from Hudson Park. She was already damp from her swim, and the fresh sweat actually felt good, although the combined odor was pretty overpowering. Her muscles, a bit shaky after her erotic encounter, quickly fell into their old patterns. She wished she'd worn something tighter or more supportive to keep her from bouncing so blatantly, but home was in the other direction and the urgency too overwhelming.

The clock on the Anchor Bank building told her it was 11:15. Time never seemed to run normally while she was with the lake. What seemed like a marathon love-making session could pass in only a few minutes. There was still traffic even at this hour, so she stopped at the corner in front of the bank and waited for the crossing signal. Hands on her hips, she paced in a tight circle, taking deep, regular breaths.

Astoundingly, another jogger emerged from the darkness across the street, dashed through the traffic, and stood bouncing in place beside her. "Hi," he said. His voice trembled with his movement. "Don't think I've seen you around here before."

"I could say the same," she said.

He smiled with shy, blatant interest. He looked barely twenty-five. His hair was dyed jet black with lighter tips. He had huge hoop modifiers in his earlobes, and the edges of an elaborate tattoo peeked from his collar and sleeves. "My name's Ace. Well, that's what they call me."

"Better than Two of Clubs," Rachel said.

Still bouncing, Ace laughed. "You're funny."

"And you're cute," she said gently. "But when I run, I only run."

"We can run together, then. Bad neighborhood for a pretty girl to be out alone."

"Are you trying to *scare* me into liking you?"

He looked confused. "No, that's not what I meant, just—"

"Ace, really, I'm not up for socializing. Maybe some other night, okay?" The crossing light finally changed, and she took off again.

He bounced in place, watching her for a moment, then called out, "Sure thing!" before heading off in the opposite direction.

"Bar time," when places serving alcohol closed their doors, was two-thirty, so the partyers were still indoors, leaving the street mostly deserted. Rachel ran past a few people, including two muscular young men who drunkenly insisted she belonged on her knees in front of them. Amazingly, she heard a third male voice defend her, saying, "Man, you guys are *assholes.*" That made her smile.

When she got within sight of Father Thyme's, she stopped in front of a darkened store that sold hemp-related products. She leaned against the wall and stretched her hamstrings, looking over her destination. From within, light glowed through the front window, which was misted a little from the air-conditioning. Someone was on-stage, seated on a stool with a guitar and facing away from the window. The patrons inside milled about; there were more than she'd expected, due no doubt to the performer.

Well, damn, she thought. She could try peeking in the window, like a passerby intrigued by the commotion, but she couldn't do it for long. No, it looked like there was no way to avoid it. She would have to go into this social lion's den dressed like a homeless hippie vagabond.

As Rachel approached the entrance, three young

women emerged. The sound of energetic acoustic guitar filled the air until the heavy door closed behind them. She could not make out their faces; two had curly hair that might be dark like her quarry's. They walked away from her toward the lanes filled with student apartments and houses. The shadowy wells between streetlights continued to hide them.

Rachel stood on her toes indecisively, keeping her calf muscles loose. Would the spirits of the lake have arranged things so that Rachel arrived just as the potential victim walked out? *Could* they? The girl she sought might still be inside, but if she *was* one of these three, Rachel would certainly lose her if she went in first.

By now the girls had reached the corner. Rachel made her choice. She stayed a few steps back, trying not to be obvious, waiting for them to pass beneath a streetlight that wasn't obscured by tree limbs. In this part of town, those were rare. The girls wore shorts or skirts, and one tottered uncertainly on three-inch cork-soled sandals. Another punched text messages into her phone. They had the air of oblivious privilege so many young women cultivated.

"...so I said, those shoes are hideous, just *hid*-ee-us," one girl said.

"Well, all her shoes are," another responded.

"What about her hair?" the third added. "Whoever told her those bangs worked should be shot."

"Maybe that stupid slut with the guitar could sing a song about it," the second girl said. "God, I *hate* those emo dykes. Wear some lipstick, why don't you?"

"It was your idea to come here," the third girl pointed out.

"Oh, fudge!" the first girl said. "I forgot, I have an Ethics in Medicine exam tomorrow."

Rachel still hadn't gotten a good look at them, and they were leading her farther away from Father Thyme's. She thought about running around the block and approaching them from the front, but that would take time, during which anything might happen.

Then she had an idea. She pulled a crumpled dollar bill from her pocket. "Excuse me?" she called.

The girls stopped and turned. They regarded her with the same disdain all beautiful young girls had for someone older, especially one so sloppily dressed and bedraggled. They probably thought she was one of the downtown homeless people, strayed from her normal haunts.

Rachel held up the dollar. "Did one of you drop this?"

The girl with the ethics exam said immediately, "I did."

Rachel kept the irony to herself. None of these girls was the one from her vision. "Well. Here you go," she said, and handed over the dollar. Before they reached the next corner she heard them giggling in minor triumph.

She clenched her fists in annoyance. What did these girls know about the value of anything, let alone someone else's money? They'd been pampered and privileged all their young lives and now assumed they were simply due anything they wanted, even a single dollar that they knew belonged to someone else. A whole generation of young adults, all content to mock any sincerity and with no appreciation of anything's intrinsic worth. Rachel wanted to dash after them, smash their cell phones and iPods, make them know some hint of the pain a real human being could feel. "Suntans and brassieres," she muttered bitterly to herself.

Her fury was cut short as a pickup truck drove slowly by, its headlights out. In the dark its color was hard to discern, but it certainly *could* have been red. She stepped back into the shadows beneath a tree, her heart suddenly thundering. As it passed, she saw the word FORD across the tailgate and the license-plate number beneath it. She repeated it in her head, trying to ensure she'd remember it.

The truck crept along the curb behind the girls. They were deep in animated conversation, arms and hands slicing the air for emphasis, and either hadn't noticed the truck or didn't care. They turned the corner, and the truck followed.

Rachel felt her chest constrict and wondered for an instant if this was what a cardiac arrest felt like. It was simple fear, though, the terror of realizing the man who'd attacked three women recently might be mere yards away preparing to snag his fourth. *So what?* her bitter self demanded. *None of them is the girl you're looking for.*

But that wasn't enough reason to send anyone into the terror she had glimpsed. She took a deep breath, recalling Lady Macbeth's admonishment: *Screw your courage to the sticking place.* Well, if hers tightened any further, she'd snap like an overwound watch. She rushed to the corner and peered down the street.

The truck still rolled silently behind the three oblivious girls. Rachel started forward, when suddenly the truck's high beams blazed to life, pinning the girls in illumination.

The girls screamed in surprise, then the one who took Rachel's money slammed her palm flat against the front fender. "Goddammit, Andy, you scared the piss out of me!"

A dark-haired boy leaned out the driver's window and said mockingly, "I don't see any puddles."

"I'll show you puddles, you dickhead," she shouted, and slapped at him through the window. The other girls laughed.

From one of the nearby houses a voice shouted, "Keep it down, will you?"

"Get it up, why don't you?" one of the girls shouted back. The boy in the truck revved his engine for emphasis. They all cackled.

Rachel almost fell to her knees in relief. These girls were in no danger at all. She pushed sweaty hair from her face, furious and embarrassed. She'd come within moments of humiliating herself before these shallow, useless *bitches*. She wanted a shower, a drink, and a few hours' sleep.

But as she turned away, two more people emerged from Father Thyme's. The man and woman walked toward her, holding hands, and she nodded as they passed. The coffeehouse door opened again, this time for three scruffy college boys. The slash of light cut across the sidewalk and then disappeared as the door closed.

One look around inside, she decided. Enough to satisfy her conscience. That wouldn't take long, and then she could go home. The spirits in the lake could do their own damn good deeds.

CHAPTER TWELVE

THE LOCK was simple. He couldn't believe his luck. And despite the warning stickers on the windows, there seemed to be no alarm system attached. He wondered how many other small businesses merely put up the stickers without actually buying the protection.

The door opened and the man stepped into the darkened kitchen. It was silent and still. He carefully closed the door and listened for any movement in the apartment above. There was nothing. Rachel's car was outside, but he knew how seldom she drove it. The lights in the apartment were dark and had stayed dark for the entire time he'd watched. She was definitely not home.

He saw the door that led to the stairs. He imagined Rachel ascending them, weary after a day at the diner, unbuttoning her blouse and stripping it off as soon as she got to the top. He tingled as he fantasized about the look on her face when she saw him waiting inside, the knowledge of what he intended to do to her making her eyes grow wide. And then the satisfaction, utter and complete, of wiping that superior smirk off her sweet, sweet mouth.

But that could wait. He had other things to take care of first. He placed his toolbox on the counter and used the tiny flashlight on his key chain to search for the things he needed to make Rachel pay.

RACHEL ENTERED the coffeehouse through the side door. The tiny place was packed. Worse, the air conditioner was losing the battle against the summer evening, so the air was thick with sweat and coffee. The crowd made her immediately self-conscious about her unkempt appearance, and she ran her fingers uselessly through her hair. She backed into the wall beside the door, near the rack of free local magazines, and tried to look inconspicuous. It was as good a place as any to scout the room for the curly-haired young woman.

Lots of girls sat around the tables, or stood over them as they spoke to seated friends, or clung to blank-faced boys while they watched the show. The girl she sought had dark hair, so that ruled out over two-thirds of them, but she couldn't keep up as they ebbed and flowed from the service counter to the bathrooms to the seats.

The crowd politely applauded the musician onstage as the latest song ended. People rose to get fresh drinks between songs, and the murmur of conversation started up almost at once.

Rachel was making another visual circuit of the room

when she suddenly gasped, then mentally kicked herself. How dense could she be? The girl onstage, who strummed a chord and said, "Thank you so much," in a low, sensitive voice, was the very one she sought. She was even bathed in the right golden light, and from this angle the patch of wall Rachel had glimpsed in the vision was behind her. The lake spirits couldn't have made it any easier if they'd hung a sign around her neck.

She was younger than Rachel originally thought, maybe not even twenty. She had wide hips and wore a broom skirt that emphasized them. Feet clad in little satin slippers poked out beneath it, ankles crossed in front of the stool. Her blouse, low cut and dark, set off her pale skin. Her short nails were also dark, and she sported several rings.

Rachel frowned as she studied her. She was cute, certainly, and had a fragile quality that encouraged either protectiveness or annoyance. But she did not get the sense of importance from her that she'd had in the vision. She seemed to be, as the harsh girl outside had said, just another emo dyke with a guitar. They were thick on the ground in Madison, and, to her ears, at least, their songs were indistinguishable. Where was the treasure in that?

Still, this was her. And now Rachel had to at least warn the girl to be careful, in some general, indirect way that wouldn't make her sound like a lunatic. But before she could approach, a voice said, "Rachel, is that you?"

She turned. Larry "Cat" Arnold, a man she'd known for years and once briefly dated, stood looking at her in surprise. He had his arm around a girl young enough to be his daughter, but no father took his child out dressed like that. The front edge of Larry's long hair was receding up his forehead, while the back grew longer as if to compensate. He went by "Cat" for his weekend jazz show on a local radio station and milked this minor-celebrity status for all it was worth.

"Well, hello, Larry," she said fake-cheerfully. She could not call him "Cat" with a straight face.

"Surprised to see you here..." He glanced down at her clothes and added, "...this late."

"Couldn't sleep," she said flippantly, "so I thought I'd jog down and get some coffee."

"To help you sleep?"

"Decaf, silly. Didn't know I'd find a concert here."

"It's been all over the radio this week. Or don't you listen to my show?"

"Just like I always have," she assured him. The irony was all hers.

He turned to the girl. "Rachel, this is my friend Anna. Anna, this is Rachel Matre. She runs that diner I told you about."

"Oh, hi," the girl said. She barely glanced at Rachel, instead checking out the other, younger men. "Nice to meet you."

After an awkward moment Larry said, "Well, we're on our way out."

"Yeah, it *is* late for a school night," Rachel said, with an absolutely straight face. Larry and his date quickly departed.

Rachel sighed and rubbed her temples. Larry had tried

to make their first and only sexual encounter into something deep and spiritual, lighting incense and putting on Gregorian chants. He even read her some poetry that he'd written. When he brought out the body paints, though, she knew it was a mistake and never went out with him again. The memory of him saying, in his best FM-DJ voice, "Let me be your canvas, my darling," still made her giggle.

She looked around at the crowd. She saw several people with familiar-looking faces and one man who bore a passing resemblance to her ex-husband. *That* made her jump. But she saw no one else she actually knew.

Then a voice said, "Hello, Ms. Matre."

She turned. A gaunt middle-aged man, long gray hair falling out from under a Green Bay Packers hat, stood looking at her. His gaze was steady, not exactly a stare but definitely a bit unsettling on a night like this. He looked familiar, but she could not place him. "Hi," she said.

"I'm surprised to see you here. Out late again?"

"Well, you know how it is."

He laughed. "I sure do. See you around."

He moved through the crowd toward the exit. Rachel stared after him, still trying to put him in some context. His pants looked darker from the knees down, as if they were damp, but in a town full of artists that was hardly an extreme fashion choice. Just as the door closed behind him, she pegged it: He was the man who'd left the diner immediately after the altercation between Ethan and Caleb.

Rachel knew she'd have to wait until the end of the set to approach the girl onstage, so she pushed through the people milling at the counter and ordered an espresso. The long-haired barista frowned a little and tried not to sniff blatantly, but Rachel blushed anyway. Even with the room's accumulated body odor, her lake-tinted scent stood out. When she paid for her drink, Rachel asked, "So who's the girl playing?"

"Patty Patilia," the man said, and nodded at a flyer taped to the front of the counter. It showed the girl with her chin tucked down and eyes raised to look mysterious beneath her dark, curly hair. Her considerable cleavage dominated the shot. Her latest CD was called *The Sister and the Saracen* and was available directly from the artist for ten dollars, a percentage of which went to the local women's shelter. Six discs were also stacked on the counter. The covers had been signed in silver Sharpie ink, the *i*'s dotted with little hearts.

Rachel sipped her drink and worked her way back to her wall spot as Patty Patilia whisper-sang through her latest number. The flyer tried to make her look sexy, but in person she really wasn't. She was soft, feminine, and pretty but did not radiate that ineffable quality that made men drool and women envious. Without it, Rachel suspected she was witnessing the girl's career peak. Unless you could be sold as physically "hot," music nowadays had no use for you, no matter how talented you were. Madison was full of great musicians who proved that.

And yet the lake spirits called her a treasure. Could there be hidden depths in the girl's music? Was Rachel about to experience a musical epiphany, like the writer Jon Landau on the night he first heard "rock and roll's future," Bruce Springsteen?

The song ended to low-key applause. "Again, thank you," Patty Patilia said. "For my next song, I'd like to do something new. Something I hope will touch you and make you think. As you know, in the last few days three young women have disappeared in Madison, most likely raped and murdered. I didn't know them and they didn't know me, but any time a woman is a victim of violence, I feel like it's happened to a sister."

A woman in the audience said loudly, "That's 'cause men *suck*." A few people laughed.

Patty ignored the comment. "So, for my missing sisters, in sincere hope for their safe return, I offer this."

She strummed a deliberately Chinese-sounding riff and began to sing.

A girl from faraway Asian shores
Came to Wisconsin to learn some more
She looked up in wonder at the towering trees
And danced in the fall with their tumbling leaves
Now she's missing, and no one can find any trace
Of the black-haired girl with the shy little face

The night has swallowed you whole
The shadows took you away
You left us without any reason
And no clue how long you will stay . . .

And she held the note for a long moment before ending with, *"Gone."*

Nearby, a skinny young man with a small ring in his lip leaned close to his girlfriend and said loudly, "I've heard cats screw with more melody."

She nodded, displaying the spiderweb tattoo on the side of her neck. "It's inane," she agreed.

"Hey, shut up," said another young man, with a sparse, curly beard. He spoke softly, but his eyes burned with outrage and obvious unrequited passion for the singer. "She's not insane."

"I said *inane*," the girl snapped. "Like your soul patch."

Curly Beard blushed, his anger smothered by the pretty girl's disdainful certainty. Then he found a last reserve of courage. "Yeah, well, if you don't want to listen, go somewhere else, but some of us are enjoying it."

"Then you're, like, beyond help," Lip Ring said. "Come on, let's find something we can dance to." Spiderweb wrinkled her nose as she passed Rachel and followed Lip Ring to the door.

Rachel slid into their vacated spot closer to the stage. She'd listened to a lot of music in her life and understood the source of their disdain. Patty Patilia didn't sound like anyone else, and most of her songs embodied both her youth and her meager technical skill. But there *was* a spark. It was there in a distinctive chord change, a throaty bit of phrasing, a surprising lyrical choice. Maybe that potential, buried for now like all treasures, was what the spirits meant.

She forced her attention away from the girl and onto

the crowd. Something had just occurred to her. Was the man who would shortly terrify Patty Patilia—the kidnapper, or rapist, or killer—in this room right now? Was it the scraggly-bearded defender of Patty Patilia's honor (*Jesus*, she thought, *why does every man feel he has to protect a girl he likes from even the slightest trouble*)? Was it the guy with spiked hair, watching sullenly from a table near the other door? Or the older man with the bookish faculty air whose eyes never left Patty's ample boobs? There was no shortage of suspects.

And what if it wasn't a man at all? She assumed sex was the motivating factor, but what if it was jealousy or revenge? Or, hell, it still *could* be sex. These days girls were all over each other too.

Patty ended the song with a return to the Chinese melody.

Will we find you alive with flowers in your hair?
Will you be on the news clutching a teddy bear?
Are you hiding but safe, of your own accord?
Or do you lie decomposing in a muddy fjord?
We light our candles and say our prayers
Hoping once again to see your black shiny hair.

She stopped and said solemnly, "For you, Ling Hu." Then she looked down dramatically.

The crowd again applauded politely.

The longer Rachel listened, the more she liked Patty. There was an appealing gentleness in her pure, sincere voice, and she played with the enthusiasm of someone who believed she had something to offer. And she seemed genuinely grateful for the restrained clapping after each song. Rachel felt an unexpected spark of anger that someone wanted to change this sweet countenance into the terrified, screaming face she'd seen in the second part of her vision.

Then she laughed, softly and to herself, over the irony. Just like the scraggly-bearded boy, just like Marty Walker's brother, Ethan, she wanted to protect a damsel in distress. Look at her now, running around in the middle of the night, determined to slay the dragon and save the princess.

She sipped the espresso to counteract the physical weariness she felt. She'd been awake for nearly twenty hours straight, and between working a full shift and being energetically used by the lake, she was *beat*. But here was her girl, the one the lake spirits wanted her to protect, or warn, or *something*, and as long as she stayed in Rachel's sight, she could come to no harm.

Rachel hoped.

CHAPTER THIRTEEN

PATTY PATILIA'S SHOW ended at 12:15 A.M., and by then Rachel was ready to scream. The espresso mixed with her nerves to make her tenser than usual, and the constant uncertainty of not knowing which saccharine-laced tune would be the last set her temper on edge. It would've been bearable had the ratio of good to bad songs been higher.

As the crowd thinned, she took a seat at a wobbly table, and by the end of the set there were only five other people left, plus the barista, who looked asleep on his feet. She studied each of them as closely as she could without being blatant; none had the obvious look of a kidnapper. Two were college boys, two more were the girls with them, and the final patron was a gray-haired man with an asthma inhaler in his pocket. She couldn't rule him out, but he certainly seemed fragile and soft for someone who had overpowered three young, athletic college girls. Of course, a gun and the element of surprise might easily compensate.

At last Patty finished her final song, a long ode to a former downtown bookstore, the lyrics filled with literary references. She nodded to the remaining patrons and said, "And that, my beautiful friends, is the end. I hope you've enjoyed yourselves. Please, support your local artists and don't file-share."

The two young couples stood and clapped. Rachel sensed that they were Patty's friends, along for moral support. The older man with the inhaler stood and toddled— no other word for it—toward the men's room.

Rachel sat, fingertips drumming on the table, until the friends finally left. Patty then wiped down her guitar, placed it in the case, and folded the little stand she used to hold her songbook. Rachel stood at the edge of the riser and said, "Hi, I really enjoyed your show."

Patty looked up and smiled. *My God, she's a baby,* Rachel thought. Behind the eyeliner and lipstick she looked like a little girl masquerading as an adult. "Thank you," she said with guileless sincerity. "I saw you come in earlier, and I could tell you didn't expect the show. It means a lot that you stayed for the whole thing."

"There was no cover charge," Rachel said. "Wait, I'm sorry, that wasn't what I meant."

"It's okay. In a town full of music, sometimes the only way to be heard is to give it away for free. I do charge for the CDs, though."

"I didn't bring enough cash, I'm afraid."

"Excuse me," another voice said.

The old man with the inhaler stood politely, hands clasped behind his back. "I'm sorry for interrupting," he said, "but I wanted to catch you before you left. I think some of your lyrics are extraordinary."

"Thank you," Patty said, and bowed her head.

"Of course, some of them are utter tripe," the man continued. "In New York many years ago, I was fortunate enough to see an early show by a ragged-voiced young man from Minnesota named Robert Zimmerman. He, too, had glimmers of genius among the tripe. Through hard work, he learned to emphasize the genius and get rid of the rest. And I think you can do the same."

"Did he ever record anything?" Patty asked.

The old man smiled. "Yes. Under the name 'Bob Dylan.'" He touched his forehead, the gesture somehow chivalrous. "And with that, I'll say good night."

They both watched him pick his way through the disarrayed chairs scattered in the empty room. "Wow," Patty said after the door closed behind him. "Do you believe him?"

"That he saw Dylan? Sure, why not?"

"No, that I could be as *good* as Dylan." She looked up at Rachel with sincere interest.

"Everyone starts somewhere," Rachel said with a smile.

Patty reached into her bag and pulled out one of her CDs, along with a silver Sharpie. "Well, anyone as riveted by my music as you were deserves to have it, money or not. If your conscience bothers you, buy one at my next show and give it to someone as a gift." She took off the cap with her teeth and said around it, "Who should I make it out to?"

"Just Rachel."

"Rachel. That means *innocent,* doesn't it?"

"My father always told me it was a female sheep."

"In Hebrew, they represent the same thing."

"Then I guess *ewe* got it."

Patty giggled at the pun and handed her the CD. "Thank you again. I'm here next month, on the tenth. I hope to see you then. Bring some friends too."

Rachel did not move. Patty frowned and said, "Is something wrong?"

"No, I just . . . I want to tell you something."

Patty perched on the stool like an eager little girl and rested her elbows on her knees. "What?"

"I just . . . well . . ." Despite all the mental rehearsal, Rachel couldn't get the words out, knowing how weird they would sound.

Patty smiled sympathetically. "It's okay, Rachel," she said in a soft, patient tone. "I think you're lovely too. But I should tell you, I'm really not gay."

Rachel blinked, flushed, and said quickly, "No, that's not what I meant. I—"

Patty gently touched Rachel's arm. "I have to go. It's late, and I want to do some writing still tonight. More genius than tripe, I hope. Thank you again." She stood and deliberately turned away to put things into her bag.

Rachel was speechless. She quickly went outside, completely nonplussed. What should she do next? She started to toss the CD into a garbage can but at the last moment stopped. She turned it so she could read the inscription in the streetlight. *To Rachel, who stayed to the end. Love, Patty.* With a little smiley face.

Shit, she thought in annoyance. *Shit, shit, shit. Now I can't just throw it away. Or leave. Shit.* She tucked it into the waistband at the small of her back, found a shadowy place beneath a tree, and waited for Patty to emerge. No one would grab the girl in the coffeehouse, and if Rachel could at least ensure she got to her car okay, she'd feel as if she'd done her duty. And if she was caught following the girl, she could spend the rest of the night explaining why she *wasn't* a lesbian stalker. What could be better?

The traffic along Willie Street was light; in a couple of hours, when the bars all closed, the streets would flood with drunks and be truly dangerous. She wondered idly which of the half dozen vehicles parked nearby might turn out to be Patty's.

MARTY WALKER LOOKED across the table at his brother. "Why am I here?"

Ethan took a swallow of his beer. "Kinda deep for this place, isn't it?"

They sat in the Sparkler, a pizza restaurant directly across Willie Street from Father Thyme's. Run by an extended Hmong family, it was well regarded by the late-night-munchies crowd and equidistant between Ethan's home and Marty's. The staff always chattered away when they saw Marty, convinced he would eventually understand, despite his protests that he barely knew any of their language. They seemed disappointed at his thorough Americanization; sometimes, so was he.

Now, though, his disappointment and annoyance were

directed entirely at his brother. "It's after midnight, Ethan. I should be at home, asleep. So should you. So why did you call me?"

Ethan looked down at the tabletop and mumbled, "I couldn't sleep."

"So take some NyQuil."

"That's not why. I..." He took another swallow. "Okay, here it is. I can't get the woman from the diner out of my head."

"Rachel?"

"Yes, Rachel. I want to see her again, but she practically threw me out when I was there before."

" 'Practically'?" Marty said.

Ethan's eyes narrowed. "Have you talked to her since?"

"I go in there all the time. It came up."

"What did she say?"

Marty sighed, shook his head, and deadpanned, "I can't repeat it, it was too harsh. My virgin ears are still burning."

Ethan smacked him lightly on the side of the head. "Don't make me come over there."

Marty laughed and took a swallow of his own beer. "Man, you *are* tense."

"*What* did she *say*?"

"She said that she was sorry for throwing you out, and that if you came back, the first cup of coffee was on the house."

Ethan looked like a schoolboy granted a reprieve by the principal. "Really?"

"Cop's honor."

Ethan tapped idly on his beer bottle and looked out the front window. "So do you think I should go?"

"Can you keep your balls under control this time?"

"Look, the guy was an asshole, and—"

"And the diner is *hers,* not yours. You have to let people handle their own stuff."

"Even if they do it wrong?"

"Wrong or just different?"

Ethan sighed. After a moment he said, "Want to know something else? I called Julie earlier."

Marty's eyebrows went up. "No."

"Well, she called me first. I saw her number on my phone. I didn't talk to her or leave a message or anything. But she'll know."

"You don't need to get caught up in that again. Seriously. It was okay before you went overseas, but after that, something really fundamental changed in both of you. Once you got back it was like watching two sharks fighting over the last minnow."

Ethan looked away from his brother's steady gaze. The change, he knew, had been in him; Julie simply reacted to it. "I know. I'll ignore her next time."

"Good. I don't like to give advice—"

Ethan laughed. "You love to give advice."

"Okay, I love it, so listen to it, why don't you? Stay away from Julie. Go talk to Rachel. Move forward, not back."

Suddenly Ethan looked past Marty, out the window. His expression was so odd, Marty turned to follow his gaze. He saw nothing. "What?"

"This may sound crazy," Ethan said, "but I thought I just saw Rachel across the street, outside Father Thyme's."

THE COFFEEHOUSE DOOR opened with a loud squeak, and for a moment Patty stood silhouetted in the light. "Good night," she called back inside, then stepped out and let the door close. She'd gone halfway up the block before Rachel realized that she wasn't going toward any of the vehicles. She was *walking* home, alone, in the middle of the night.

Rachel slapped her palm against her forehead. This whole neighborhood was made up of students, for blocks and blocks in every direction. How could she not have thought of that? And each of those darkened houses and tree-shrouded streets represented a potential ambush.

"THAT *IS* CRAZY," Marty agreed. "It's going on one A.M., and she opens her diner at seven."

Ethan nodded, accepting Marty's explanation. But his reflexes, honed by the constant readiness necessary in the Middle Eastern desert, told him he'd been right.

Those same reflexes froze him in his chair when the Sparkler's door opened and Caleb Johnstone entered. The gray-haired man was out of breath and sweaty and did not notice Ethan. He walked to the counter and spoke to one of the Hmong girls, who took his money and handed him a pizza. Without looking Ethan's way, he went back outside and walked off down the street. He kept looking around, like a guilty man haunted by past misdeeds, until he turned a corner down the block.

"Now what?" Marty asked, waving his hand in front of Ethan's face. "You're awfully jittery tonight."

"That was the guy I ran out of Rachel's," Ethan said.

"Caleb?" Marty said. "Well, he's allowed to eat pizza too."

Ethan glanced back across the street, toward the coffeehouse. He was certain of what he'd seen, but there seemed no point in making an issue of it. Rachel was entitled to a late-night cup of coffee in someone else's establishment, and she had been alone. That, at least, was reassuring.

When he went to the counter to get his next drink, he noticed a tiny red smear on the floor that hadn't been there before. The only patron he'd seen near the spot was Caleb. He started to call Marty over, to see if the red stain was paint or blood, but then decided that would *really* sound paranoid. Besides, it was most likely just pizza sauce.

RACHEL MOVED AS silently as possible behind Patty, using the pools of shadow as she'd done earlier. Patty seemed oblivious to her presence, whistling and practically skipping up the sidewalk. She turned left, went down two blocks, crossed the street again, and headed up a slight hill toward the big houses that overlooked Lake Mendota. These were old structures now sliced into small apartments, the outsides covered with networks of wooden stairs.

A couple of cars passed but no other pedestrians. Rachel's exhausted calves burned with the effort of following the girl uphill. She slipped on a discarded beer can, and the noise of metal scraping on concrete tore through the relative silence.

Patty stopped and turned. Rachel dove into the shadows beside a car parked on the street, hoping this one didn't have a proximity alarm. Her breathing sounded like an industrial compressor in her ears, and she felt her pulse thump in her temples.

Patty stayed very still for a long moment, silhouetted beneath a streetlight. Then she resumed her trek.

Rachel crouched against the car. This was *nuts*. She'd done all she could, and that was that. She'd barely have time for a shower and nap by the time she got home, and she was too old to keep staying up all night this way.

Then, just as she was about to abandon Patty, the lights of another vehicle swept the empty street. She dropped back against the car as a Ford pickup rolled slowly past.

Rachel's throat constricted. She somehow knew, with utter certainty, that this was the truck she'd seen outside her diner and that it meant Patty harm. She tried to see the license plate, but the spot on the bumper was empty. She realized too late that the plate was displayed in the cab's back window.

The girl had reached the top of the hill and turned along the lakefront road. The truck was almost at the corner as well. Except for Rachel, there seemed to be no one around.

Rachel knew this was the moment. She had to do

something; she couldn't just let Patty be snatched off the street. She looked around for any inspiration and found it in a red Wisconsin *W* bumper sticker slapped haphazardly on the car hiding her.

She stood and ran up the hill, deliberately letting her feet slap the sidewalk to make as much noise as possible. "Whooo-EE!" she yelled as if drunk. "Go Badgers! *YEAH!*"

Patty turned toward her, then walked on more quickly. The truck stopped, turned in the opposite direction, and drove rapidly away. Rachel reached the corner in time to see Patty rush up the steps to one of the apartment houses. The door slam echoed in the night.

Rachel put her hands on her knees and bent over, stretching her hamstrings and gasping. Okay, *there:* princess saved, dragon thwarted. That should make the spirits happy. Now all she had to do was run three miles back to her apartment and grab what little sleep she could before it was time to open the diner again.

She listened once more for the truck's motor but heard nothing. Satisfied, she jogged wearily toward home.

CHAPTER FOURTEEN

RACHEL, HEAD DOWN, watched her own feet slap on the sidewalk. It was a bad habit, one of the main ones she'd tried to break since taking self-defense classes in college. *Walk with your head up,* the instructors had warned, *as if you can handle anything that comes your way. Looking down implies weakness.* And usually she did so, but tonight she was just too tired.

Which was why she didn't notice the truck pacing her, lights out, until it was almost too late.

Her mind was whirling with the night's events. What did it mean that the lake spirits could pull her from her body at will and send her wherever they wanted? Would it happen again? And why, after displaying only scenes from the past, did they now show her a glimpse of the future? Did it signal some change in the dynamic that had sustained her all these years?

A tire crunched over a discarded plastic soda bottle. Rachel looked up sharply and saw the truck. Its lights were out, and the dark shape behind the wheel radiated malevolence.

The outline alone was enough to spook her. With no conscious decision, she ran, cutting across a yard and tearing down the sidewalk toward home. She didn't glance back to see if the truck followed. By the time she stopped beneath a tree, huddling in its shadow, the vehicle had vanished. She waited to make sure it didn't reappear.

Had it been the same truck? She couldn't be sure. She began to tremble, delayed shock looking for a foothold in her system. She refused to give it one, though, and instead took off toward home, running as fast as her weary legs would go.

As she ran, her common sense took the time to berate her for being a fool. Was she a detective? A bodyguard? A night watchman, even? No, she was a restaurateur, for God's sake, a glorified fry cook. All she could do, all she should be *expected* to do, was pass on information so that the people trained and paid to deal with these problems would know where to look for them. All along she'd assumed the spirits were omniscient, or at least had access to more information than her limited human consciousness. Now she knew better. Who sent a fry cook to do a bodyguard's job?

IT SHOULD'VE BEEN enough terror for one night.

She stopped a couple of blocks from the diner to walk and cool down. Because it was late, and quiet, and she still twitched from adrenaline, anything out of the ordinary stood out in sharp relief. So the black truck parked in front of her diner, engine running, muffled music audible, might as well have been under a spotlight.

She ducked into the shadow of the old battery factory. Luckily the night's other events had pretty much burned out her need to panic; now she was only weary and annoyed.

What next, an alien invasion?

But this wasn't the same truck as before. It was newer, a Nissan, and had some sort of writing stenciled on the door. She was at the wrong angle to read it, though.

She wiped sweat from her eyes with the tail end of her shirt. If she went back to the corner, she could cross the street, go up two blocks, and approach the diner from the other side. Then she could slip in through the back kitchen door, and whoever sat in the truck would never see her. She would, as always, be safe and secure.

Part of her, though, wanted to force the confrontation, to see the face of whoever was waiting for her. She was angry now and at the end of her patience.

After the last stalking incident with Curtis the obsessed delivery driver, she swore she would never tolerate such behavior again. She had done nothing to encourage him, yet he left her flowers, sent her cards, and finally began driving past the diner at all hours. She learned to recognize, and dread, the sound of his truck's diesel engine. Still, it did not terrify her until he began showing up just at closing or right before opening, his angular face pressed against the glass, a smile more predatory than seductive splitting his face. She'd called the police, notified his company, and sworn out a protective order against him. The new driver on his route told her he'd left the state. It had been weeks, though, before she truly felt safe again.

She had a gun in her apartment, bought right after the Curtis incident. She kept it loaded, cleaned it once a month, and told absolutely no one about it. Not even Helena knew. Given her other secrets, keeping this one was a snap. But she'd always wondered if, in the moment, she could pull the trigger on another human being.

If they pushed things tonight, she knew. They'd go down. *Et tu,* babycakes.

She quickly circled the block and, staying in the shadows, crept to the kitchen door. She slipped her key in the lock and turned it. There was no resistance; the door was unlocked. Only she and Helena had keys, and Rachel never forgot to lock up.

She opened the door enough to peek inside. It was dark and silent. "Helena?" she hissed. There was no response. More loudly she said, "Helena, it's me. Are you here?"

She got no answer. She entered quietly and closed the door behind her, careful to lock it. Then she stayed in the shadows, crept to the front window, and peered out. The truck was there, engine idling, music playing. She still could not make out the words on the door.

She rushed up the stairs to her apartment. *That* door was still locked, and she opened it in record time. Without turning on any lights, she went to the dresser. Tainter, sensing her mood, halted midway through his bound of greeting and scampered aside.

She lifted the gun, reassured by its weight in her hands. It was a short-barreled .38 revolver, the classic Colt "ladies' gun." The smell of metal and oil gave her a rush of power. She purposefully strode to the window, the weapon held against her thigh. Carefully, she turned the handle on the blinds so that they slowly angled down.

She had a clear line of sight at the driver-side tires, and the windshield gleamed with reflected street light. She might not be able to see who was in there, but she could surely take him out.

Her thumb flicked the safety off. In her mind, her ex-husband, Don, her stalker, Curtis, her lecherous uncle Hammy, all stood before her. *You just need to do it until you learn to like it,* Don said. *I can't wait to put my tongue all over you,* Curtis panted. And worst of all, Hammy, saying in that tone adults use when kids are being stupid, *It's just so you'll know what to do to your boyfriends when they kiss you, honey.*

None of them believed she'd shoot. They were about to learn different.

Whoa, she thought suddenly. *I am panicking. This is anger, not sense. I'm pissed off because of the other things, not this thing. I should handle this thing differently, before I really mess things up.*

The anger dissipated almost at once, leaving behind a sense of chagrined calm. She closed her eyes, counted slowly to ten, and made sure the rage was gone for good. Then she flicked the safety back on, replaced the gun in her nightstand, and dialed 911. She gave a concise report of the truck sitting outside her building. The operator assured her a car would be sent immediately. She snapped the phone closed, dragged her old bar stool to the window, and waited.

It took ten minutes, but finally a police car did pull up beside the truck, and its blinding spotlight shone into the cab. After a moment the driver's window rolled down and her stalker leaned out into the light. She could see only his dark hair and wide shoulders. But when the door swung open and he stepped out of the vehicle, she immediately recognized him.

Ethan Walker.

She gasped as her body, despite all the night's drama, responded to this realization.

ETHAN SQUINTED into the policeman's light and waited politely. Never speak first, Marty always told him. Nothing pisses a cop off worse than a mouthy perp, and a pissed-off cop is more likely to hurt you.

The thick-bodied black woman looked at Ethan's driver's license and saw that it was the same name as written on the door of the truck. She said, "Sir, have you been drinking?"

"No, ma'am," Ethan said. The buzz from the pizza place had faded, and he'd picked up a cup of coffee from Denny's on his way here.

"Then what are you doing out here?"

He took a deep breath. There was no point in making anything up. Sheepishly, he said, "I met a girl here yesterday. I don't know how to get in touch with her. I just sort of . . . I don't know, I just wanted to come by. Visit the scene of the crime, you know?"

"Crime?" the officer repeated.

"Yeah, you know." He grinned. "Where she stole my heart."

For a moment she kept her stern, straight face. Then she busted out laughing. "You're serious, aren't you?"

"Halfway," he said with a shrug.

"That might be cute, if you were fourteen. But by all appearances, you're a grown man."

"Yes, ma'am."

"I'd think you'd be able to handle a schoolboy crush a little better than this."

"Crush" doesn't do it justice, he wanted to say. Instead, he said, "I suppose you're right. I didn't think it through very well."

She handed him back his license. "Okay, Romeo. But this is a pretty quiet neighborhood, and with all these girls disappearing, people are skittish. They see a big black truck sitting out here in the middle of the night, engine running, and they call us. So why don't you toodle on home and try again tomorrow, during the day? Maybe bring her flowers?"

Ethan smiled. "Yes, Officer. Sorry for the bother."

"No bother, as long as you're telling me the truth and I don't catch you back here again."

"You won't."

"All right, then. Good night," she called as she walked to her car.

Ethan put his wallet back in his pocket, climbed into

his truck, and sat there feeling more stupid than he had since high school algebra class. It was one thing to have sexual fantasies about a woman you barely knew but another entirely to sit outside her place of business as if she might magically appear, answering the same carnal call of the night. Was he suddenly a love-struck adolescent again?

He put the truck in gear and sped away.

RACHEL WATCHED his truck vanish into the night. She was shaking again, but not from fear. The god-awful lust had returned, just as bad as before, as if the night's tryst with the lake had not even happened.

She went into the bathroom and started a cold shower. Her fingers shook as she peeled off her sweaty clothes. And as the icy spray first touched her, something she'd completely forgotten rose from her memory, adding an emotional chill to the water's effect.

Back at Father Thyme's, the man in the Packers cap had asked, *Out late again?* She was not a regular at the coffeehouse, and she visited the lake in secret, so how did he know she was out late *again*?

CHAPTER FIFTEEN

A KNOCK ON THE DOOR awakened Rachel. She was sprawled facedown on the couch, the TV playing softly in the background. She wore only a man's undershirt, and when she moved, every muscle protested. She stood with a groan, dislodging Tainter from the small of her back, and grabbed sweatpants from the floor in the bathroom. Without removing the security chain, she opened the door.

Helena stood there, her expression odd. "What time is it?" Rachel asked sleepily.

"It's five A.M., but . . . something awful has happened."

"To you?"

Helena looked like she might cry. "No, it's . . . Can you please open the door?"

Rachel closed the door, removed the chain, and opened it all the way. "What?"

"You better come downstairs and see for yourself."

Rachel followed Helena downstairs. When she came into the diner, she froze, eyes wide.

The dry-erase walls were covered in enormous, sloppy red writing. *Fuck you bitches* was written in two-foot-high red letters along one wall. *Kiss my ass whores* took up another wall. One of the counter stools had been wrenched from its base, and red paint had been poured into the toaster and coffeemaker.

"Jesus Christ," Rachel whispered. "How did... When..." After the events of the previous night—hell, she though bitterly, of just a few *hours* ago—she lacked the stamina to control herself much more. She felt tears surge up, and it took everything she had not to let them fall.

The kitchen door opened and Jimmy entered, whistling. When he saw the writing he stopped in mid-note. "Holy shit. What happened?"

Helena shook her head. "I don't know. What time did you get home last night, Rachel?"

She said nothing, but the evening's events rushed through her head. The door had been unlocked, but she hadn't turned on the lights when she went to look out the front window. She had been so focused on the man in the truck that she hadn't even glanced at the walls. Had Ethan done this? No, that made no sense at all. If not him... then who? The man she'd chased away from Patty? Some random gang of teens?

"Okay, here's what we're going to do," Rachel said. She caught Jimmy staring at her breasts, which the baggy undershirt did little to hide. Crossing her arms, she said, "Jimmy, go down to the Ace Hardware across from St. Vinnie's thrift shop and get three gallons of red paint and three of those long-handled rollers. Do it fast; they open at five-thirty. Helena, you go out to Target and get us a new toaster and coffeemaker; they're open twenty-four hours. When Jimmy gets back, we'll paint over those lovely comments and get ready for our customers. I'll order some replacement wall panels and a new stool today too. In the meantime, put a *wet floor* sign over that spot so nobody gets tetanus from those broken screws."

"On it, boss," Jimmy said, and left. Helena put her hand on Rachel's shoulder and said, "Are you sure? Shouldn't we call the cops or something? Maybe not open today?"

Rachel shook her head. "I'll talk to my insurance company and see if this is covered. If they need a police report, then I'll call the cops. But if we don't open, then whoever did this wins."

Helena started to say something else, thought better of it, and followed Jimmy outside.

When she was alone, the morning sun just lighting the tops of the trees outside the window, Rachel sighed, bowed her head, and allowed herself to cry for five minutes. Who could have done this? Who could hate her that much?

Only one name came to mind: Don Talley, her ex-husband. He was petty enough to do this, but would he? She recalled the truck that followed her on the way home. She hadn't looked closely to see if it was, in fact, the same truck that had menaced Patty. Could it have been Don, intending harm only to her?

That marriage had been the single biggest mistake she'd ever made. She had met him at a wedding she catered back when she ran Soirees to Go, and at first he'd seemed so easygoing, likable, and charming that she thought, briefly, he might understand her relationship with the lakes. He'd dazzled her with his attention, and before she knew it she was Mrs. Rachel Talley.

By the end of the next six months, she was ready to commit murder or suicide, whichever opportunity presented itself first. Don had hidden a mass of insecurities the size of Australia behind that charming exterior, all of which he now felt free to expose. At first she'd tried to reassure him and assuage his ego, but it was just too much. And it all coalesced and eventually centered around one thing: her inability to have an orgasm with him.

She'd mentioned she liked to skinny-dip and planned to tell him the whole truth soon after their honeymoon. But almost at once he became fixated on making her come. He insisted that if he had just five more minutes, even when they'd stretched things out to nearly an hour, she would've gotten "there." He blamed everything on her lack of regular orgasms, and since he also kept her away from the lakes, she grew more tense and snippy as well. Their home became a battleground and their bed the Russian front: cold, brutal, and the site of unbelievable carnage.

But Don hadn't contacted her in years. The last she heard, he was in Hong Kong. What could have brought him back after all this time, seeking revenge only now for some perceived wrong?

She looked up at the graffiti. It was impossible to

identify the handwriting. And if Don had come all this way, would this be *all* he would do?

That thought made her carefully look around for more damage. She found none, but perhaps this was merely the beginning of something. Would she have to be on her guard constantly now, like she'd been for Curtis?

"No," she said aloud, hands on her hips. "No one will terrorize me. Not Don, not Curtis, not anyone." Her words echoed off the empty, defaced walls.

Then she headed upstairs to get ready for the day.

THEY MANAGED to cover the words before the first patron, Mrs. Boswell, arrived. She looked at the patchy painting, scowled a bit at the smell, but said nothing. She took her usual seat, opened her newspaper, and began to read. Helena poured her coffee and took her order as if nothing unusual had happened.

Suddenly Mrs. Boswell exclaimed, "Oh, my goodness. Oh, this is awful. Did you see this?"

She pointed at a photo on the front page. "That poor Chinese girl who disappeared—Ling Hu. They found her body last night, or, rather, early this morning."

Rachel looked up from the sink where she was wiping down the new coffee carafe. The name cut through her hazy, sleep-deprived brain, carried on the half-remembered melody of Patty Patilia's song. She rushed from the kitchen, sat on the counter, and swung her legs over it to the other side. She peered at the newspaper over Mrs. Boswell's shoulder.

"I knew it would end like this," Mrs. Boswell said. "But it's still just so awful."

The byline was by Julie Schutes. The lead paragraph read:

Fishermen found the body of missing UW–Madison student Ling Hu in Lake Mendota before dawn this morning. Police say at present they know neither the cause of death nor how long the body had been in the water.

Rachel scanned the rest of the article. With nothing new to report, it simply rehashed the previous coverage. This included reprinted quotes from people who knew the girl, photos of the original crime scene and apartment building, and of course a photo of the girl herself, the image significantly smaller than the one showing her covered body being loaded into an ambulance.

Rachel felt hollow as she stood up. She knew nothing about this girl, she'd had no visions regarding her, and had gleaned her *Lady of the Lakes* info from the usual cop scuttlebutt. But there was Ling Hu, smiling in one picture and dead under a sheet in the other. The other two missing girls would no doubt soon meet a similar end. But at least she'd saved Patty.

"That's so *sad*," Mrs. Boswell said. "She was such a lovely little thing."

The door opened, and Elton Charles entered, sweaty from his morning run. "Did you see the news? They found one of those girls who disappeared." He did a double take at the red walls but, like Mrs. Boswell, said nothing.

"I was just reading about it," Mrs. Boswell said, holding up the paper.

Helena put a large glass of orange juice down in front of Elton, then turned to Rachel. "Are you all right?" she asked quietly. "If you need to go upstairs for a while..."

Rachel shook her head. "I'm just really tired," she said, and went into the kitchen and began scrubbing red drops of paint from a pot, just to have a task. She was too exhausted to cry again, but she knew it would come tonight when she was alone—tears for a total stranger. And then there was the practical consideration: What would *The Lady of the Lakes* have to say about this?

HELENA WATCHED her boss with concern. She couldn't imagine why this news bothered Rachel so much, when she'd taken the vandalizing with such equanimity. They didn't know the victim, and while it was sad, the world was full of sad things.

Before she could ponder it further, though, the bell over the door jangled and Marty Walker entered. He hung his suit jacket on the wall peg and took his usual seat at the end of the counter, nodding at Elton and Mrs. Boswell. Then he stared at the red walls.

"Surprised to see you in here," Helena said as she put coffee in front of him. "Shouldn't you be at Lake Mendota with all the other cops?"

"I have been. Now it's all about waiting for test results

and other lab things." He nodded at the red wall. "What happened?"

Helena glanced back toward the kitchen. "Spur-of-the-moment experiment. What do you think?"

"It's a little . . . ragged around the edges, isn't it?"

Helena shrugged. "That's what I thought too. Way too modern art for me. But there was no way to know without doing it. I bet we go back to the white walls pretty soon."

Marty looked at her oddly, then looked past her at the kitchen doorway. "Is Rachel back there?"

"Yeah."

"Could you ask her to come out here a moment?"

Helena turned and called, "Hey, boss! You got a visitor."

When Rachel approached, Marty stood and said, "Can we step outside for a moment?"

Rachel glanced at his shoulder holster. "Your gun's showing. Am I in trouble?"

"No, nothing like that. Just something I'd like to discuss in private."

RACHEL FOLLOWED Marty outside. It was already warm, and the air hung with mist the sun had not yet burned away. She put her hands on her hips and said, "Yes, Officer?"

"I want to apologize for my idiot brother."

"Again?"

"Apparently. I talked to him this morning about his little, uh . . ."

"Covert surveillance?" She said it without a smile, because it certainly wasn't funny.

"Let's say overzealous approach."

"Let's say stalking."

"Rachel, I'm really sorry. So is Ethan. He was just lonely and sleep-deprived and not thinking things through. He wanted to come with me and apologize himself, but I said it'd be better this way."

"Did he really?"

"Yes," Marty said. "Ethan takes things to do with personal honor very seriously."

"That whole once-a-soldier thing."

"No, he's always been that way. I admit you've seen the less admirable aspects of him, but, really, he's a good, decent guy. He didn't mean to step on your toes when he chased away that troublemaker, and he didn't realize parking outside the diner would freak you out."

Rachel looked down as she pondered this. Someone had spray-painted a small stencil of a broken heart on the sidewalk, and it was faded but still visible. At last she said, "He probably didn't even know I lived here, did he?"

"Probably not. I didn't tell him."

"And he *is* your brother."

"All my life."

"And I *did* invite him back. Although I kind of imagined it would be during business hours."

Marty smiled.

She blew a curl from her forehead. She had been passive in responding to everything that happened last night; here, at least, was a chance to be direct. "Okay, Marty, tell you what. Give me his number and I'll call him and talk to him. If it's like you say, just a string of misunderstandings, then everything's cool. But if he does one more weird-ass thing, he's out. For good, end of story, restraining order filed. I mean it."

Marty handed her a business card. "That's his office and cell number."

She read over the card. "He runs his own business?"

"Well enough to support our father's farm too. Because God knows Dad isn't making any money at it."

Rachel put the card in her pocket. "Okay. But I'm serious: no more weirdness. I don't need it, and I won't put up with it."

Marty held up his hands. "It's between you and Ethan now."

JULIE SCHUTES sipped stale coffee as she read through the text on her screen. She desperately wanted a shower but didn't trust the office to let her know if any new information came in. She wasn't some blank-skulled TV reporter, after all; she was a whole lot more than her pretty face and top-rate legs, although she was not above using whatever it took to get the story. Her coworkers, especially the female ones, saw this as an unfair advantage and took any chance to sabotage her.

The call about Ling Hu's body had come in at 3:30 A.M., and she was at the crime scene fifteen minutes later. On the way there, she'd called Sam Garnett and told him to hold the morning edition, that she'd have the story within an hour. It had taken a Herculean group effort to get it done, and she'd actually been impressed with the way Garish stroked everyone's ego so that the end result was important to them all. Maybe he wasn't such a putz.

She'd written the story on her laptop in the car, then pasted in sections from her earlier stories to reach an acceptable word count. Now she had to write a *real* story for the next day's edition. She had her contacts at the coroner's office primed to notify her as soon as the cause of death was determined, far in advance of any official announcement. Using her most sympathetic, gosh-I'm-nearly-in-tears voice, she'd left messages with Ling Hu's friends, seeking comments. She'd written the outline and all the prose around the comments, so now she just had to wait for the phone to ring.

She saved her work, then switched over to the Internet. *The Lady of the Lakes,* curiously, said nothing about Ling Hu. That struck her as odd; how could a person or group know about every cat stuck in a tree and yet *not* know about this? Did he/she/they just not care? Was it a racial or political thing, because the victim was Chinese?

This lapse was a clue, she realized, to the identity of the mysterious blogger. She made a note in the special file she kept, one more tidbit that would, someday, allow Julie to unmask this erstwhile Lady. Then her phone rang with the first of many returned calls.

———

LATER, AS SHE stood on State Street, Rachel wondered what would really qualify as "weirdness." She was exhausted after last night's adventures and really should be at home, resting and dealing with the vandalism, instead of standing downtown in the summer heat. She certainly shouldn't be wearing a vaguely provocative spaghetti-strap top, a tight khaki skirt, and high-heeled open-toed shoes. And she definitely didn't need the splash of red lipstick that, she knew from experience, accented her mouth in a way that made most men a little nervous. Yet here she was, gazing at the tasteful sign that said *Walker Construction,* while Helena and Jimmy prepared for the lunch crowd and got the estimate to replace the damaged dry-erase wallboards and the ripped-out stool. Some boss she was.

She could've just *called* Ethan, of course. His cell-phone number was on the card Marty gave her. That would've been enough for most people. But something in her practically screamed to be in his presence again, and she figured that during the middle of the day, in public, would be the best way to keep from making a fool of herself. Well, a *bigger* fool.

She went inside and took the stairs instead of the elevator. When she emerged onto the third floor, she easily found the right door. She opened it and saw a sparse office suite with a young Indian woman at the receptionist desk.

The woman looked up and blinked with slow, dramatic disdain; obviously she felt Rachel was in the wrong place and the distraction annoyed her. She said, "May I help you?" but for a moment it wasn't clear if she was speaking to Rachel or into her headset mouthpiece. After a moment she added, "Yes, miss, you standing right there."

"I'm looking for Ethan Walker," Rachel said.

"He's not in at the moment. May I take a message?"

What message could she leave? *Came by your office to see if I still get weak-kneed at the sight of you?* "No, thanks, I'll try back later."

"He won't be in the office at all today," the receptionist said.

"Thanks," Rachel said, and turned on her heel. When she got to the stairs again, she stopped, leaned against the rail, and took several deep breaths, surprised at how nervous she had been. What did she expect to happen? That he'd appear, throw her across the nearest desk, and act out the fantasy that kept replaying in her mind?

A sudden wave of weariness made her sit on the top step and lean against the painted concrete wall. She licked her lips, tasting salt from sweat unrelated to temperature. Then she dialed the cell-phone number on the business card.

It rang twice before a confident masculine voice said, "Ethan Walker here."

"Is this Ethan Walker?" Rachel asked before she could stop herself.

He chuckled. Some sort of engine rumbled in the background, and voices shouted in Spanish over it. "Yes. And who's this?"

Grateful that he could not see her blush, she said with extra dignity, "This is Rachel Matre."

"I'm sorry, there's a lot of machinery here. Who?"

"Rachel ... Matre," she repeated, her voice echoing in the stairwell. "I own Rachel's Diner, off Willie Street."

There was a long pause, during which she heard more Spanish and the sound of metal pounding on metal. Finally Ethan said stiffly, "What can I do for you, Ms. Matre?"

"Uh, actually, I thought I could do something for you."

Did she imagine the little catch in his voice when he asked, "And what's that?"

"Buy you lunch."

"At your diner?"

"Well, that's an idea, but I'm in the stairwell of your office building downtown, so it might be closer, and maybe better, if we meet on neutral ground."

Again the silence and the noise of whatever construction he was supervising. Then he said, "Yeah, okay. Do you know where the Angelic Cannery is?"

"On Johnson Street?"

"That's it."

She looked at her watch. "I can be there in five minutes."

"It'll take me thirty."

"Okay, I'll meet you there."

"Okay."

"Bye."

"Bye."

She snapped the phone closed and put it back in her purse. She was breathing quickly and shallowly all of a sudden. There was no way this could go well; at most she would end up with a clear conscience, knowing that she had tried and could therefore look Marty Walker in the eye when he asked what happened. Besides, she was certain Ethan Walker didn't date women like her. His type was probably blond, professional, with an immaculate wardrobe and a solid golf swing.

Someone like that *Cap Jo* reporter, she bet.

ETHAN STARED at the phone in his hand. Had that just happened? He opened it again and pulled up the recent calls. Sure enough, there it was. She *had* called him, and they *had* made a lunch date. Son of a gun.

He ran a hand through his hair. He'd committed himself without thinking it through and suddenly felt both foolish and, inexplicably, afraid.

His foreman, Richie, stopped a few feet away. "You all right? Did you get some bad news?"

"Huh? Oh. Yeah, I'm okay. I just . . . I have a meeting downtown in half an hour. I'll be back around two. Keep things moving, will you?"

"As if you were an angel on my shoulder," Richie assured him.

FAITH LUCAS and Carrie Kimmell looked silently at each other over their duct-tape gags. The basement was sweltering again, and the dim light that filtered around the edges of the tiny blacked-out window allowed them to just make each other out. Both women were exhausted, thirsty, and starved, and their bodies burned with pain. Their captor would bring them water soon and maybe another handful of saltines, just enough to keep them alive. But their thoughts were entirely focused on the fate of the Asian girl who'd been taken away and had not returned.

Faith sat with her bare shoulders against the wall. Her wrists were raw, and she felt blood trickle from the furrows cut into them by the handcuff ties. The slippery lotion smeared on her skin made her thighs slide together, but the pain there was so insistent that she sat awkwardly bowlegged, her tied ankles crossed. She slowly worked her hands back and forth, gasping behind the duct-tape gag whenever the plastic strip worked into a sore spot. She was no longer terrified, she was simply numb, her feeble escape attempts now a mere reflex. The plastic would not break; she would not escape.

Suddenly the basement door banged open. Both girls jumped, and Carrie inchwormed back against the wall, her shoulder against Faith's. Their captor stood in the door, breathing heavily, and clearly alone. There was no sign of the Asian girl taken away the previous evening or the bottles of water they'd been expecting. Instead, the hand that pointed at Carrie trembled with either weariness or fear. "Now. You."

Faith sighed with relief. Carrie began to cry.

CHAPTER SIXTEEN

WHY DID SHE HAVE *to wear that skirt?* Ethan thought as he stepped into the air-conditioned restaurant. Those exquisite legs as she rose from the bench beside the door made his own knees wobble. And, worse, the cold air had the usual effect it did on women's nipples, and he had to force his eyes to remain above her neck. "Ms. Matre," he said with a smile, feeling unaccountably like he had on his first date back in junior high. Christ, he thought, should he have brought her a corsage?

RACHEL'S STOMACH did flips as she stood. He was silhouetted in the doorway like a chiseled statue, and as he moved into the amber-tinted interior light, his skin seemed bronze. Again she realized how young he was; he couldn't yet be thirty. Was she metaphorically robbing the cradle, or at least the middle school?

When he touched her hand, she got a sudden intimate

tingle that almost choked her voice. This was no little boy. "Call me Rachel," she said, glad the shiver hadn't reached her throat.

They followed the greeter to a table in the back, near the glass wall that displayed the huge beer vats. Ethan tried to hold her chair for her, but it was so unexpected that she ended up knocking it to the floor, where its crash echoed through the restaurant. Blushing, glad for the dim lighting, she picked it up and sat.

"Sorry," Ethan said as he took his seat opposite her. "Habit."

"It's a nice habit," she said too quickly. "It's just something I don't get very often."

The waitress brought menus and water. Rachel's mouth was dry, so she drank most of hers in one swallow. She ordered a beer; Ethan requested a martini, extra wet. "I have to go back to work later," he explained. "You know all those warnings about operating heavy equipment? They're there for a reason."

After both had ordered their meals, Ethan said, "First things first. I apologize for last night. I just ... I was out, you crossed my mind, and I drove by the diner to just ... I don't know. I didn't realize you lived there too." He spread his hands helplessly and smiled.

"I've had some bad experiences with men being a little too pushy, so I'm probably oversensitive. If I'd come outside and said something to you at the time, we could've cleared it up without the police." She took a deep breath. "And now it's my turn. I'm sorry for throwing you out the other day. That was an overreaction. You meant well, and no harm was done."

"Thank you," he said with a nod.

They sat in awkward silence until Rachel finally said, "So you're in construction?"

He nodded. "It's a small company, but we've gotten some nice contracts. Condos around the lakes and such. Might lead to bigger and better things."

"Are things that are bigger necessarily better?" Immediately she winced at her choice of words, but he seemed not to notice.

He said, "No, I don't think size is the *only* criteria for something's value."

"I've seen a lot of beautiful property replaced by things that were bigger and heard all the reasons it was better. I'm not convinced. The old battery factory needs to be torn down, but God only knows what they'll replace it with. More of your condos, probably. Homes to keep people from ever having to meet their neighbors."

He kept his tone light. "Well, everyone's idea of beauty is different, I suppose."

She leaned slightly toward him, her eyes intent. She tried to keep her tone from growing shrill, but this was an issue she had strong feelings about. "Beauty? You call those new McBuildings beautiful? If we're not careful, everyplace will look like everyplace else. If I see one more Walgreens go up where something original and special used to be, I'll turn corporate terrorist."

He sat back, reacting to her intensity. After a moment he said lightly, "Good thing I don't build Walgreens, then."

"I know, but you do *build*. Whether there's a need for it or not."

"If you're going to start by ripping me a new one over my chosen career, then we won't have much to talk about," he pointed out.

She paused, then smiled and looked down. "I suppose you're right. I actually *do* have manners, I promise." She looked back up, tossing her head to get a stray curl from her eyes. "So, to be fair, is there anything you want to get off your chest about diners?"

"No, I generally approve of them." He paused, then added, "And the beautiful women who run them."

Their eyes met. A long moment passed before they simultaneously looked away.

Finally Rachel said, "And own them."

"And own them," he agreed.

She smiled. "Thank you."

He drank from his martini. "I guess it's not really news if I say that I find you very attractive and would like to get to know you better."

"No, I've caught on to that," she said coolly, hiding all the volcanoes erupting within her.

"How do you feel about it?"

She took a swallow of her beer. "I guess . . . well, I'd be lying if I said I hadn't also been thinking about you."

"So it's mutual?"

"It is."

He smiled.

"But I should warn you, I don't have a great history with relationships."

"With men in general, or just builders?"

"Oh, it's everyone. I was married once, and that ended badly. I haven't really dated much, because I tend to attract—no offense—men who want to turn me into something else. And I have a lot of other . . . issues." *To put it mildly,* she thought.

"I've hit some relationship speed bumps too," he said. He might've turned red as well, but she couldn't tell in the uncertain light. "I think the trick is to start slowly and make sure we don't cross any lines prematurely."

She nodded. "Okay. So how do we start?" Her body knew exactly how it wanted to start, and finish as well. But she kept that to herself.

He thought for a minute, in that exaggerated way that meant he already knew the answer. "Why don't we try dinner tonight and then see what happens?"

She looked at him closely, suddenly seeing things she'd missed. He was physically big and had the confidence that went with that, but there was also something quieter, an assurance that came from self-knowledge more than any external source. He was who he was, and he was content with that. There was none of the self-pity the other men in her life had worn like a badge. The realization was almost like a breeze on a hot day.

"Why don't we, then?" she said at last, and smiled.

THE BOY WAS looking for a quiet, shaded place to study for his upcoming physics test. He left the park's worn path and climbed down the bank to where the big gray rocks marked the shoreline of Lake Monona on the isthmus's southern edge. The century-old oaks blocked the sun, and the only sound was the irregular slap of the waves. He found a comfortable spot, kicked off his sandals, and prepared to open his laptop.

Then he noticed the clothes.

Jeans, shoes, socks, bra, and sleeveless T-shirt. No panties. The boy, an avid reader of *The Lady of the Lakes* blog, immediately suspected what he'd found and called 911 on his cell phone. Thanks to the driver's license and debit card tucked into a pocket, the police quickly determined that the clothes' owner was, or had been, Patty Patilia. She had last been seen leaving her nearby apartment three hours earlier. She'd been snatched in broad daylight barely four blocks from the state capitol.

CHAPTER SEVENTEEN

THE MAN CLOSED the basement door and got a beer from the refrigerator. It was so hot down there that he always felt like he needed a shower after each visit. His sweat-soaked underwear made him itch. Yet his beauties repaid him for their water by the way their skin glimmered and trembled in the light, and that was worth any discomfort. He discovered it was ridiculously easy to forget the Asian one who'd died.

He sat at the kitchen table, lit a joint, and looked at his watch. It was only dinnertime, nowhere close to night. He longed for darkness, for the time to get behind the wheel of his truck again and go cruising for Rachel Matre. He'd learned her habits well enough now to know she would be out late, jogging along the lake, just as she'd done the night before. Finding her was just a matter of patience and luck, the former of which he could control. He trusted fate for the latter. After all, with the exception of the Chinese girl dying on him, everything had gone perfectly. And even that hadn't really been his fault.

He took a long drag off the joint. His fingers tingled as the chemical lethargy settled in. It would be time soon enough; for now, he could luxuriate in the anticipation.

"THAT WAS NICE," Rachel said as Ethan opened his truck's passenger door for her.

"You sound surprised," he said as he took her arm and helped her down. She saw him admire the way the summer dress crept up her thighs; she appreciated the arm muscles visible past the cuff of his short sleeves.

"Well, with all the misfires between us, I wasn't getting my hopes up," she said. She smoothed down her dress, a bright green floral pattern that she knew brought out her eyes. It stopped just above the knee, not far enough to be scandalous but certainly well within the come-ahead-Fred range. In a pinch, though, it could also mark the no-way-José line. She was still uncertain how to designate it for the evening, although the moment of truth was approaching fast.

Ethan clicked the key chain, and the little chirp told him the truck was locked. She smiled at this little act of faith. What would he do if she left him stranded on the doorstep after a quick peck on the cheek?

When she turned to face him, she tottered a little, as if the dress shoes were unfamiliar, and saw him suppress a chuckle. What he didn't know was that the stumble was completely unrelated to the shoes. Instead, she was struck anew by his masculine silhouette, by the way his chest and arms strained against the polo shirt's fabric while his waist didn't even touch the material where it dangled over his belt. There was nothing threatening about this either, like with some muscular men. It simply made her knees wobble and filled her with the desire to run her hands over his chest.

How will I get through this, she wondered, *with my dignity intact?*

DINNER AT MADISON'S unique Ella's Deli had been a delight, not least because Rachel didn't have to cook any of it. Afterward, Ethan took her for a ride on the old-fashioned carousel outside. Finally they stopped at the Harmony Bar for drinks and left when the live music started.

They'd both learned their lesson at lunch. All evening the conversation had steered mercifully clear of politics, religion, or anything remotely controversial. Instead, they discussed favorite songs, movies that made them laugh, and books that meant a lot to them. She was pleasantly surprised that he was so well read and delighted that he loved John Mellencamp's "Cherry Bomb." And, most surprising for a male, he hated anything involving Adam Sandler. She told him about running and listened politely while he described his weight-training routine.

The physical tension between them could've lit a cigarette, but she didn't mention it. She forced it down, afraid of disconcerting him with the intensity of her erotic response. But she sensed that it was reciprocal, and by the time they arrived back at her diner's door, she was sure they both wanted to simply rip off their clothes, throw themselves onto a bed, and get at it.

Rachel put her key into the lock and stopped in mid-turn. This was the moment when she would decide what the hem of her dress represented. Taking a deep breath, she turned to face him. "I really enjoyed tonight, Ethan. Really."

"Me too."

She fingered one of her shoulder straps and looked up at the indigo sky. The Wisconsin summer sun stayed obstinately around until 9:00 P.M. Watching the last pink clouds to the west, avoiding his eyes, she said, "I know it's still early, but part of me wants it to end right now, so that it'll stay a good memory."

She could hear his disappointment, but he said, "I can understand that."

She forced herself to meet his gaze, faking an assurance she didn't remotely feel. "Other parts of me are recommending somewhat . . . bolder action."

He put one hand on the doorjamb and leaned in close. Since she was on the first step, their faces were at the same level. He said, "Will you think less of me if I admit that the same thought has been on my mind most of the evening?"

"Only most?"

"Well, that steak was *really* good."

She laughed. She felt his breath on her lips, smelled the slight mix of beer, beef, and the Altoid he'd chewed on the way here. Then their eyes locked, and the moment seemed to go into that thicker realm of time where instantaneous events pass slowly enough to really absorb them.

When she spoke at last, her voice was ragged, soft, yet certain. "I want you to come inside."

"I want to," he said, and rested his hand lightly on her waist.

It felt huge to her, and powerful, a hand that could hold her down and make her do anything. No, she corrected, make her *want* to do anything. She took a deep final breath before her courage failed. "I have to warn you, though, there are things about me that are a little...no, they're *very* weird."

"Are you secretly a man?"

She giggled. "No, not *that* weird."

"Then I can probably work around it. I have some dark things too."

She felt dizzy with desire and wanted nothing more than to fall against him and feel those strong arms lift her up. But she held on to her dignity. "Can we talk first?"

"We can talk *only.* If that's what you want."

She could tell by his eyes that he meant it. It was more than she'd hoped, and now she was even more apprehensive. But she turned and opened the door before she could change her mind. His hand slid to her hip as she moved, and she felt the brief touch all the way to her toes.

Neither noticed the lone figure slumped in a Ford pickup parked down the street, invisible in the dark evening shade of an old birch tree.

———

THEY KISSED in the stairwell before she even turned on the lights. He spun her easily to face him, but his initiative was swept away by the hungry embrace she threw around his neck. Off balance, he fell back against the door and slammed it shut. She kept him pressed there in the dark, standing on her toes to reach his mouth with her own. She felt his response through his jeans, and his hands were on her ribs, thumbs stroking the sides of her breasts.

She broke the kiss long enough to gasp, "We're not talking."

"No."

"I lied back there, when I said I wanted to talk, you know."

"And I'm lying right now, when I say I don't want to see you naked."

She giggled. "It'd be way too much like Cinemax to do it for the first time on the stairs up to my place, wouldn't it?"

"Well, we *are* adults, and this *is* your building," he said, moving his hands to fully encircle her breasts. She sighed at the pressure of his strong fingers kneading her through her dress. "Technically, we're already *in* your place."

She kissed him again, her tongue hungrily raking his. "It'll be more comfortable upstairs," she said against his lips.

"Smells like you just painted down here too."

She nodded. "And I need to pee."

He chuckled. He moved his fingertips back to her hips, running them along the band of her thong panties beneath the dress. "Then apparently we're meant go upstairs."

They kissed intensely as they worked their way up the steps. At the top landing, she kicked off her shoes and ground herself wantonly against him, delighted by his response and her own eagerness. She felt the beer just enough; she was far from drunk but relaxed enough to quiet the second-guessing commentary in her head. Whatever happened, she'd chosen this of her own free will, and, by God, she'd follow through and enjoy it, even though she knew there would be no climactic moment for her.

She opened her apartment door, turned on the light, and felt the expected rush of mild embarrassment at her decor. But thoughts of shame of *any* sort vanished the moment he spun her around and kissed her again. This time he backed her up to the wall, and there was a fleeting moment where she remembered the *other* time a man had done that, when it had not meant desire or tenderness or lust but an attempt at possession. But, again, the intensity of the moment pushed those memories of Don back down out of sight. She lifted one leg and rubbed her bare thigh against him, his rough denim delicious against her soft skin.

"Excuse me for just a moment, okay?" she gasped.

"Okay," he said, and stepped back. He made no effort to hide the erection distending the front of his jeans. She closed the bathroom door and stood still for a long moment, simply catching her breath.

ETHAN FOUGHT the panic coursing through him. He'd stood upright while bullets struck the sand all around him, walked knowingly across a mined bridge, and never faltered. But those acts had not depended on his damn *dick* staying upright. At the moment he could barely remember how it felt when it wasn't tumescent, but he knew from experience that its attention could flag at a moment's notice.

He noticed the cat curled up on an arm of the couch, one paw dangling. He smiled, grateful for the distraction. "Well, hi there," he said softly. "You must be Tainter. Rachel told me about you. Yes, she did."

The cat's eyes did not open. He slid slowly off the arm and landed on all fours, then slunk under the couch.

Ethan took a long breath and slowly let it out. Maybe he should leave now, before he disappointed her and humiliated himself.

IN THE BATHROOM, Rachel flushed the toilet, then pulled the dress over her head and hung it on the bathrobe hook. She wore only dark blue panties beneath it. She turned on the water and looked in the mirror, trying to see herself the way Ethan would. She was slender, firm-breasted, her hair a bit disheveled. She had tan lines, and the tattoo below her navel drew attention to that area.

But she had to admit, for a woman her age she held up pretty well. He might not be winning the lottery, but she was no cheap parting gift either.

She reached for her robe, then stopped. That was pointless; she was already naked in a way that had nothing to do with clothes. No need to be a hypocrite.

She turned off the light and opened the door. He stood in front of her couch, contemplating the Frida Kahlo poster above it, until he realized she'd returned. The look on his face was everything she'd hoped for.

He finally said, "I'm . . . speechless."

She smiled. "Good. We decided not to talk, anyway."

She guided him into the bedroom and closed the door to keep Tainter from interrupting. The only light came from the streetlamp outside the window. She pushed him down on his back and peeled him like fresh produce in the diner, starting with his socks and working up. When she slid his jeans down his legs, his erection announced itself through his Jockey briefs. With a moan of desire that made him shiver, she pulled off his underwear and knelt over him, her fingertips lifting him to her mouth.

He closed his eyes and arched his back. "Oh, God, Rachel—"

"Shh!" she ordered. "Just . . . enjoy."

She wanted him to know what it felt like to be engulfed in something, to experience what she did when the lake spirits claimed her. She wanted to *take* him, to possess him, and she knew that at this moment his whole being was concentrated in what she now kissed, licked, and sucked.

———

HE RAISED his head enough to watch her rhythmically bob over him. She still wore the midnight blue thong, and he desperately wanted to rip it from her and show her what she'd done to him, what she'd made him newly capable of after months of failure. But he held back, waiting for an indication that she wanted it too. If, he thought with a shiver, he lasted that long.

He clamped his eyes shut against the vision, the memory, that hovered just beyond his consciousness. The poor dead girl, and the soldier standing over her, *grinning* at what he'd done to her body—

Yet with one artful stroke of her tongue, Rachel sent the image back into the darkness and replaced it with healing images solely of her.

SHE TOOK HIM to the very edge, then, with a final kiss on his swollen tip, she stretched out beside him, running her hands over his chest. "Did you like that?" she whispered.

"*Now* we're talking?" he said with a shudder in his voice.

"Not really," she sighed. His belly was tight and sweaty, the light hair around his navel damp. Her hand moved lower, encountering more hair and the residue of her own kisses.

"Then, yes, I liked it. It's been . . . a while since I felt so good. I liked it very much. Do you want me to show you how much?"

She nodded against his shoulder.

In one explosive movement he had her in his arms—no, in his *hands*, those huge paws around her waist, lifting her and turning her onto her back as his mouth slid down her torso, lingering over her nipples and then moving lower, his fingers sliding her panties from her. Before she could say anything, beg for him to wait so she could explain that this was ultimately pointless, he lifted one of her legs and draped it over his shoulder, while his hands spread her thighs and allowed his tongue the access it sought.

The first stroke made her cry out; it had been years since she'd experienced this, and all the desire for it seemed to burst forth from a forgotten reservoir within her. She heard her own voice gasping, whimpering, and almost sobbing as he worked on her. He knew where to nibble, when to bite, and what to suck on, drawing her into almost a rage of physical need. And he got her so close, closer than anyone ever had. *Oh, God, if only,* she thought.

Finally he rose above her and said, "I don't want to wait anymore."

"Condoms in the nightstand," she gasped. He rolled one on with trembling fingers.

She fell back, legs spread, weak from the things he'd already done to her. She felt him position himself and reached down to help guide him in, feeling the hard, hot presence *within* her that was completely different from the way the lake spirits felt. Her awareness was so heightened that she could barely breathe.

He stayed in that position, his arms trembling, looking down at her. Sweat gleamed on his forehead, but he remained still, as if afraid his size would injure her.

"Don't be gentle," she said, her hands running over his shoulders, her legs wrapping tightly around him. "I'm not fragile. Just *fuck me.*"

He pushed down with his hips, driving himself deeper, and the mattress groaned along with her. She arched her back, knees wide, and rolled her hips to let him have all he could take. Her hands roamed his flesh, amazed at the layers of muscle she encountered. She'd expected him to be strong—*cut,* in gym parlance—but this was more than that.

She put her palms against his chest as he lowered himself again, and she felt the muscles sliding beneath his skin. She moved one hand to his buttocks, already slick with sweat, and squeezed as much as the hard muscles allowed. He moaned in response and raised his head to gasp for air.

She nipped at his chin, then his neck, and finally took one of his nipples in her teeth. He cried out and again drove deep into her, using one hand to tangle in her hair and pull her head back. His mouth crushed against hers, his tongue penetrating with the same forcefulness, and she clung to him as he began to truly *fuck* her.

When he rolled onto his back and she was suddenly astride him, the deeper penetration made her scream. She arched her back and pushed with her hips, riding him with all the fury she could muster. His cries grew animalistic and urgent, which just made her grind against him even harder.

She felt a rush of emotion that, while not a true orgasm, nevertheless left her with a feeling of such feminine power that she wanted nothing more than to submit to him. She crawled off him, onto her belly, and raised her hips. She looked back, offering herself to him in total submission, as he got to his knees and positioned himself. He lifted her off the bed with the intensity of his entry.

Finally, simultaneously exhausted and infuriatingly incomplete, she pulled away, rolled onto her back, and again spread herself for him. He returned to her and she wrapped him in her arms and legs, holding him tight.

"I'm not good for much more," he breathed between grunts. "It's been a while since..."

"Go ahead," she sighed into his ear, stroking his sweat-damp hair. She almost wished they hadn't been so responsible, so she could feel his release deep inside her.

"What about you?"

"I can't, baby. Just go ahead."

"No, whatever you need me to do, I can—"

"Please, just *do* it," she said, suddenly desperate for the feeling, the knowledge that she could inspire that in him. He didn't argue. He rose above her, all his weight and strength pressing her down into her mattress, and then she felt it. He swelled within her, then twitched, and his contained lust strained against the latex. It almost brought her to the same release, but her orgasm hovered just out of reach, the tingles building and spreading but never quite digging in and taking hold. She pumped her hips desperately, wanting it more than she'd ever wanted anything, but it withdrew as always, leaving the ache that could be sated only one way.

Finally they collapsed side by side, each sweaty and out of breath, looking up at the ceiling. Tainter scratched at the door with a plaintive, worried *meow.* They turned and looked into each other's eyes for a long, serious moment, each knowing that something fundamental had changed. This could be no simple one-nighter.

Neither moved for a long while. Tainter went away, and the air-conditioner compressor kicked on. Finally she rolled onto her side and put her hand on his chest. His heart thudded against her palm. "I need to tell you something, Ethan."

He started to speak, but she touched his lips and added, "No, I promise you, it isn't what you think, no matter what you *do* think. Just let me get this out before I lose my nerve."

"Okay," he said, and stroked her cheek with his fingertips.

She took a deep breath and began her story.

CHAPTER EIGHTEEN

T HE SUMMER I was fourteen, my sister, Becky, and I were swimming in Lake Monona. Our parents were on the bank watching us. There were lots of other people around. Then some drunk in a speedboat, trying to get into the Yahara channel locks, cut across the swimming area. He came up behind me; I never even saw him. He went right over me. The boat knocked me out, and the propeller cut my scalp down to the bone."

She tossed her hair to one side and he put his hand on her head. She felt him slowly trace the raised line of the scar.

"I was underwater for two hours," she continued. "The police came, and rescue boats. Everyone at the lake that day helped look for me. Well, except for Becky, who just lost it. She blamed herself. Anyway, they finally found me floating in the weeds more than a mile away. Naturally they thought I was dead. God knows, I should've been. But I wasn't."

She paused, recalling that day with all the clarity only

life-changing trauma can provide. She'd spoken of it so seldom, she found herself searching for words. "They had to do CPR and get all the water out of my lungs, but I wasn't dead. No one could explain that. They also couldn't explain what happened to my swimsuit."

"They found you *naked*?"

She nodded. "My suit was one of those one-piece numbers my mom insisted on, about as sexy as a cabbage. It did turn up, but it wasn't torn or ripped. It looked like I'd simply taken it off, which of course made no sense given the situation."

She shifted on the bed and felt the fabric pull away from where it stuck to her sweaty skin. This was harder than she thought, more so because she couldn't see Ethan's face clearly enough to gauge his reaction. "They took me to the hospital, stitched me up, and I recovered. But something was different."

"What?"

She rolled onto her back and crossed one ankle over her knee, staring at the ceiling. Now she was glad it was dark and he couldn't see her face, because she felt the burn of a blush. "Can I ask you something personal first?"

"Sure."

"How old were you when you first started . . . well . . . masturbating?"

He was silent for a moment, then said, "Eleven or twelve, I guess. Why?"

"Well, me too. Only, after that day at the lake, I couldn't . . . you know."

"Masturbate?"

"No, of course I could do that, it was just . . . I couldn't have an orgasm. I could get close, right up to it, but never quite there."

"And that's why—"

"Wait, I'm not done. I couldn't tell anyone about that, of course. If you ever meet my family, you'll understand why. And that didn't make it any easier to put up with. I was a two-a-day girl back then, even though I was still a virgin. The thing is, whenever I'd try, I kept having this urge to go skinny-dip back in the lake where I nearly died. When I'd get close to . . . you know, *coming,* I'd remember the way the lake water felt on my skin. It became kind of an obsession."

She paused again. After a moment he quietly prompted, "So what did you do?"

"Put up with it until the next summer. I spent that whole winter begging my folks to promise they'd take me back to the lake, told them some b.s. about needing to 'face my fears.' I was constantly so horny I bit off everyone's head who spoke to me. I started drinking and smoking dope, just to deaden the way I felt. It was a tough winter."

"So did your parents take you back to the lake the next year?"

"They did. I had to promise a thousand different ways that I'd be careful, watch out for boats and everything else. But I had my own priorities and, by then, I was so desperate I would've said or agreed to anything. As soon as I could that day, I slipped away, took off my swimsuit in some bushes where I hoped no one could see, and . . ."

She trailed off. The headlights of a passing car swiped across the ceiling. The next few moments would determine everything. What if he jumped up, grabbed his clothes, and ran? What if he went and told Marty, and his other friends, about the crazy woman who ran the diner? It was more than a personal revelation; it was something that could damage and destroy every aspect of her life. Did she trust him that much?

"What happened?" he asked softly, nothing but kindness and curiosity in his voice. She could dimly see his face. He wasn't laughing or scowling, just looking at her with interest and concern.

"I disappeared for two hours again. I stayed underwater the whole time, apparently. And something in the water . . . made love to me. It took my virginity."

She waited for the laugh, or at least the derisive snort. But he said nothing.

"When they found me, I was bleeding . . . down there," she said. "They thought someone in the park had molested me, then thrown me into the lake to drown. My mother was absolutely hysterical. But I knew that whatever had done it wasn't anything . . ."

Oh, boy, she thought, *here it is.* She forced the words out. "It was nothing human. It was in the lake. It *was* the lake. The water itself was my first lover."

She closed her eyes. Her heart was pounding, and she felt sweat spring up all over her. No one had ever heard this story before, even though she'd rehearsed telling it countless times. Not even Don, but then, she had no doubt how *he* would've reacted. But she really knew nothing about Ethan. She'd just exposed herself, in every possible way, to a man who was basically a stranger.

They were both silent for a long moment, conscious of every sound, from the street outside to Tainter's muted scuffing in his kitchen litter box. Then, in the same warm voice, Ethan said, "Then what?"

"I learned that only whoever or whatever lived in the lake could make me come," she said. Despite the fear, there was the power of release in just saying the words. "I could get close to it with myself or with someone else. But only the lake could get me there."

"Only Lake Monona."

"Actually, either of them, Mendota or Monona. Something about Lake Wingra gives me the creeps, so I've never tried it there."

He touched her hip with his fingertips. "You seem pretty well adjusted, for having gone through all that."

She shrugged. "Fall down or keep moving. What would you do?"

"Keep moving." He slid his hand along her belly, idly tracing the outline of her tattoo. "Do you have any idea *why* this happened to you?"

She shook her head. "I've read everything I could, talked to everyone who might know. The Native Americans believed something unusual lived in the water, but the tribe that put up the effigy mounds isn't here anymore. There are references to a tribe called the Lo-Stahzi, who were powerful shamans, but they died off or disappeared long before the current tribes came to this area, and that was way before any Europeans did. So, no, I don't have a clue. I don't even have names for them. But in a sense . . . they own me."

" 'They'? There's more than one?"

She nodded. "Several. I know because they behave differently." How could she really describe the way one would gradually bring her to the height of need, while another used her with such violence she was always surprised when she wasn't bruised the next day? Some caressed her in ways that made her giggle, others pummeled her into whatever position they wanted. Most times more than one used her simultaneously. And always they gave her fulfillment of such exquisite thoroughness that they more than made up for any brief discomfort. Then, at the end, whether she'd been tenderly loved or willfully taken, she was brought back to the surface, to her world, with soft watery kisses to express their thanks.

"Why do you say they 'own' you?"

She turned and smiled at him. "Come on, Ethan. If you could get off with only one woman, wouldn't you feel like she owned you too?"

"I don't know. But probably," he added.

"Yeah, well, there's my story."

He shifted on the bed and rested his head on his hand to look at her. "Have you ever seen a doctor about this?"

"What kind of doctor?"

He shrugged. "I don't know. Some kind."

"I'm not crazy."

"That's not what I meant."

What kind of whore constantly wants sex and won't let herself get off? Don had roared. *And why do you sneak off to*

the goddamned lake all the time? Who are you meeting there?
"I know how it sounds. I don't know why I'm even telling you about it." She sat up and swung her feet off the side of the bed. She covered her breasts with her arms. "Look, maybe this was a mistake, maybe—"

"Maybe," he interrupted as he stroked her back, "you shouldn't assume how I'm going to react."

His touch sent oddly comforting tingles down her spine. "You don't believe me," she insisted obstinately.

"Did I say that? I'm surprised, I'll admit. And it does sound out of the ordinary. But I *do* believe you."

"Yeah? Why?"

"Because . . ." Now he looked uncomfortable. "Up until now, since I got back from my tour in Iraq eight months ago, I couldn't . . . stay up."

She wasn't sure how to respond and settled for simply, "Oh."

His voice grew flat and distant. "I saw something happen there. A soldier in my squad raped and killed an Iraqi girl. I walked in and saw the body and saw what he'd done to her. So whenever I'd get close to . . . being with a woman, I couldn't get that image out of my mind. I . . . wasn't able to perform."

She turned so she could see him better. She wanted to touch him, to comfort him, but wasn't sure how. "I'm sorry, Ethan."

"From the moment I saw you, though, it's like . . . I've been hard as a rock. I was terrified it wouldn't last, that I'd get right to the point of needing it and then lose it, but . . . I didn't."

"So you just wanted to prove something with me?"

"No, that's not it at all. I just . . . I haven't felt safe since then. But when I came with you . . . I did. And . . ."

She brushed a stray strand of hair from his forehead, almost choking on a wave of tenderness. She knew he was strong physically; now she saw how deep that strength really went. She realized he was voluntarily as naked as she was. "What?" she prompted when he did not continue.

He sat up beside her. "I have an idea."

CHAPTER NINETEEN

Fifteen minutes later they stood naked, holding hands, at the edge of the lake in Hudson Park. The bushes shielded them from view, and mosquitoes swarmed their salty skin. It was an overcast night, and occasional heat lightning sheeted across the clouds.

Rachel smiled nervously up at Ethan. The sweat made highlights on his chest and abs; the smooth curves of his shoulders and biceps gave him a Greek-statue look. "I've never done this before," she said as shyly as a nude woman could.

"A guy always likes to hear his date say that."

She stepped close to kiss him and felt his arousal announce itself against her belly. Knowing she had brought him to life again so soon sent a thrilling sense of power through her. "I should warn you, I really don't know what will happen."

He caressed her hair and shoulders. "And you never will, standing here."

She nodded, then stepped into the water. He followed. She moved with the authority of experience, while he tottered awkwardly on the uncertain bottom. The night was silent except for the lapping of the small waves on the lake and the city noises that served as a dim, omnipresent backdrop.

ETHAN FELT momentarily foolish with his erection preceding him, but one look at Rachel's silhouette in the night made it the only possible response. He could see her perfect breasts, the nipples dark and erect. The swell of her hips below her narrow waist made him tingle deep inside.

The water rose to their knees, then their hips, then the middle of their chests. Finally Rachel stopped and turned to face him, expression lost in shadow.

She put her arms around his neck. Her breasts were soft against his chest. "Are you sure about this?" she said softly.

He shifted his weight on the silty bottom until he was steady, then slid his hands up under her arms, simultaneously lifting her and kneeling. She spread her thighs. For an awkward moment the correct position eluded them, and neither had a free hand to help. Then he found her and lowered her onto him. She wrapped her legs around him and made a sound halfway between a growl and a sob as he entered her. For a long moment neither one moved.

————

RACHEL WAITED for some indication of the lake's approval. The water engulfed her lower body but did not form the hands, lips, and other things that meant the spirits were present. Was she doomed yet again to the awful frustration?

But the immediate feeling of clinging to this iron-strong man as he impaled her intimately pushed any doubts aside. Even if she couldn't come, this moment was something to cherish. "Oh, God," she breathed, kissing his neck and shoulders, rolling her hips forward and back against him. His hands cupped her rear, effortlessly supporting her weight.

The slow grinding gave way to harder undulations, more-demanding thrusts. Water shot up between them and drenched their faces. The splashing sounded unbearably loud, and she feared at any moment flashlights from shore would pick them out, followed by mocking catcalls. But she couldn't stop.

Please let this happen, she begged the spirits. *I'm not abandoning you, I'll never leave you, but I need this.*

As if in response to her unspoken plea, the unmistakable feeling built within her, making her gasp and strive harder to reach it. "Oh, my God, Ethan, I'm so close," she whispered, and took his earlobe in her teeth for emphasis. Her cries changed from grunts of carnal effort to pleading, keening whines of desperation. Nothing the lake did for her could compare, truly, with the hot physical presence inside her. Would they know this and prevent her from reaching the moment of ecstasy hovering just beyond reach?

Please, she implored. *Please...*

ALL ETHAN could do was stand and let her pound against him, which was more than enough for him. Despite their earlier activity, he was just as hard and realized he was also getting close. Worse, he'd neglected to bring any protection, so he was completely dedicated to resisting his own orgasm. The need grew stronger with each moment, though, and he knew he was doomed to lose. He'd never wanted to come inside a woman the way he wanted it now.

Her movements grew more urgent, and the waves lapped at them like extra hands coaxing them on. Her arms were wrapped tight around his neck, her ankles locked around his thighs. She grunted a little with each slam of her pelvis, and the sensation built around him until he almost couldn't breathe.

"No condom," he whispered urgently, his body straining for control. "Trying not to—"

And then he could tell: *It* happened. Suddenly Rachel's muscles tightened, her limbs clamped around him, and her spine arched, creating a tension that held her immobile. Only her hands moved, alternately raking and grasping his shoulders. He couldn't see her face, but he heard her little choking gasps, as if she could barely catch her breath.

———

HER EYES OPENED wide as the longest, most powerful orgasm of her life raged through her. Not even the lake spirits had brought her to this height. It was no mere physical response centered between her legs either; this was something that took over her whole being, the way a man in the electric chair responds to the surge of voltage. She had no idea she was even *capable* of this feeling, and it seemed to choke all but the most necessary breath from her.

Finally, with a cry, she went limp. Her arms hung uselessly down his back. She was exhausted, spent, and nothing mattered at all.

HE FELT HER shuddering, possibly sobbing, but he had his own problems. He had only moments of control left.

"Can't hold back much longer," he whispered, his voice shivery. "Really, I'm not kidding. . . ."

She leaned back enough to look into his eyes. "Don't try," she said raggedly.

"Are you sure?" he gasped. He was there, right there, ready. It was time to fling her away or—

"Yes!" she choked out.

And then it didn't matter; he couldn't have held it back if he'd wanted to. He came inside her, furiously and with more intensity than even back at her apartment. It was as if that earlier time hadn't even happened, he was so full and desperate. She shuddered in his arms as he poured forth; then she spasmed tight again, keening into his shoulder to muffle the cry as she, too, came again.

———

THEY STOOD TWINED together for a long time, their breath coming in gasps. When she moved to stand, their sweaty skin stuck together and pulled loose with a slick, muffled *pop.*

She peered up at him. He looked dazed, and Rachel was certain she did as well. Her legs could barely hold her, and she was glad he was sturdy enough to lean on. She said, "That was...," then trailed off. No words seemed adequate.

He nodded. "Yeah."

She caressed his arms and shoulders, her cheek against his chest. His heart rumbled like some powerful engine. "I don't know how to explain—"

"No," he said. "You don't have to."

She swallowed raggedly. "Will I ever see you again?"

"I..." She could tell he was struggling to find something to say, some way to put into words what he was feeling. Her own emotions swelled at the knowledge that the transcendence had been mutual. Finally he shrugged and said with a smile, "Yes. Yes, you will."

It was enough. Rachel stood on tiptoes in the mud and kissed him as if the world might end.

FIGHTING THE GIGGLES, they reached the bank and retrieved their clothes. Before she pulled on her shirt he kissed her again, hard and possessively, luxuriating in the way her breasts pressed against his chest. Then they scrambled back to his truck.

ONCE AGAIN, neither noticed the *other* truck, parked on the street behind a Saab belonging to one of the huge, expensive lakeside homes. The figure inside the truck had witnessed, though not completely comprehended, their tryst in the water and seethed with fury and frustration as Rachel covered her bare skin. As the lovers drove away, the figure sat pondering, knowing that the final aspect of the plan must be implemented soon, for sanity's sake if no other reason.

CHAPTER TWENTY

MARTY WALKER GAZED at the report on his desk, his eyes slightly unfocused. It was the coroner's preliminary results from the autopsy on Ling Hu, and it put everything he thought he knew about the case into limbo. He was forcing himself to go back to square one, to look at the disappearances of Faith Lucas and Carrie Kimmell as unrelated crimes instead of the sequel events he, and everyone else, assumed they were.

Because Ling Hu had not been murdered.

"Penny for your thoughts," Julie Schutes said as she approached. At this time of night, the rest of the squad room was empty, except for one man at the far end playing solitaire on his computer.

Marty stood, and they shook hands. "Awfully late for a pretty girl to be downtown alone, isn't it?"

She sat on the edge of his desk. "I'm no 'girl,' Detective. But thank you for the rest of it."

He returned to his chair. "What brings you around?"

"Maybe I just wanted to talk to an old friend. We don't see each other much these days."

He smiled knowingly. "Is that really it?"

"Partially, yeah. I really have missed you and Chuck. But it's also work-related. I know you've gotten the autopsy results on Ling Hu by now."

"And why do think I'd let you see them?"

"Because I'm irresistible, even to gay men. And you know eventually they'll be made public, so holding them back is just petty."

"Julie, you are a piece of work. Most people would be home watching TV by now."

"Most people, Marty. Not us."

"Besides, the final report will be out for all to see in a day or two. Why do you want to see the preliminary one now?"

"Because news goes bad faster than Chinese food. No offense."

"I'm not Chinese."

"So can I see it?"

He shrugged and nodded toward the file. "I didn't show it to you."

"I found it in the garbage," she agreed as she perused the report. He watched her frown, then scowl. "So she *wasn't* murdered?"

"Died of an acute asthma attack. She didn't even drown; she was dead before she hit the water."

"And she had a recent, partial tattoo." She paused and frowned again. "Who gets a *partial* tattoo?"

"As you can see from the photographs, it was going to

be pretty extensive. I'm guessing that it takes more than one session to color in that whole design." He shook his head and added sadly, "Guess she won't be making those appointments, huh?"

"Recent ligature marks on her wrists and ankles. She'd been tied up multiple times. That's something."

"Or not."

"How do you mean?"

"Her boyfriend—one of her boyfriends, I should say—told us she liked things a little rough. Enjoyed being tied up, coerced, that sort of thing."

Julie closed the file. "I didn't know that," she said with genuine surprise. "That's not how her friends described her to me."

"There's friends, and then there's friends."

"What about the *boy*friends?"

"One was at home chatting online at the time she disappeared. Not a suspect. The other was a football player and might be, but my instinct says no. And if you keep reading, you'll see there's no evidence of either sexual assault or consensual sexual activity within the twenty-four hours prior to her death."

She put the file down and chewed her lip thoughtfully. "So *is* this related to the other disappearances?"

Marty shrugged. "Ling Hu was a wild girl. I'm inclined to think she was sneaking around behind both boyfriends' backs and things got out of hand. Whoever the guy was, he panicked and dumped the body. We'll catch him and charge him, but not with murder."

Julie sighed and shook her head. "So much for the next Ed Gein."

"Sorry to disappoint you."

She stood and smoothed her skirt. "You never disappoint me, Ethan."

"Marty," he corrected.

She controlled her expression but could not restrain the blush. "Sorry. Marty."

"Any message?"

"For Chuck?"

"Or anyone else."

She smiled. "It's nothing personal, I always wear my Freudian slip with this skirt."

"Sure."

"Thanks for not showing me the report, Marty."

"Anytime," he said, watching her go.

He picked up the phone and started to call Ethan, then saw the clock. It was after midnight. Whatever Ethan was up to, Marty knew he wouldn't want it interrupted this late.

Then he opened the file on Ling Hu. Something nagged at him about it. There was no disputing the cause of death, but some detail wasn't quite right. It would come to him eventually, he knew. But he had three other missing girls to worry about first.

ETHAN AND RACHEL lay in her bed after a giggly shower together, kissing and touching. Finally Ethan asked, "Do you want me to go home?"

"No, that's silly. It's nearly one in the morning."

"If it'll make you more comfortable—"

"Stop. If I wanted you to leave, I'd tell you."

He kissed the tip of her nose. "This has been a heck of a first date, I'd say."

"Would you?"

"Will there be a second one?"

"Are you sure you want one?"

He ran his thumb over the end of one nipple. "Pretty sure."

"Even if it's not as intense as this one?"

"I was having a good time *before* we took our clothes off too."

She nestled against him, his arm around her, her leg draped across his. After a few minutes his steady breathing told her he'd fallen asleep, and, shortly, light snoring confirmed this. In the dim light she watched his features soften, which made him look positively boyish. She wanted to awaken him for another round of kissing and fondling, but that seemed thoughtless given all he'd been through. He'd certainly earned a few hours' respite from her attentions.

Rachel, though, found she couldn't rest. Elation, and energy, and a new vivid knowledge of herself coursed through her, and she was wide awake. She lay perfectly still, tried meditation and mental relaxation exercises, but sleep simply would not come. When the clock on her nightstand read 2:00 A.M., she gave up.

She carefully disengaged from him and padded into the kitchen. Tainter glared his puritanical disapproval. By the light of her cell phone, she wrote on a Post-it, *Gone for a walk. Nothing's wrong, just too wired to sleep. Back soon.* Then she tiptoed back and put it over the numbers on the clock, so he'd be sure to see it.

She paused and looked down at him, at the unbroken line of skin visible from ankle to shoulder as he rolled onto his side. His muscles had softened with sleep but still stood out beneath his skin. Normally she couldn't abide bulky gym-rat men, but the memory of how strong he was, how he'd borne her weight and exertions with no apparent strain, made her grateful for his dedication. A weaker man, a man more like her ex-husband and the others she'd dated, would have never been able to stand it. And a lesser man never would have joined her in the lake in the first place.

She realized her hands were absently rubbing her thighs. She smiled, risked waking him with a soft kiss on the shoulder, then dressed and slipped out into the night.

She barely felt the pavement beneath her feet as she ran along the empty sidewalks. The big houses were mostly dark, except for two where she glimpsed shirtless young men playing computer games. She wanted to laugh, she was so happy, but she kept silent due to the hour.

She dashed across Hudson Park and down to the water. She whipped off her shirt, tossed it and her shoes into the bushes, then stepped out of her panties and shorts. She dove into the water, heedless of the loud splash, and swam with limbs that should have ached from her earlier exertion. She'd never felt so strong, though.

She reached the drop-off and stopped. She sank slowly,

arms and legs spread, looking down into the great black space where her other lovers dwelled. She'd promised never to leave them, and she wanted them to know she meant it.

For one long, terrifying instant, she feared she'd been abandoned. She heard uncharacteristic silence in her head and was afraid to let out that final breath. Surely, if they disapproved, they would've let her know, wouldn't they? That couldn't possibly have been their good-bye, could it?

Then, with a surge of relief, she felt the water solidify around her, cradling her and pulling her onto her back. Hands moved over her, caressing her in the darkness in the same firm yet gentle manner. Her weary body somehow found the strength to respond, and she was soon lost in a semiconscious haze of sexual satiation. But the voices spoke with an uncharacteristic urgency completely at odds with their languid manner. The words barely penetrated her fuzzy brain.

You must find strength, they seemed to say. *You must reach out to the man who treasures you as we do. You must calm your fear and trust your love.*

She writhed and moaned as the spirits managed to wring one more climax from her satiated body. It was a small one, a gentle rush that drew her body taut like a satisfying stretch first thing in the morning. Only as it faded did their uncharacteristic urgency register, and she could not recall exactly what they said.

When she emerged from the lake, her legs literally wobbled. She was thoroughly, utterly *spent* and knew she would now sleep like a baby when she crawled in beside Ethan. Just the thought of that made her smile, and she put the spirits' odd words down to her own fuzzy brain. She simply must have heard them wrong.

As she slid her panties up her legs, a bright flashlight sprang on directly in front of her, blinding her. She dropped the rest of her clothes and crossed her arms over her chest. She waited for the official voice and frantically ran down in her mind all the excuses she'd accumulated over the years for just such an emergency. She said demurely, "I'm sorry, Officer, it was just such a warm night I got carried away. It won't happen again."

But the light did not move, and no one spoke. Mosquitoes and midges danced in the beam. "Officer?"

She felt a sudden chill of utter terror as she realized the truth. *Oh, my God, this is* him. It was the man from the burgundy Ford truck, who had kidnapped the others and killed at least one of them. Now he had her at his mercy. She was naked, and alone, and far, far from home.

"No, please," she whispered, and began to tremble.

"Turn around," the man holding the light said. His tone was flat and Midwestern—the voice of ninety percent of Madison. "And keep quiet."

"Hold on a minute, please," she said, trying to buy time. "I'm not as young as you think, I'm no college girl—"

Something metallic clicked behind the light. She saw no gun but recognized the sound. "Turn around and shut up, or I'll leave you dead in the mud. I've got no patience left tonight."

She did as instructed. She gazed out across the water, its surface dark and shimmering. There was no wind, so the ripples were small and quiet. Even the waves that lapped at the bank sounded muted, as if the lake was also afraid. Her own shadow, cast by the light, stretched out ahead of her before it, too, blended with the darkness. "Help," she whispered to the spirits.

Strong hands grabbed her arms and twisted them behind her back. Her assailant wrapped duct tape firmly around her wrists, then spun her around to face him. She squinted into the light, blushing from shame and terror and rising fury. Before she could say anything else, he slapped a piece of duct tape over her mouth. "If you try to fight or make any noise, I'll kill you. Nod if you understand."

What could she do? She nodded. Insects drawn to the light pelted her face around the tape.

He turned out the light. Before her eyes could adjust, he bent and threw her over his shoulder. More tape quickly bound her ankles. Her abductor was short and thin and struggled for breath as he carried her up the hill. He did not grope her or seem at all interested in the fact that she was nude except for her panties. Maybe that came later.

She looked around for any movement, any sign she'd been seen and might be rescued. There was nothing. The upside-down houses were dark and the streets empty. She strained with all her strength against the tape at her wrists, but it held fast.

He tossed her into the bed of his pickup. She landed

heavily on the metal, and what felt like nails or thumbtacks jabbed her skin. The truck's suspension creaked with her weight. When she looked up at her captor, he tossed a blanket over her. It smelled of urine, sweat, and indefinable terror. Then something pressed down on either side of her as he used cinder blocks to hold the blanket in place.

The tailgate slammed shut. When the engine rattled to life, the panic really hit. *I've been kidnapped,* she thought in a panic. *I'm going to be raped and killed and dumped in the lake like that Chinese girl!* She twisted her wrists, fingers straining to find an end of the tape. She tried to spread her ankles enough to work her feet free. But both efforts were futile. She struggled to wriggle out from beneath the cocoonlike blanket, but it held fast. Claustrophobia kicked in, but her screams were muffled beneath tape, fabric, and engine.

She could not tell the truck's direction once it made the first couple of turns. She only knew she might never see her diner, or the lake, or Ethan Walker ever again.

The visions came back to her vividly: the girl on the lakeshore, naked just as Rachel was now, and Patty Patilia's screaming face, eyes wide above the same sort of duct-tape gag that now muzzled Rachel.

Cry now, she told herself. *Get it over with. You'll need to be strong later.*

So she did.

CHAPTER TWENTY-ONE

ETHAN AWOKE, saw Rachel's note on the clock, and lifted it to check the time—3:30 A.M. Wouldn't she have to get up in an hour or so to get the diner ready for breakfast? *He* would have to get up around then, since he had to go home first before heading to work. He frowned, then went into the bathroom.

As he washed his hands, he scanned the little room for a sign that Rachel was some kind of lunatic. No strange prescriptions in the medicine cabinet, no collections of male body parts lined up in the towel closet. Everything seemed normal.

He went naked into the living room and looked around at her home. The night's events, now that his larger head was in charge, began to seem especially strange. Sure, he was relieved that he'd been able to keep it up, that the vision of the dead Iraqi girl's ripped and beaten body hadn't intruded. But sex in the lake? Sex *with* the lake? It had all seemed eminently reasonable at the time and even immediately afterward. But now that his mind wasn't heat-fogged, he began to seriously wonder about Rachel's sanity. Where was she now? Normal people didn't go for walks at 3:30 A.M.

He picked up the picture on the coffee table. It showed two girls, one clearly Rachel, the other just as clearly a close relative, likely the sister she'd mentioned before. They looked happy, content, normal. But, really, who displayed family photos where they *didn't* look that way? Just because the trauma didn't show didn't mean it wasn't there. He knew that for a fact.

He returned the picture to its spot, then crept through the dark apartment looking for other, more-recent photographs. Softly, he sang his childhood misheard version of "Sister Christian":

> *Motorhead*
> *What's your price tonight?*
> *If I am missing light,*
> *You'll pee all right tonight. . . .*

He stopped abruptly when he realized what he was doing. He felt a rush of shame and disgust. He was *snooping.*

Julie used to snoop through his place when they were together. He knew where everything should be and could tell when something had been moved. There was no pattern to her searches, she was simply looking methodically through his life, like a good reporter. Except he wasn't the subject of an article, he was her boyfriend. And now he was doing the same thing to Rachel.

He retrieved his pants, then sat on the couch. He was no longer sleepy and didn't want Rachel to find him wandering naked through the apartment when she returned. He turned on the TV and began surfing the channels, finally settling on a basic-cable showing of *Caddyshack*. Tainter emerged from wherever he'd been and curled up on the cushion beside him.

By the time the movie ended, the sky was light gray outside the windows, and Ethan realized that Rachel had not returned.

ETHAN PACED the short length of Rachel's living room as he held his cell phone to his ear. His clothes were wrinkled and his hair was a bedhead tangle. Helena watched him, arms folded across her chest. She'd arrived for work, come upstairs to see what was keeping Rachel, and found Ethan. Now, despite her initial amusement, she shared his concern. Rachel was far too responsible to simply fail to show up without a reason.

"Marty," Ethan said suddenly, making Helena jump. "Listen, can you come by Rachel's diner? Sooner would be good, soonest would be best. I may be overreacting, but I've got that creepy feeling something's happened to Rachel." He paused. "Yes, we went out last night." He paused again, then sighed in embarrassment. "*Yes,* I spent the night here. Are you coming? . . . Okay, bye."

He snapped the phone closed and turned to Helena. "Marty will be here shortly."

Helena nodded. She trusted Marty and believed he

wouldn't have vouched for his brother if Ethan had been one of those crazy woman-beating ex-soldiers all too common in the world. "Thanks," she said. "It's not like Rachel to do this."

He nodded. "Is there any coffee downstairs? I could use a cup to clear my head and help me wake up."

"Sure," she said, and gestured toward the door. As he preceded her down the steps, she glanced back at Rachel's apartment, looking for anything out of place. Ethan had had plenty of time to clean up any blood or other evidence, but if he'd hurt Rachel, there should be *some* sign. But she saw nothing. Even Rachel's cat seemed unconcerned.

Still, as she followed Ethan downstairs, she reflected on his broad, muscular shoulders and how much damage they, and his army training, could do to a lone woman in the middle of the night.

IN THE DINER'S cramped kitchen, Marty listened calmly to Ethan's story. When his brother finished he said, "Okay, let's start somewhere logical. Where would she likely go at that time of the morning? A restaurant? A coffee shop?"

"The lake," Ethan and Helena said almost in unison. Then they looked at each other, but neither laughed.

"Which lake?" Marty asked.

"Monona," Ethan said. "Hudson Park."

"Have you checked it?"

"No, I called you first."

Marty scowled a little, then said, "Excuse me," and went into the apartment stairwell to use his phone.

Ethan turned to Helena. "You know about the lake?"

"I know she goes skinny-dipping in it a lot."

"Do you know why?"

She snorted. "Hell, Rachel does a lot of things I can't explain. I think she just likes the danger element of it, being naked in the middle of town."

Ethan nodded as if his thoughts were identical.

Marty returned. "I put in a call, and a uniform's going to check. He'll call me when he gets to the park."

"Thanks," Ethan said, scratching his chin. He needed a shower and a shave.

Helena took Marty's arm. "Come on, we'll have some coffee while we wait."

Helena had not opened the diner. She couldn't run the place herself, and it seemed somehow disloyal to pretend nothing unusual was afoot. A few people came to the door and peered inside, then gave up. She poured three cups of coffee and placed them on the counter.

They all jumped when Marty's cell phone rang. He snapped it open and turned his back, barking, "Walker speaking." He listened for a long moment, then said, "Call it in, then. We'll be there shortly."

He faced them, and his expression, previously merely annoyed, was now grim. "They found clothes at the lake. We need to get down there and see if you two can identify them."

CHAPTER TWENTY-TWO

THE KIDNAPPER KEPT Rachel wrapped in the blanket as he again threw her over his shoulder and carried her from the truck. He seemed to have difficulty managing the weight and paused to shift his grip several times. Rachel fought the choking claustrophobia as the blanket pulled tight against her face. The tape holding her wrists and ankles was still secure. She recalled an old poster her dad kept in the garage, of a bikini-clad girl holding a distinctive gray roll. The caption read, *It's not broken, it just needs duct tape.*

The sound told her he carried her across gravel, then up a short set of steps. His shoulder dug painfully into her ribs. A door opened, and she sensed they were now inside. Floorboards creaked beneath their combined weight. Lights came on, filtering through the fabric.

Then another door opened and they descended more steps. These practically screamed their protest, wood and nails straining to support them. Her abductor labored as well, his breath coming in great openmouthed gasps. Five steps and they were again on the ground, and he bent to drop her on the floor. She landed on her belly, and he pulled on the edge of the blanket. She unrolled like Cleopatra.

She came to a stop on her back, her weight painfully on her wrists. A fresh rush of shame at her near-nudity made her blush. The floor beneath her was rough concrete, and the air was stiflingly hot. A bare lightbulb hung almost directly overhead, momentarily blinding her. She turned her head and saw the one thing she hoped she wouldn't.

Another woman, undressed and bound with plastic ties instead of tape, lay on her stomach. And beyond her, a second one raised her upper body to see the new arrival. This girl, whose hair was still visibly blond despite days of accumulated grease and grime, seemed to be smeared in some sort of paint. From her navel down past her knees, swirls of color, mostly red, covered her. The skin beneath and around these swaths was pale and clean, not filthy like her arms, feet, and face.

Rachel stared, trying to resolve this into something that made sense. She knew the girl's name from the news stories and flyers posted everywhere, including in her own restaurant: Faith Lucas, the *Golden Girl Gone*.

Faith squirmed into a seated position, and suddenly Rachel understood. The girl wasn't covered with paint, she was covered with *tattoos*. And they were fresh, some still bleeding, which explained the red smears as blood mixed with the antiseptic lotion covering the most recent additions along the tops of her thighs. Others, less recent, were scabbed over.

The other girl stared at Rachel over her gag. There was something familiar about her too. When Rachel took in her single garment with its pattern of little red hearts partly obscured by sweat and grime, she suddenly realized that this was Carrie Kimmell, the first girl the lake spirits had asked her to help. She, too, bore the marks of recent tattooing, this time on her shoulders and upper back.

She felt a pang of shame at her cowardly certainty that night that she could not have helped the girl. *Fuck me, I could've at least tried,* she berated herself. *Instead, all I did was* type *about it. And now look what's happened.*

Suddenly she wondered if this would give away her carefully crafted secret identity. *The Lady of the Lakes* could obviously have no comment on the disappearance of Rachel Matre; would anyone notice the omission and make the connection? She felt like Clark Kent, wondering at the meaning of that knowing look in Lois's eye, and for a moment the fear left her.

Then it returned when she realized who *wasn't* in the room: Ling Hu, the Chinese girl who vanished first. The one who'd just been found dead.

Carrie Kimmell whimpered. A similar clean space spanned her shoulders and trailed down her spine to the small of her back. There were only black lines so far, no colors, but the pain from having been inked directly along her backbone was obvious.

Then the two victims raised their bleary eyes to their captor, who stood against the stair rail catching his breath.

Time to see the monster, Rachel thought, and followed their gaze.

OFFICERS WERE IN the process of cordoning off Hudson Park with yellow tape by the time Ethan, Marty, and Helena arrived. Neighbors in bathrobes and other sleepwear watched from the nearby yards, sipping coffee and chatting on cell phones. Three marked police cars were parked at the curb along with, most disturbingly, an ambulance.

Marty whipped his car onto the sidewalk before slamming on the brakes and bouncing them all forward against their seat belts. It brought a momentary smile to Ethan's face; even after living in a city for ten years, Marty still couldn't park worth a damn. The amusement vanished almost immediately.

They followed Marty across the park, ignoring the sign that instructed people not to walk on the effigy mound. The paramedics and uniformed officers clustered at the lakeshore looked up as they approached.

"Detective Walker," a sergeant named Jimson said. He was older than Marty, with a thick salt-and-pepper mustache. "It appears to be just like the others."

Marty nodded and called out, "Mr. Dawes?"

A thin black man wearing rubber gloves and goggles stood. "I believe he's correct."

"Can we see some of the clothes?" Marty asked. "These people knew the victim and might be able to identify them."

The word *victim* rang in Ethan's mind. He watched Dawes carefully pick up something he immediately recognized: Rachel's gray T-shirt. He'd seen it hanging on the back of her bathroom door earlier before she left.

He saw by her suddenly pale complexion that Helena recognized it too. "That's hers," the waitress said, her voice catching in her throat. "That's Rachel's. It's one of her favorites for running."

"Are you sure?" Marty asked.

She nodded. So did Ethan.

Marty handed it back to Dawes. "We need to lock down a timeline," he said to his brother. "I need you to tell me *exactly* what you remember about when she left. Helena, try to think of anyone who might have it in for Rachel, some old boyfriend or something. I know she has an ex-husband somewhere."

"Don. He's in Asia, last I heard. And this isn't really his style, he's more passive-aggressive. He'd be more likely to threaten to hurt himself to get her attention."

"That may be, but anything you can give us will help. If Rachel was taken by the same man who abducted the others, what you know might help us find the common denominator among them. And then we might find the perp before anything else happens."

They all knew what he meant. Helena nodded again, and her eyes filled with tears, but they never spilled out.

ETHAN NURSED his coffee at the diner counter and watched his cell phone beside the saucer. It resolutely did not ring. He'd taken the day off from work, ostensibly due to illness; the truth would take too long and sound too weird. Now he simply waited for Marty to report anything new, while his guts wrapped tighter and tighter around themselves. It was the same feeling of rage and helplessness he'd lived with in Iraq: He'd seen that man—his friend and brother soldier—standing over the brutalized body of a *child*, grinning and laughing with no more concern than if it had been some animal. When he thought about Rachel lying beneath someone with that same evil smile...

Several times he caught himself staring at the other patrons. They all probably knew Rachel better than he did. Could one of them be the culprit, bold enough to come back to the diner after committing some unspeakable crime? What about the scruffy guy huddled over his laptop? Or the old man flipping through a worn paperback?

He closed his eyes and took several deep, calming breaths. It was just like Iraq, all right—the friends and enemies looked the same, spoke the same language, smiled the same smiles. You didn't know you'd been tricked until the bombs went off.

If any clue turned up, any revelation, Marty would alert him. Every minute that passed, though, added more time to Rachel's ordeal, and Ethan knew far too well what a man might do to a woman in that amount of time.

And to think that less than twelve hours earlier she'd been pressed against him, skin to skin, gloriously alive. The memory of her touch, her breath, the movement of her skin against his—it had been somehow *more*. Not just sex, not just physical gratification, but some connection that made all his worries irrelevant. So what if he'd only known her, really, for a day? In some ways it felt like he'd waited his whole life to find her.

And now she was gone.

He'd lost a lot of things in life, most with no protest. He wasn't losing Rachel without a fight.

OCCASIONALLY HELENA glanced at Ethan, but mostly she left him alone. She was torn between her natural suspicions of him—after all, he was the last one to see Rachel—and her instinctual sense that he really was one of the good guys. Still, worried reticence and sociopathic guilt could look a lot alike.

Helena, with Jimmy's help, had finally opened the diner for the usual crowd. But Ethan's large, silent presence unnerved them all. Helena told the others that Rachel was down with the flu, and if Ethan hadn't been stoically perched at the end of the counter, staring into space, it might've worked. However, the combination of Rachel's absence and Ethan's grim demeanor kept conversation to whispers, and people who normally sat and visited for an hour finished their food and scurried quickly out the door.

Helena looked at the clock. She hated to send Ethan away, since he had nowhere to go except home or his office, where he would be alone. But he was getting to her too.

"Helena," Mrs. Boswell said softly, and motioned the waitress closer. "You keep staring at that man down there. Isn't he the one who chased away Caleb Johnstone?"

"That's him," Helena said.

"Is he expecting another fight today?"

Helena looked at his straight shoulders and wary demeanor. "Hon, I think he always is."

ETHAN SUDDENLY sat up straight. How had he not thought of the obvious? He motioned for Helena, and when she arrived he said urgently, "That guy I chased out of here the other day—what was his name?"

"Caleb Johnstone," Helena said with a frown. "Why?"

"No reason," Ethan said as he stood. "I'm going home to clean up a little, okay? Marty knows how to reach me if there's any news, and I'm sure he'll call you too."

Helena reached across the counter and grabbed his arm. "Do I look like an idiot?" she hissed. "Marty knows to talk to Caleb. He's probably already done it."

"Marty can ask questions, sure," he said, his voice a quiet rumble. "But I can get answers." He pulled his arm free and rushed out the door.

CHAPTER TWENTY-THREE

THANKS TO THE Internet, finding the address was a snap. It was on the far west side of town, past Middleton going toward Sauk City, on a dead-end road. Ethan showered, changed into comfortable jeans and an old Bucky Badger T-shirt, and put a gun beneath his seat. It was a Smith & Wesson M&P automatic, and he had a permit for it, since he often carried large sums of money. But he had no real intention of using it. What he wanted to do—what he needed to do—could be done only with his bare hands.

As he backed out of his driveway, he thought briefly about calling Marty. But he couldn't. It would compromise Marty professionally, and he would never do that.

CALEB JOHNSTONE'S house was a small brick ranch design, built during the early seventies. An old Toyota hatchback, all four tires missing, was up on concrete blocks in the driveway, with a maroon Ford pickup behind it. The yard was ragged around the edges, and grass grew up through cracks in the concrete drive. The holly bushes along the front porch were tall and irregular. Behind the house stood a wooden work shed with a green fiberglass roof.

The house windows were all dark, reflecting the harsh afternoon sun from their smudged and neglected surfaces. The garage door was down and the front door closed behind the screen. It was impossible to tell if anyone was home.

Ethan parked on the street, in front of the plastic mailbox. The nearest houses were a half mile in either direction, far enough that a scream from inside the house might not be heard. His chest tightened as he inadvertently imagined what Caleb Johnstone might do to Rachel to elicit such screams.

Ethan knew how hard it was for soldiers to go back into society. Once they'd been through training and emerged with a soldier's mind-set, the civilian life felt alien. Ethan was lucky, in that sense. He'd done a good job regimenting and disciplining himself long before he joined the army, so the personality change wasn't as great. But for a certain type of soldier, normal life, with its ennui and necessary compromises, was frustrating and infuriating. He'd seen that frustration in Caleb that morning at the diner.

Ethan opened the mailbox and flipped through the mail. It was all junk, except one letter from the VA. All were addressed to Caleb Johnstone, so evidently he lived alone. "He was quiet, kept to himself," Ethan muttered ironically as he walked up the drive, making no effort at stealth.

He was about to climb the porch steps when he glanced again at the work shed. Something about it held his attention, the same way a particular "abandoned" vehicle had once done in Iraq. In that instance, the shivers had proved all too prescient; two insurgents burst from it, weapons blazing, and before they were both mowed down, one triggered the explosives inside it. Without Ethan's instincts, his whole squad would've been wiped out. So he would be a fool to ignore them now.

He moved silently around the end of the house and peered into the backyard. A patio with rusted furniture and a grill that hadn't been used recently were just outside the sliding glass doors, and an empty clothesline sagged across the yard. A limp wire fence marked the property's edge, with fields beyond it. Nothing spoke of recent use, except for the worn path from the back door to the shed.

He considered going back for the gun but decided it would only escalate things and might put Rachel in additional danger. Bullets flying around would make no distinction between kidnapper, hostage, or rescuer. He took a deep breath, then quickly strode to the shed and opened the door.

His eyes took a moment to adjust. The shed was a typical jumble of tools and engine parts, with an old lawn mower disassembled in the middle of the floor. But the shaft of sunlight streaming in past him revealed something far more disturbing.

Pinned to the far wall was a magazine centerfold, with

Asian throwing knives stuck into it at strategic anatomical points. On the floor beneath was a large pile of other discarded pictures, all similarly mutilated. Ethan felt a rush of both fear and triumph; clearly Caleb had issues with women, issues that could turn sexual and violent.

"What the hell are you doing here?" a voice bellowed behind him, and Ethan whirled. Caleb stood in the shed doorway, holding a long hunting knife.

Ethan was not even conscious of his movements. The next moment of awareness found him astride Caleb, with the older man facedown on the grass, his right arm bent behind his back. The knife lay several feet away. Over the blood pounding in his ears, Ethan said, "Where's Rachel?"

"The fuck are you talking about?" Caleb said through clenched teeth. "Get off me!"

Ethan bent the arm a fraction more. His shadow fell across Caleb's back, and sweat dripped from his face onto Caleb's shirt. "I'm *so* not in the mood. Answer me, or get ready for orthopedic surgery."

"I haven't seen her!" Caleb yelled. "Not since two nights ago!"

That, Ethan realized, was the same night he'd seen Caleb at the pizza place and Rachel emerging from Father Thyme's. "Tell me about two nights ago," he said.

"*Fuck* you!"

Ethan was ready to snap the man's arm when he noticed the unmistakable slanted door at one end of the house's foundation. The path to it was as clear as the one to the shed. "What's in the basement, dickhead?"

"Nothing!" Caleb cried, but with no sincerity. In a

voice so calm it was almost comical, he added, "Look, just let me go and we'll forget this whole thing, okay? I won't call the cops and I won't press charges."

Ethan stood and pulled Caleb to his feet. He held the older man's arm locked behind his back. "Why don't you show me the 'nothing' you've got down there?"

"It's just old parts and furniture and shit, really."

"I'm an antiquarian," Ethan snarled. "Move."

Caleb suddenly went limp. Reflexively Ethan's hand opened as he reached to catch him. Caleb spun and slammed the heel of his right hand into Ethan's chin. Ethan felt the impact to his toes. He thought he'd also been hit in the back of the head, until he realized it was simply his skull smashing into the ground as he fell.

Caleb straddled his chest, the big knife at his throat. He was bright red with fury, and his eyes gleamed. "All right, pretty boy, let's see how tough you are, now that you're not showing off for your precious Rachel." He slid the blade against Ethan's skin, nicking it just under his jaw. "Think she'll still like you if I slice up that pretty face?"

The pain cleared the haze from Ethan's brain. Now *he* was mad, as he'd been only a couple of times in his life.

He knocked the knife away, slicing his hand in the process. He grabbed Caleb by the crotch and crushed what he found there. Caleb shrieked, high and trilling. Ethan grabbed his throat with his left hand, lifted him, and drove him back into the house's brick wall. Caleb fell to the ground and keened his agony.

Breathing heavily, wincing as sweat stung the cut on

his jaw, Ethan yanked Caleb back to his feet. "If you've hurt her, cocksucker," he snarled, "you'll choke on your own balls." He resisted the urge to drive his fist into the man's now-pale face.

Blood from his injured hand soaked into Caleb's shirt as he pushed the man toward the basement door. The latch wasn't locked, and Caleb opened it with trembling fingers. Ethan kicked one door aside, then the other, and shoved Caleb down the stairs ahead of him. When he reached the bottom, he froze.

Three rows of marijuana plants filled the open space beneath hanging growing lights. They were thick, healthy, and damp from the misting humidifiers scattered around them. He saw no doors that might lead to other rooms.

"This is it?" Ethan asked.

"What did you expect?" Caleb croaked, still unable to stand upright.

Then a new voice said, "Don't either one of you dumb shits make a move."

CHAPTER TWENTY-FOUR

IT *HAD* TO be anticlimactic, Rachel thought, but this was ridiculous. The kidnapper who'd riveted the city with his reign of terror was a short, gaunt man with a fringe of hair that grew to his shoulders and failed to compensate for the bare skull above it. His bald forehead shone with the sweat of his exertions. His too-large T-shirt nearly hung off one shoulder, *Flashdance*-style, revealing ropy muscles beneath sickly skin. He appeared to be in his forties, with graying stubble on his chin. His eyes were hidden in shadows. Elaborate tattoos curled up his arms and peeked from his collar.

Then Rachel blinked in surprise. She *knew* this man. She'd seem him twice recently without recognizing him, but now that she saw the ink on his arms and neck, she pegged him immediately. But he wasn't her ex-husband, or Curtis, or Caleb Johnstone.

Arlin Korbus—the man who'd slipped out of the diner after Ethan faced down Caleb and who had approached her at Father Thyme's, where Patty Patilia was playing.

And the man who, three years before, had given her the tattoo below her navel.

Without a word, Korbus turned and climbed the stairs. The door slammed shut, and the dead bolt on the other side clicked into place. The three women lay still on the basement floor, listening. Above them they heard footsteps, muffled TV voices, the sounds of a refrigerator compressor bumping on and off. Water sluiced through the pipes that ran along the ceiling.

The room was like a sauna, filled with the nauseating scent of bodily odors and functions. By squirming and pushing with her bound feet, Rachel managed to sit up against the wall. Then she instantly regretted it, as the damp concrete seemed to crawl with mold and other, more-mobile things that scurried against her skin. She leaned forward, her own breath loud in her ears. Her shoulders and lower back ached.

Arlin Korbus. A man she hadn't seen in years and wouldn't remember now except that she'd spent a long, semidrunken evening staring at him as he drew the effigy tattoo beneath her navel. His studio was called Korbus Inks, and he'd been recommended by several diner patrons back when she'd first taken over for Trudy. At the time she'd felt no discomfort or ickiness with his hands so near her most intimate area, which had been her biggest worry. And she hadn't knowingly seen him since.

No, that wasn't true, she suddenly remembered: She *had* seen him, or glimpsed him, on the news one night as he came out of the courthouse. He'd held his hands to cover his face, but they'd also shown his mug shot and his name. What had he been charged with again? She couldn't recall.

She had no idea how the legal case finally ended, but his shop, which she passed occasionally on her way to the downtown farmers' market, closed soon after. Later it re-opened as an Asian grocery. That had been around six months ago.

He'd been a trim, friendly man when he'd worked on her and Helena, laughing and teasing them. Now, though, he seemed wasted and cold, with eyes like those of the sharks she'd watched on The Discovery Channel. Something about him seemed *rancid,* as if his personality had gone rotten like a head of lettuce left too long in the crisper. Before, she'd actually gotten a secret tingly thrill from the way his rubber-gloved fingers lightly stroked her skin; now the thought of him touching her at all filled her with disgust.

Sweat covered her now, and she winced as it trickled into her eye. There was no way she could stand up with her ankles bound across each other, and he'd been too careful to leave anything available that might let her cut the tape.

She studied the basement. Pipes ran along the ceiling, but apparently even the water heater was upstairs. The walls and floor were empty of anything except mildew and the occasional small insect. Water seeped in along one edge of the floor and made a puddle about an inch deep. The back of the room was pitch-black, out of reach of the feeble light above her. They were trapped in a barren concrete box.

But why was *she* here? What connection did she have with young girls like Faith Lucas and Carrie Kimmell?

In the darkness, something announced its presence with a soft scrape against the floor. A shape formed from the shadows, pale and indefinite, and for a moment Rachel's heart threatened to squirm up her throat and burst through the tape gagging her. Then the image resolved itself into another prisoner huddled in the shadows, knees drawn to her chin. Big eyes peeked out from beneath dark bangs. Rachel stared and felt something inside her twist with renewed despair.

It was Patty Patilia. Not only had Rachel not saved her, now they were to share the same fate.

Rachel slid sideways to the floor and allowed herself to cry again. The sound was muffled and impotent. The tape across her mouth itched, and the taste permeated everything. She had never felt so helpless, and never hated it as much.

She cried only enough to relieve the emotional pressure. It was a skill learned in the wake of her stalker, and it served her well now. She took several deep, calming breaths through her nose. Then she tried scraping the tape from her cheek by catching an edge on the concrete floor, but that merely left another raw spot that stung when sweat trickled into it. She finally gave up and worm-scooted on her side back to the wall. She was exhausted by the time she managed to sit up again and found it hard to catch her breath through the tape. Fresh perspiration trickled down her face and along her spine.

She made eye contact with Carrie Kimmell. Rachel

could do nothing against their plastic ties, but if one of the others could make a tiny rip in the tape holding her, she could possibly escape and bring help. Through grunts and nods, she indicated what she wanted.

Carrie shook her head and scooted away, huddling beside Faith against the wall. Both girls had the dazed, glassy look of captives with no fight left in them.

Rachel turned to Patty in the dark corner. Patty's eyes were clear, but she made no effort to move. Tears cut fresh tracks through the dirt on her face.

With a muffled cry of exasperation, Rachel squirmed along the wall toward Patty. It was difficult, and within moments she fell painfully to the floor. A sharp-edged sliver of glass poked into her shoulder.

Suddenly the door opened and Korbus stood silhouetted at the top of the stairs. He carried what looked like a whip looped in one hand.

Faith and Carrie huddled more closely together, as if they could escape his notice. Patty Patilia began to cry in earnest, the way a terrified child might.

Korbus came down the stairs and perused his captives like a pet owner admiring his animals. He'd changed shirts, and his hair was tied back in a ponytail. He stopped at the bottom, clearly a little winded.

His gaze settled on Rachel. She lay awkwardly on her side, her head twisted around to watch him.

He had the determined look not of a criminal but of someone with a large task ahead. "Looks like you've got a lot of initiative," he said. "Trying to get someone to help you get that tape off, aren't you? Seems like I got here just in time."

She put all of her hatred into the glare she sent his way and was pretty sure her *Fuck you!* carried clearly.

He smiled. "Might as well get you caught up with the rest," he said, and pulled a knife from his pocket. He flicked it open with a practiced twirl of his wrist, and the blade gleamed hotly in the light.

Korbus brought the knife down slowly and slipped it under the tape at Rachel's ankles. She felt the flat of the blade against her foot. Then he cut the tape with an effortless *snick*. She winced as he yanked it free of her skin.

He put away the knife, grabbed her arm, and pulled her up. She got her feet under her and stood, freshly conscious of her nudity as her breasts swayed with the movement. She unsuccessfully fought the blush creeping up her shoulders and neck. Korbus glanced at her, and for a moment there was the male predatory appreciation she'd expect from a man who kept naked women in his basement.

But almost immediately it faded to the cool, clinical gaze of a technician at work. He unrolled the whiplike strip in his hand, revealing it to be a dog leash with a choke collar attached. Before she could react, he had the chain-link collar around her neck and the leash clipped to it. She glared at him, fury rising past fear.

He wrapped the leash's other end around his fist; to choke her, he only had to tug. "Come on," he said, and turned toward the stairs. She spread her feet and braced herself as the collar tightened against her neck.

He stepped close and spoke in a cold whisper. "Be sure you want to pick this fight, Rachel," he said. "If you give me too much trouble, I'll bend you over a table and show you what women are good for. Only I won't use my dick, I'll use whatever's handy. Understand me?" He snapped her panties' elastic waistband for emphasis.

The use of her name frightened her the most. She choked down a whimper but looked away from those paradoxically dead yet ravenous eyes.

"Then you'll cooperate?"

She gazed at the floor, at her own bare feet now smeared with sweat and dirt. She nodded.

"Good. Up the stairs, then. You go first."

She glanced at Carrie and Faith. Their incomplete tattoos told her exactly what was in store. Then the leash tightened, and she preceded him up the stairs. Her bare feet felt tender against the wood.

CHAPTER TWENTY-FIVE

THEY EMERGED INTO the kitchen. Dishes were stacked neatly in the drain, and magnets held magazine photos of tattooed women to the refrigerator. Korbus paused to close and lock the basement door.

Rachel looked around for a phone or computer, but if he had either, they weren't in this room. She saw no sign that anyone else shared the home. The windows were all covered with heavy blinds, so there was no chance a neighbor might spot her. If there *were* any neighbors, that is; they could be in one of Wisconsin's thousands of isolated farmhouses. The door that looked like it might lead outside was dead-bolted and chained.

Korbus led her down a short hall and into what at first she took to be a bathroom. It certainly *had* been once, but he'd knocked out the wall between it and a small bedroom, making a single space with a sink, counter, and toilet. The walls were painted bright white and reflected the fluorescent lighting so that, after the basement, Rachel was almost blinded. Where there had been a bathtub was now a table that slanted at a forty-five-degree angle from the floor, made of rough-edged wood and stained with what could have been either ink or blood. The renovation work appeared to be recent, hurried, and rather sloppy. That made it no less effective, though.

He closed the door, locked it, and put the key in his pocket. There were no windows. She could hear nothing except her own heart and Korbus's labored breathing.

At last he turned to face her. His expression was weary and pale. "I'll cut your hands loose," he said, "and you can go to the bathroom, if you need to." He looked evenly at her until she nodded. Truthfully, her bladder was killing her. "But if you try anything funny, you'll be pissing your panties from now on. Understand?"

Again she nodded. What else could she do?

"Turn around, then."

First he removed the collar. Then she felt the knife slip between her wrists and cut the tape. It yanked painfully on her arm hair as she separated her hands. Then he slipped the leash off over her head. She crossed her arms over her breasts, expecting him to grab her at any moment.

Instead, he turned on the tap and faced the door. "I'm not watching. I'm not one of those golden-shower guys. Do your business."

This was her chance, she thought. He had his back to her, and she was free. But she was also weak, sore, and naked. And he still had that knife.

She slid down her panties and sat on the toilet. The running water masked the sound, at least. As she urinated, she carefully pulled the tape from her mouth, wincing at the numb area it left. She worked her lips and jaw back to life.

She finished, pulled the panties back up, and said raggedly, "Mr. Korbus?"

He did not turn around. "Flush, please."

She pulled the handle. In the quiet, apparently sound-proofed room, the noise was like the Death Star exploding. When it faded, he turned to her and said, "You can climb onto the table, or we can fight about it." He held up a thick baton with a gleaming metal tip. "One jolt of this gets a cow into the slaughterhouse chute, so it's a good motivator."

She swallowed hard, connecting the prod with his threat in the basement, and wrapped her arms tight around her torso. "This isn't going to work. You know people will look for me."

He nodded toward the floor. "People are looking for them too. Cops, friends, parents." He smiled, a cold yet somehow pathetic expression. "They won't look here."

Although she hated it, she let her tears flow, hoping she would seem more sympathetic. She hunched down, making herself as small and pathetic as possible. "Why are you doing this to me?" she said in her best little-girl's voice. "I never hurt you. I never did *anything* to you."

He smiled again and shook his head. "You don't remember either, do you? Just like the rest. I'd hoped that since you weren't some airheaded college girl, you might be different."

"I *am*," she said, ashamed at the whining tone she used. "Really, I am. Please believe me."

He sighed, both bored and annoyed. He gestured with the prod and said, "Get up on there or I'll use this. I mean it."

Still sniffling, she stepped up to the table. She laid her back against it, arms still crossed over her chest. The wood was rough and cold against her shoulders. There was a lip at the bottom for her feet and two straps to secure her ankles.

"I'm going to buckle your feet," he said. "You try to kick me, or hit me, or anything, then you get zapped." She stayed very still as he secured her ankles with Velcro straps bolted to the wood. She struggled to keep her thighs together.

He stood with a groan. One of his knees popped loudly. He put the cattle prod aside and said, "Put your arms down. If you cooperate, I'll shackle them at your side, which isn't that uncomfortable. Give me a hard time, and I'll tie them behind your back again. And," he added, leaning close as he'd done in the basement, "I know how to pierce pretty much every body part. Some of them hurt more than others."

She lowered her arms. He'd already seen her, after all. He fastened her right wrist, then walked around the table for the left one. When she felt the strap pull tight, she was suddenly claustrophobic, and her heart began to thunder. "Please, don't do this, whatever it is. Let me go," she said, breathless. "Please, this isn't right, you can't do this—"

"Calm down," he said firmly, the way he might snap at a panicky child. "I'm not going to kill you."

"What about Ling Hu?" she almost shouted. She frantically pulled at the bonds on her wrists, rattling the table. *Don't freak out!* her rational mind cried, but it couldn't be heard over the terror. "You killed *her*!"

He grabbed her jaw firmly and slammed her head back against the table. She froze. He leaned so close that she could smell his minty, vaguely antiseptic breath.

"Let me tell you a little story about Ling Hu," he said. "I saw her in a convenience store down on Willie Street. I remembered this amazing design I did for her, something that would be a real work of art. She didn't want it, though, she just wanted a tramp stamp like all the other girls. So, anyway, I complimented her tattoo, thinking she might remember me, thinking she might even thank me for it. You know what she said? 'Fuck you, creep.'"

He released Rachel's jaw. "So I grabbed the stuck-up little bitch off the street, brought her back here, and decided to give her that tat whether she wanted it or not. I won't be around in six months; my work deserves better than that."

"Are you sick?" Rachel asked quietly. "I mean . . . ill?"

He ignored her and instead turned to his worktable. "So I looked back through my shop's old records. There were eleven of you bitches who turned down designs I'd worked really hard on. And five of you were still in town. I decided that if God hated me so much He had to destroy both my career *and* my life, then I'd make damn sure I left my mark anyway."

He paused and chuckled to himself. "I mean, hell: I grabbed Ling Hu right off the street and no one saw me. If that's not a sign, I don't know what is."

"So what will you do to us...afterward?"

He shrugged. "I don't really give a fuck. I suppose I thought at first I'd just let you go. By the time any of you got to the police, I'd be dead, and I figure at least one of you will decide to leave my art alone. But now..."

He stopped and tapped his fingertips on the table. "I did *not* kill that Chinese girl. She had asthma or something that I didn't know about, and the sleeping pills I was giving her must've aggravated it. I actually feel a little bad about that, and that's why *you're* wide awake."

"Do you feel bad enough to let me go?" she whispered.

He sighed and shook his head. "When life takes all your options away, you go with what's left, whether you like it or not." He put a strap across her throat, then stepped to a cloth-covered workbench and examined a row of small metal tips. He pulled surgical gloves from a box dispenser and expertly put them on. "I won't kid you, this is going to hurt. Maybe a lot; my hands aren't as steady as they used to be. But the less you fight, the faster it will go."

The reality washed over her like a cold wave. Her body, her skin, was about to be *defiled*. Soon he would use her, not sexually perhaps but still as an object with no more importance than a sheet of poster board. And she could do nothing to stop him. "Please, don't," she whispered.

He turned to her, a tattoo gun in his hand. "My advice..." And here his smile turned frightening. "My advice is to simply lie back and enjoy it."

RACHEL LAY LIMP and whimpering on the table. Her throat was raw from screaming, and her muscles exhausted from straining against the straps holding her. The insistent pain became the only thing that penetrated her haze-lathered mind.

She realized with sudden clarity that both the buzzing sound and the burning sensation had stopped. She opened her watery eyes and croaked, "Are you done?"

Korbus swabbed his work with antiseptic. "For now," he said, and wiped sweat from his own face. "I can't work too long at one time."

She began to tremble uncontrollably, and her skin felt cold and clammy. Was she going into shock? What he'd done to her certainly qualified as an injury.

After she was clean, Korbus took a picture of his handiwork. He's taken one at the start too, the first time in her life that Rachel had been photographed naked. Then he'd uploaded the photo to his laptop and printed out the first of the stencils.

She'd seen these stencils before. She recalled sitting in Korbus's tattoo parlor with Helena, half drunk and giggling as he showed her the same design he was now imposing on her. She'd asked for a simple silhouette of the Hudson Park effigy mound, but instead he presented her with an elaborate image of a forest scene that would fill the space between her sternum and pubic bone with half-nude natives dancing along her ribs. There was no way she was getting *that* done—not least because being top-less for the tattoo guy was just trashy—so despite his best efforts to persuade her, she got only the one design. She'd always liked the result and never once thought about his insane idea again.

Now, though, it was *all* she could think about. The smell of ink and antiseptic, the odor of microscopic bits of skin and blood burning, made her almost pass out. But merciful unconsciousness eluded her. She felt the blood trickle in tiny rivulets down her skin and the cool bite of alcohol as he wiped it away.

She had no sense of time in the windowless, clockless room. At one point Korbus was gone for what seemed like several minutes. She fought with all her strength to break free, straining arms and legs against the table and straps. She screamed for help. She did not look at what he had done to her.

When he returned, he settled back into work without even a word. Finally he sat back, face sweaty above his surgical mask, and said, "That's the biggest part. We'll start on your boobs tomorrow."

She glared at him, trying to channel her fear and shame into rage. He did not look away. Instead, he said, "I stayed up all night working on this design. Inspiration, you know. No sense of time, didn't stop to eat or sleep. My mojo was working. And then you laughed at it. I expect that from these other spoiled bitches, but you, you're a grown woman. You're supposed to have..."

He waved his hand in the air as he sought the word. "Manners."

Despite her anger, Rachel blushed anew, because he was right; she and Helena, half drunk and giddy, *had* laughed at it, with Korbus right there. He'd laughed, too, at the time, as if their scorn were no big deal. But that was no justification for this.

Still playing helpless, she choked down her fury and said meekly, "I'm sorry, Mr. Korbus."

"Doesn't matter," he said. His tone was not bitter or angry, just resigned. "Doesn't matter a damn now."

"I didn't mean it, Mr. Korbus," she said. And it was true, she hadn't intended to hurt anyone's feelings.

He laughed, cold and mirthless, like the sharp bark of a coyote standing over fresh roadkill. "You asked me before if I was ill. I'm close to my expiration date, for sure." He ran a finger along the fresh line and flicked the tip of one breast for emphasis. "But I haven't spoiled yet."

He rummaged on the table, then held up a long plastic tie, the kind used to bind the other victims. "I'm going to tie your hands again. You've been reasonably good, so I'll tie them in front this time. Then I'll give you some water before I take you back to the basement. I imagine you're thirsty."

She nodded. Her thoughts, though, were on escape. With her arms tied in front she might struggle, but not while her ankles remained strapped to the table. And he kept the cattle prod within reach. He'd perfected his little procedure, all right.

In moments he'd released her arms and bound her

wrists, tight enough that she worried about the circulation. Then he held out a bottle of water. She took it in her
hands and drank gratefully. Between drafts she asked,
"What about food?"

He slapped her behind. "Crackers when I feel like it.
This isn't a hotel."

She drained the bottle, and he took it away. When he
tore off a fresh piece of duct tape, she said, "Do you have
to? I won't scream, I promise."

He smiled sarcastically. "Right. Stockholm syndrome
in record time, eh? Sorry." He pressed the tape to her face.

CHAPTER TWENTY-SIX

ETHAN SAT ACROSS from Marty's desk. It was as disorganized and cluttered as his room had been when they were kids. And just like then, Marty knew exactly where everything was.

Ethan had a Band-Aid on his jawline and a gauze bandage on his hand; neither injury needed stitches. However, he was certain he'd have to replace all his trousers; they would no longer fit, now that Marty had effectively and thoroughly chewed his ass off.

"The *only* reason you're not in jail right now is that you were the one bleeding, and Caleb had enough pot in that basement to make what he was doing a felony," Marty told him in the car coming back to town. "Not to mention that he confessed to vandalizing Rachel's diner. He'll make a deal to drop charges against you if we lower the charges against him."

"How do you know that?"

"Gee, could it be because I'm a cop?" Marty almost shouted.

"I'm sorry," Ethan mumbled.

"I think everybody knows that by now. Christ on a stick, Ethan, don't you think Caleb was one of the first people we talked to? He had a solid alibi. If there had been any holes in it, any doubt at all, we'd have hauled him in for questioning, or at least had someone watching him."

"Yeah," Ethan said.

"Yeah, no shit." Marty sighed, tapping his hands on the steering wheel as they waited for a light to change. "You're coming back to the station with me, so I can keep an eye on you. I'll bring you back to get your truck later. And I don't want to hear a god*damned* word out of you, do you understand?"

"Yes," Ethan agreed. He looked down at his knees, unable to meet his brother's gaze.

"I know you're worried, man. I don't blame you. But this isn't like war. Or maybe it is, I don't know, but the rules are different. You'll have to trust us, trust *me*. Can you do that?"

"If I have to, I have to," Ethan said flatly. "How'd you find me?"

"Helena called me. And you better thank your sorry white ass that she did, because if any other cop in the *world* had found you, you'd be in jail right beside Caleb."

Now it was late afternoon, and nothing had changed. There were no leads, no tips, no clues. The evening news would carry the story, but neither man held out hope for a break based on that. Being on TV hadn't helped the others—especially Ling Hu.

Marty dug under a pile of loose printouts for a folder. "You know, I think this is the most frustrating case I've ever worked on," he said. "Five girls, one dead that we know of, and all taken from the middle of town, without a single substantial clue except their abandoned clothes. No one saw anything, no one heard anything, and none of the victims seem to have anything in common. I tell you, the hardest thing to track down is a truly random criminal."

"Did you check *The Lady of the Lakes?*" Ethan asked.

He nodded. "Nothing. Not even a mention of this. I sure wish I knew how they got their information and why they know all about some things and nothing at all about others."

Ethan looked at the picture of Marty and his longtime partner, Chuck, in sweaters before a cozy fireplace. They seemed happy to simply be in each other's presence, similar to the childhood picture of Rachel and her sister. "Do you think she's dead?"

"Honestly, Ethan, I don't know. Ling Hu died of an asthma attack, according to the preliminary report, so she wasn't murdered. She also wasn't sexually assaulted, even though we found her nude."

"But she could've died before the kidnapper got around to either of those things."

Marty nodded. His computer chimed to announce an e-mail, and for a long moment the only sound was his typing a response. Across the room, the phone rang at another desk, and a gruff, unsympathetic voice answered it.

Finally Marty said, "I hate that I brought you into this, you know. Sending you to the diner like I did. I just thought you and she..." He ended with a shrug.

"We did," Ethan said. "That's the worst thing about it. She was great. Funny, sexy, smart..." He ran his hand through his hair. "Like Julie, except without the bitterness and paranoia."

"It's not paranoia if people *are* talking behind your back," Julie said.

Ethan spun around in his chair. Marty stood and said formally, "Ms. Schutes, what a surprise. Normally the desk sergeant calls up to announce visitors."

Julie was immaculate in a summer blouse and skirt, her bag over her shoulder. Her blond hair was pulled severely back, and she wore black-frame glasses. Her face twisted for a moment as her personal reaction battled her professional detachment. The latter won. She kept her gaze resolutely on Marty and said, "Actually, I wasn't here to see you, Detective Walker. I thought I'd stop by to say hello on my way out of the building. But since I *am* here, I'd like to ask you some questions about the latest disappearance."

"And I'd like to answer them, but I can't."

"No comment, then?"

He sat again. "No comment. Except to tell everyone, especially women, to use extra caution."

"Is this latest disappearance connected to the others?"

"He said no comment, Julie," Ethan snapped without looking at her.

Julie started to bark a reply, then noticed his bandages. "What happened to you?"

"I cut myself shaving," Ethan said through clenched teeth.

She moved to the side of his chair. "I hear you reported her missing too. The anguished lover waiting desperately for news is always good for a few paragraphs of filler. Care to comment?"

Ethan stood and glared down at Julie. For a moment he seemed about to strike out, if not physically then with a verbal tirade. A couple of other officers at nearby desks stood as well, ready to intercede at the signal from Marty.

But Ethan clamped it down. "If you'll excuse me, I need to visit the men's room."

He pushed past her, shoving the chair aside to avoid physical contact.

JULIE WATCHED him depart, then turned back to Marty. The cocky chill was replaced by real emotion as she said, "You could've told me he was involved. I had to find it out from the P.R. officer. And then here he is, big as life."

Marty sighed. "There's not enough hours in the day for everything I could've done, Julie."

"So he *does* know the last victim?"

Marty nodded. "She disappeared after a date with him. Their first date."

Julie turned again and looked down the row of desks to make sure Ethan was truly gone. She tapped her fingers on the chair back and said finally, "Doesn't that make him a suspect, then?"

"No," he said sternly. "And this is all off the record, Julie. Seriously."

"I don't blame you. This whole thing doesn't make the police look very good."

"You mean it doesn't make *me* look very good. Are you going to hang me out to dry in your article?"

She tried not to smile, but it still crept out. "You're a shit, you know that?"

ETHAN WANDERED numbly through the police station. A few officers squinted at his visitor's badge as he passed, but for the most part they left him alone. He'd visited Marty before, and word of his contretemps with Caleb Johnstone evidently hadn't reached the rank and file.

He opened the door to the fenced parking lot and went outside. A half dozen white police cruisers waited for their patrolmen to return, some with their engines idling. The metallic squawk of the dispatcher rang through open windows.

He went to the chain-link fence and stood with his fingers threaded through it, his forehead against the metal. It was warm from the sun. Just beyond the fence, past the narrow bike path and gently sloping bank, stretched Lake Monona, southernmost of the city's lakes.

The afternoon sun made the highlights on the lake sparkle. A Jet Ski bounced across the wake of a fishing boat, and in the distance he saw a small sailing craft making for one of the big houses on the far shore. Bicyclists and joggers passed within arm's reach, but none paid him a second glance. No doubt they assumed he was a cop, and no one wanted to make eye contact.

He turned toward a distinctive *whirrrr-snik* sound. An elderly man sat at the water's edge, casting his rod and reel into the lake. He let the lure settle, then wound it in with slow, methodical movements. When it emerged from the water empty, he didn't seem disappointed and immediately threw it back again, repeating the process.

"Are they biting this time of day?" Ethan asked.

The man turned. He had dark eyebrows and unruly white hair. His face was lined and suntanned. "You talking to me, Officer? I got my fishing license right here."

"No, I'm not a cop."

"If you're a prisoner, then that's a terrible bit of escaping."

Ethan laughed. "No, I'm just here visiting."

"I had a friend whose son was just visiting, for five to ten."

"My brother's a cop."

"Oh. Well, no, the fish aren't biting." The lure came up out of the water again, fish-free. "The spirits aren't with me today."

Ethan perked up at the use of the word. "Spirits?"

"The spirits in the lake. If they aren't with you, you could toss dynamite in there and not have a single fish float to the surface."

"I didn't know there were spirits in the lake."

"Where'd you grow up?"

"Monroe."

"Do you fish?"

Ethan nodded.

"And you never heard about the lake spirits?"

"Not until recently."

The old man shifted so he could look at Ethan directly. "You know about the animal mounds in the area? The people who built them did it to honor the spirits in the lakes. If you want to do any good fishing here, you better bring along something to honor them too. They decide they don't like you, you might never get back in their favor."

"What sort of things do they like?"

"I bring 'em beer." He nodded at the cooler beside him. "The first drink is always for the lake."

Just as Ethan was about to point out that his offerings seemed to do little good, the man's rod bent sharply and he jumped to his feet. Within moments he'd landed a walleye that looked to weigh well over five pounds.

Ethan was about to congratulate the man, when Julie said behind him, "Isn't watching someone fish the only thing lamer than actual fishing?"

He turned. She stood with her arms crossed, the light wind tousling loose strands of her hair. A pair of uniformed cops stood by their car and grinned as they appraised her. If she knew, she didn't seem to care.

"I'm not your story, Julie," Ethan said. "Go away."

"I'd say a local builder and Iraq war vet who gets in a

fistfight with another veteran over a dope deal gone bad would make a hell of a story," she said blithely.

"You wouldn't *dare*. You know that's not true."

She smiled in smug triumph. "But all the facts fit."

"What do you want?"

She looked down and shook her head. The maliciousness left her face. "I'm sorry, Ethan, that was...thoughtless. Just when I think I'm over things, they come back stronger than ever. I didn't expect to see you down here, and to find out you've moved on...it stings a little."

"Well, I'm going home, so you'll have the place all to yourself."

As he walked past, she touched his arm. He stopped. She said, "I do miss you, you know."

He did not look at her.

"I still say we could've made it work," she continued.

He whirled toward her angrily. "Is that some kind of joke?"

"What? No, I didn't mean...Look, I'm sorry for that too."

He saw the genuine regret in her eyes, and after a long moment he nodded. "Everybody's sorry for something."

Her blue eyes fixed on him with all of her fierce, intelligent intensity. "Are you?"

Ethan recalled his grandfather's admonition: *Never apologize; it's a sign of weakness.* He'd believed that for most of his life. Now he knew it wasn't true. But he didn't want Julie to know he knew. So he turned and walked back into the building.

"That's what I thought," she called after him.

Inside the building, he found a secluded hallway corner and dialed his brother's cell phone. When he got voice mail, as he hoped he would, he left Marty a message saying he was going home. But he had other plans for the evening.

CHAPTER TWENTY-SEVEN

RACHEL PRECEDED Korbus down the basement steps. Her hands were bound in front, her mouth taped, and the choke collar again encircled her neck. She felt the strap bounce between her shoulder blades.

She stumbled on the last step and fell to her knees, then forward onto the concrete. With her wrists tied in front, she was able to stop herself from landing on her face. Still, her elbows and forearms scraped painfully on the cement.

Korbus grabbed her arm and yanked her to her feet. He swiped at the dirt clinging to her oiled skin. She pressed her arms against her nipples and glared over the tape.

"Don't get any dirt on that while it's still bleeding," he said. "Wouldn't want an infection or anything, would we?"

He guided Rachel to the back wall and gestured that she should sit against it. When she did, he pulled her legs out straight and put a plastic tie around her ankles, binding them across each other. Only then did he take the choke collar from her neck.

His bald head gleamed with sweat as he looked at the others. Their eyes were wide above their gags. Faith and Carrie still huddled together, while Patty remained far back in the corner. They waited to see who he'd pick for the next session, but instead he yawned, went back upstairs, and closed the door. The bolt slammed home on the opposite side. Then, unlike before, the single dangling bulb went out, leaving them in darkness.

Faith and Carrie began to scream through their gags. Rachel awkwardly got to her knees, sat back on her heels, and tried not to hyperventilate. The room was close, hot, and damp, and the darkness made it completely unbearable. She twisted her wrists uselessly; the plastic ties were unbreakable. And there would be no way of working her ankles free.

She closed her eyes and tried to ground and center, to fight the panic. The pain from the tattoo made it easier than she thought. Instead of adding to her fears, it helped change them to anger. She had been defiled in the worst possible way, permanently marked by the will of a man who treated her body as nothing more than a canvas. How *dare* Korbus think he could force his precious designs on the flesh of unwilling victims? His captives weren't even people to him, just tools to be used like paint and needles. Their feelings meant nothing.

As her eyes adjusted, she realized some light was actually seeping in from a small window overhead, where the basement ceiling met the wall. The glass had been painted black, but in spots the edges had flaked off. The illumination was weak but definite, sending narrow beams of faint light—moonlight? sunlight?—that, combined with her memory of the room, allowed her to see enough to move around.

Rachel crawled uncomfortably on her hands and knees over to Patty. The girl was absolutely wide-eyed with terror, her face sweaty and streaked from crying. She looked soft and achingly vulnerable; Rachel could not imagine anyone being aroused by the pitiful, slightly plump body normally hidden by clothes, now brutally displayed against her will. *I'm so sorry I failed you,* she thought. *I should've done more. Then I might not be here either.*

She lightly touched Patty's face. The girl whimpered and jumped. Fresh tears sparkled in the dim light.

Rachel couldn't just let this go on. These were *kids,* unprepared for this and entirely unable to cope. They might have read about brutal things, seen online videos of cruelty, but they'd never experienced it firsthand. They could never extract themselves from this, and she had no illusions that Korbus would release them once they were covered with his obscene art. He would bind them, photograph them one last time, and then probably masturbate to the pictures. Or, as she suspected, die quietly in bed of whatever illness racked him, leaving his body and theirs to be found only when the smell of decomposition grew too great.

There was no time to lose. She reached up and peeled the duct tape from her face. It hurt even worse on the already-raw skin. Then she leaned close and whispered, "Patty, can you hear me?"

She felt the girl's greasy hair brush her cheek when she nodded.

"We can't wait for someone to find us, we have to rescue ourselves. Do you understand?"

This time the ends of Patty's hair slapped her face as she rapidly shook her head *no*.

Rachel grabbed the girl's hair roughly and yanked it tight. "He's using us as his damn *canvas,* Patty," she hissed. "And he won't be able to let us go when he finishes. Is that what you want? You have to be *stronger* than this!"

By now Rachel's eyes had adjusted so she could see Patty clearly. The black tips of Korbus's new design curled over her shoulder. The girl's expression changed subtly from helpless to the first glimmer of anger. She still had some courage left, Rachel realized, with a rush of sisterly pride.

Suddenly Rachel felt a chill unlike anything she'd ever experienced. The black tips on Patty's shoulder began to *move,* becoming spindly black extremities that climbed out of the darkness and reached for Patty's face.

Rachel awkwardly jumped back and, forgetting that she was no longer gagged, shrieked.

The sound rang through the basement. The other girls echoed it with their muffled cries. Then her mind interpreted the tableau and told her what she was seeing. It was no alien creature or hell spawn emerging from the depths; it was a *spider,* black and shiny, now crawling down Patty's shoulder toward her chest.

A wave of nausea driven by stress and discomfort swept over Rachel. The spider wasn't *that* big; she just had a natural aversion to crawly things, and its sudden appearance had surprised her. She closed her eyes and took several deep breaths, trying not to vomit what little remained in her stomach as the sudden adrenaline rush faded.

Then, just as Rachel began to relax, the arachnid slipped on Patty's sweaty skin and tumbled momentarily into a tiny sliver of direct light. Rachel caught a glimpse of the distinctive red hourglass on the spider's hard, smooth body.

A *black widow.*

New horror rose in her. She recalled the family stories of her uncle Speck in Ohio, bitten by one of these in a tractor shed. Since no one, including him, actually saw the spider bite him, the doctors were hesitant to start treatment; using the wrong antivenin could simply speed the fatal process along. By the time the doctors decided it was now or never, her uncle's chest was swollen and hard as a barrel due to the toxin's effect on his muscles. He was treated at the very last minute and ultimately survived, but he was never the same.

Now an identical creature righted itself and crawled delicately back up the curve of Patty's bare breast, which jiggled as she trembled. Rachel looked around for something to swat the spider away, but the basement was as bare as its captives. "Don't move, Patty," she whispered, "Just be as still as you can."

Patty was rigid, eyes wide above her gag, her body

arched and pressed back against the wall as much as her bonds allowed. The spider scrambled for purchase on her collarbone, and she rolled her eyes downward desperately, trying to see it. It tapped its long front legs against her vibrating flesh in an unmistakable sign of belligerence.

Rachel tried to slap it away, a moment too late. The creature's legs waved just at the edge of Patty's vision, and her composure fled. She screamed again and tried to buck it off by convulsing her whole body.

The spider rolled forward, the tips of its legs now arched inward to pin itself to the spot, and Rachel saw the striking motion even as she swung her clasped hands at it. She hit Patty instead, startling the spider even more and causing it to bite a second time. Rachel's next blow finally managed to knock it to the floor, where it lay with its legs curled into its belly, stunned.

Knowing she risked a bite herself, Rachel balled her fists and smashed them down as hard and fast as she could. She felt the spider's body crumple and spurt beneath the blow, and pain shot up her arms from hitting the concrete. She looked frantically through the spider's gooey remains on her hands for evidence of a bite but found none. Finally she glanced over at Patty.

The girl was sobbing, mucus trailing from her nose down onto the gag. Rachel crawled back and ripped the tape from Patty's face. For a moment the crying stopped and she stared; her face sported a red splotchy rectangle where the tape had adhered. Then she screamed.

Rachel again grabbed her by the hair. "Stop it!" she hissed, staring at the bites. They were small red bumps, barely noticeable, but she knew worse would come soon. How long, though? "Listen, you have to calm down. Panic will make it worse."

"That was a black widow, wasn't it?" Patty sobbed. "They're poisonous, aren't they? I'm going to die! Oh, God, I'm really going to die like this, down here, no one's going to rescue me—"

"No, you're not!" Rachel snarled. "He's counting on us being too scared to fight back, and so far he's been right, but we can't just lie here and *take* it anymore."

Growling with frustration, Rachel turned toward the door. She writhed in slow motion to the stairs and then wriggled her way up them. It was tedious going, and she repeatedly banged her knees on the edges of the steps. Her panties snagged and tried to roll down her legs as she moved, and the ragged wood left tiny jagged splinters in her bare skin.

Exhausted, she reached the top and banged weakly on the door. "Mr. Korbus!" she called. "A black widow spider bit one of us! She needs a doctor!"

She waited for a response, but there was nothing. No creak of floorboards, no annoyed muttering. Had he gone out? Or, worse, had he *died*?

"Korbus!" she yelled again, her voice suddenly breaking as the strain took its toll. "Please, she's really in trouble!"

There was still no response. She looked down at Carrie and Faith. "Come on, you two, get those gags off and help me yell!"

The two girls looked at each other, then reached up to

remove their gags. Carrie peeled hers slowly, while Faith yanked hers off in one quick move.

"Help!" Carrie said, her voice thin and hoarse.

"Help us!" Faith echoed.

"Help!" Rachel called, balancing enough to raise her hands and pound higher on the door. She drew back for another blow, then felt her center of balance shift. She tumbled backward and slid down the stairs, the momentum driving splinters into her back and buttocks.

She landed with a sob at the bottom. Even the agony from the fresh tattoo paled next to this. She rolled onto her side and saw Patty still crying, while Carrie and Faith mechanically cried, "Help," over and over. Rachel felt her own tears swell behind her eyes.

Then she spotted something in the darkness beside Patty, something she'd noticed before but forgotten. She reached her bound hands toward it and felt a shiver of hope.

She crawled toward it.

CHAPTER TWENTY-EIGHT

LAKE MONONA WAS large enough that, after dark, many parts of its shoreline were hidden from casual view. Ethan had scouted this particular lakeside lot for a bid several weeks earlier, so he knew there was enough overgrown shrubbery to hide his truck. Now, shielded by the trees and bushes, caught between an incomprehensible urge and the common sense he'd always prided himself on possessing, he crept carefully down to the water.

Marty had called and left a message telling Ethan to stay at home. Julie had *not* called, thank God. The evening news showed a picture of Rachel when it mentioned the case, and the sight made his heart throb in his throat. But there was no real news, and not even *The Lady of the Lakes* had any information. Like the others, Rachel had fallen down a rabbit hole and vanished from this universe.

He'd taken a cab from the police station and retrieved his truck from the street outside Caleb Johnstone's house.

Then he'd gone home until dark, when he could come to a spot that he knew afforded privacy.

A car drove down the street behind him, its thumping stereo Doppler-shifting as it passed. He waited to make sure it was gone. He'd already removed his shirt, shoes, and socks and was now unfastening his belt. He was almost dizzy with a combination of worry, fear, and something very like eagerness. He wasn't the lake's "chosen one," though; would he do anything other than get soaked?

He stepped out of his jeans and Jockey shorts, then removed the bandages from his jaw and hand. Naked, he faced the lake, watching the waves smack against the big gray stones. He would have to climb down those to reach the water—climb down nude and barefoot. The thought was suddenly daunting.

When he felt the first touch of liquid on his toes, he stopped. He knelt at the edge of the water and opened the bottle of Heineken Dark. It was his favorite beer, the one he saved for special occasions, and it seemed an appropriate offering. He said quietly, "This is a gift, because I need your help." He poured the dark liquid slowly into the water. When the bottle was empty, he put it aside on the rocks. He took a deep breath, glanced one last time through the trees to make certain no one was around, and stepped out into the night.

He felt incredibly vulnerable—more so than in the middle of a war with bullets and shrapnel flying at him. He scowled at his mincing, uncertain steps as he negotiated the rocks and sighed gratefully when the hard surface gave way to silken mud. When the water was knee-deep, he slid forward on his stomach, ignoring the water's bite at his fresh injuries. Then he drifted forward toward the drop-off, kicking his feet against the bottom. Every inch of his skin was alive with anticipation.

Suddenly his feet found nothing to kick against. He had a brief, odd thought that, since the lake spirit or ghost or whatever it was had taken Rachel, it might be a totally male spirit, uninterested in him. Or, more awkwardly, it might be a male spirit that *was* interested in him. This made him smile; Marty would certainly find this amusing.

He put his face under the water and looked into the darkness but saw nothing. From here on, it would be literal blind faith. He took a final breath, closed his eyes, and let himself slip beneath the surface.

RACHEL CAREFULLY dipped a fingertip into the water that had seeped in along the floor's edge. As soon as she did so, the intimate tingle that shot through her assured her that this was no leaky pipe. This was groundwater seeping into the basement; this came from *the lakes*.

Fresh sweat popped out all over her. She hoped the dim light hid the flush across her shoulders and neck from her fellow prisoners. Even in this crisis, there was no denying or resisting the water's effect. And if her plan worked, she'd be a lot more embarrassed than she was right now.

Just touching the water might be enough; for all she knew, the spirits were aware of her already. But she couldn't take that chance. The strongest connection she felt with them was always at the point of orgasm, when she could almost sense their thoughts, just as she knew they could read hers. She needed to reach that moment of abandon, and she had to do it fast.

She lay down on her side, her back to the others. Then, eyes closed tight against embarrassment, she slid her wet fingertips inside her panties.

She moaned softly at the touch, her fingers' destination already hypersensitive and ready. She tried to keep her thoughts focused on calling for help, but her body's response soon had her engrossed in more-immediate concerns, one hand working, the other opening and closing in response.

ETHAN SURFACED, treading water. He looked back at the shore, then out across the water.

Nothing had happened. Nothing unusual, erotic, or even a little bit strange. Apparently the spirits didn't care for Dutch beer. Or they simply didn't like men.

He was about to swim for the shallows when, abruptly, with no warning, he felt something touch him *there.*

RACHEL WHIMPERED as the tension built within her. She knew she might not be able to reach orgasm, that this could be yet another time when she got right to the edge, right *there,* but couldn't make it all the way. But she'd passed the point of no return and could barely have stopped if their captor had opened the basement door. All her noble, desperate goals of saving Patty and rescuing herself and stopping Korbus had faded into the hot, damp desire to *come.*

ETHAN FROZE, thinking absurd thoughts like gar, snapping turtles, or even trout. He sank slowly until the water closed over him again. He kicked his feet enough to stop his descent and waited. His lungs throbbed with the tail end of his last breath.

He remembered he'd once read that the emperor Caligula kept small boys around to swim with him and nibble like minnows at his genitals. But this touch was light, and knowing, and played along his growing erection with an intent no natural lake denizen would share. It felt unmistakably like *fingertips,* and he grew hard under their ministrations.

He fought the urge to surface. The spirits kept Rachel from drowning, and he could only hope for the same. The watery fingers encircled him, then solidified into something that surrounded and engulfed him—a familiar sensation that allowed him the resistance he needed to penetrate . . . whatever it was.

It felt incredible, and he gasped reflexively. When he realized his lungs had actually expanded and filled, he looked up at the twinkling stars through the surface distortion. *I should be drowning,* he thought, but he had no difficulty breathing. He looked down, but his body was hidden by the darkness.

Something slid around his waist, strong and muscular like a woman's lean thighs. He felt the swell of firm breasts against his chest. The tingles of his orgasm began, and he fought to hold it back until . . . until what?

Suddenly his perceptions changed. He smelled the distinct odor of sweat and another scent it took him a moment to classify: the musk of female desire. He could not only smell it, he could *taste* it, and knew it was some evocation of the previous night, as he supplicated himself to Rachel's needs. He closed his eyes, and then vividly, as if right there before him, he saw the flat plain of her belly, her navel a dark pit on the sweat-glistening surface, the dark tattoo beneath it, above the delicious curls. . . .

At that moment two things occurred simultaneously. First, he realized the tattoo was in fact the clue he'd been seeking, although he had no idea what it meant. And second, he came with a rocketing intensity second only to the way he'd come the night before in this same lake.

ACROSS TOWN, in the dark and damp basement, Rachel gasped and her eyes opened wide. She felt someone inside her, the unmistakable sensation of a male organ filling her, moving and responding. It was uncannily like Ethan, and with that realization she climaxed, clenching her teeth against the sound, muscles trembling with the effort not to thrash. The moment hovered, spread, and engulfed her, until it finally faded to a dull roar.

It was nothing like she'd experienced before. She could almost feel Ethan's body against hers, his weight pressing into her, his erection filling her even as her own fingers did. *Ethan, help me,* she wanted to scream. *It's the tattoo man. Ask Helena about him. She was there!* She knew no real words had left her lips but prayed that the magical, sensual connection was real and that the lake spirits would function as a conduit.

Then it was over. She fell limp, hands between her thighs, gasping and sweating. Something had happened, she knew, but she wasn't sure what. She could only wait.

Patty moaned—not like Rachel had, but in pain. Rachel sat up and turned as much as she could. If the poison was working, time was running out.

She glanced at Carrie and Faith. Both stared at her with expressions that mingled contempt and disgust, and Rachel felt herself flushing. But she ignored them as she got to her knees. "Korbus!" she yelled furiously. "Goddammit, Korbus, get down here! Do you hear me?"

Again there was nothing, the house above them as silent as the proverbial grave that might await them all.

CHAPTER TWENTY-NINE

ETHAN?" MARTY SAID, his voice slurred from sleep. "Where the hell are you? You said you were going home. I assumed you'd have sense enough to stay there."

"Never mind," Ethan said breathlessly. He sat in his truck, wet beneath his clothes; he'd dressed quickly and rushed back to his cell phone. He started the engine and said, "I'm on my way to your office."

"Whoa, calm down, I can't understand you."

"I'm on my way to your office," he said distinctly, and backed the truck out from behind the shrubs. He pulled out onto the street with a *thud* as his undercarriage bounced on the curb. "I think I have something."

"Besides a hole in your head?"

"About the case, Marty."

All the sleepiness left his brother's voice. "Did Rachel contact you?"

Like you wouldn't believe, he thought to himself, but he said, "No, but tell me: Did all the girls that disappeared have tattoos?"

"*Tattoos?*"

"Yes."

"Oh, son of a *bitch*!" Marty yelled. Ethan heard the sound of bedsprings as his brother jumped up. "Goddamned son of a *bitch*!"

Ethan pulled the phone away and looked at it, just to verify he had, in fact, called his brother. When he put it back to his ear, Marty was saying, "...goddamned clue was right in front of me and I missed it all this time!"

Marty seldom lost his temper, and when he did it was usually a situation exactly like this, with all the fury directed at himself. "What are you talking about?" Ethan asked.

"Ling Hu!" Marty bellowed. "She had a fresh tattoo on her back! I mean *really* fresh, with scabs and everything. I should've fucking *seen* that! The only way she could've gotten it was if whoever kidnapped her *gave* it to her!"

"Okay, okay, calm down," Ethan said. It was just like when they were in high school and Marty belatedly realized he missed an easy question on a test. "I think that's what the connection is. Can you check to see if the other girls had tattoos and, if so, where they got them? Helena can tell you where Rachel got hers."

"Oh, so you're the detective now?" Marty snapped. Ethan could tell by the banging and rustling that his brother was frantically getting dressed. "Well, you couldn't do a worse job than I have. I'll meet you at my office. Hopefully I'll have the answers by then. God*dammit,* I'm an idiot!"

"You're not an idiot."

"Yes, I am. Now shut up so I can call the station and get all this checked out."

Ethan closed his phone and shook his head. And to think he'd been worried that *he* would sound like a lunatic.

"It hurts," Patty rasped, her breath shallow. She squirmed stiffly against the wall, and her face drew into a grimace. "It's getting hard to breathe...."

"That's just panic," Rachel said, knowing it wasn't. She rubbed her hands up and down the girl's arm for reassurance; the touch of skin on skin helped her work through the last of her post-tryst shakes too. "Try to stay calm. You're not alone, I'm right here."

"Why did you...What made you..." Patty couldn't find the words she wanted.

Rachel leaned close. "When we get out of this, I'll tell you all about it."

"What if we don't?"

"We will, sweetie. And that's the only way you'll believe me."

Patty nodded at Rachel's fresh tattoo, which had bled anew in places, leaving black streaks down her belly. "Does *that* hurt?"

Rachel smiled wryly. "I'd forgotten all about it, actually. Thanks for bringing it back up." Truthfully, the splinters driven into her hips and buttocks hurt far worse, especially when her weight pressed on one.

"And that's why he kidnapped us? To give us tattoos?"

"Apparently. I think we all turned him down at some point when he wanted to get fancy on us, and we hurt his feelings. Now he's terminally ill, so this is his last hurrah."

"When I got mine done, he wanted to do more, to do wings on my shoulder blades. I told him no." Her lip trembled. "The design was beautiful, though. Really. I just felt like *I* wasn't pretty enough for it. Maybe I should've said yes."

"*No,*" Rachel said firmly. "None of this is your fault. Don't ever think like that. What he's done to us is awful, disgusting, and wrong."

Patty smiled. "You came to my show the other night, didn't you? I gave you a CD."

"That was me," Rachel agreed.

"And... this is weird to ask: Did you follow me home?"

"Actually, yes. And when I explain the other thing, it'll explain that too." She added dryly, "But I'm really not into girls."

Patty managed a small, hollow laugh. "I'm not either, but under the circumstances, if we get out of this, I'd feel like I owed you."

"Just try to stay still," Rachel said, and turned toward the door at the top of the stairs. No light showed underneath it. "The more you move, the faster the poison will spread."

At the word *poison,* Patty's smile vanished. "Are you a nurse?" she whimpered. "Is that how you know?"

"No, I... I run a diner."

"You're a cook?"

"*Head* cook. And bottle washer."

"Then how do you know about spiders?"

"Honey, you'll just have to trust me on that. It's the land of the blind and I'm the one-eyed man."

Suddenly Patty winced and arched her back as much as her bonds allowed. The dim light fell across the bite, now dark and swollen.

Rachel turned to the others. "She's going to die if we don't do something," Rachel said.

"Help," Carrie called mechanically. Faith said nothing; she just continued to glare at Rachel.

Rachel spat her disgust, but truthfully she had no other ideas. She looked around the dark room one last hopeless time. No doors, no reachable windows. Nothing to cut their bonds. Nothing to throw or use as a weapon. And no sign that her desperate Hail Mary to the lake spirits had done anything at all, except that she was sure she'd somehow connected, however faintly, with Ethan. But was it enough?

Just then a distant door slammed, and the floor above them squeaked beneath someone's steps. Rachel's heart pounded in her ears. If she was going to do something, she'd have to do it now. But what?

Only one idea came to her. She looked back at Patty. "Hang on. Try to stay calm, no matter what happens."

"I will," Patty sniffled.

Rachel crawl-scurried across the floor to the steps and began working her way up them again. Her desperation and fury overrode all the pain. Above her, someone moved through the house with the slow familiarity of a resident.

WHEN ETHAN entered the police station, he found Marty waiting in the lobby. His brother's jet-black hair stuck out at odd angles from beneath a baseball cap, and his khaki pants were wrinkled. "Come on," he snapped with no preliminaries. "We've got a name."

Ethan followed his brother through empty hallways toward the garage. "Who?"

"A guy named Arlin Korbus did Rachel's tattoo, Patricia Patilia's, and at least one of Ling Hu's. I don't know about the other two, but three out of five is enough to justify talking to him."

"Now?"

"Yes. I have a spider sense, and it's going off like crazy. He lives out in Fitchburg, so I'm going to pay him a visit."

"I'm coming too."

"Have I tried to stop you? Just promise me you'll stay back and let us handle it." He paused outside the garage door and frowned. "Why are you *wet*?"

"Er . . . I fell in the lake."

"Are you okay?"

"Yeah."

In the garage, Marty unlocked the unmarked cruiser and they climbed inside. Before he started the engine, he turned to his brother. Marty knew what Ethan had seen in Iraq and would have given an eye to spare him a second experience like that. Quietly, he said, "There's no telling what we might find there, Ethan."

Ethan nodded, looking straight ahead through the windshield. "I know."

Marty roared out of the garage, simultaneously calling for two other patrol cars to meet him at the address.

RACHEL REACHED the top of the stairs again, careful not to lose her balance this time, and drew breath to yell. Then she stopped. Even if Korbus had told the truth about the Asian girl's death, he wouldn't dare summon medical help for Patty. The girl would die in the same slow agony that had almost claimed Rachel's uncle.

She heard his footsteps on the other side of the door. His shadow blocked part of the line of illumination along the bottom of the jamb. She waited for him to open it, but nothing happened. He was listening, she realized, to see if they were moving around.

She licked her lips and, in a ragged voice she hoped sounded like a whisper, said, "Hurry, keep digging! We have to make the hole big enough to get out! He'll be back any minute."

Below, Faith looked puzzled and Carrie opened her mouth to speak, but Rachel quickly put her finger to her lips. She hadn't heard Korbus walk away. Faith sat up straighter, watching with wide eyes.

"Are you out?" Rachel hissed. "Good! Now you, go out after her!"

The light came on downstairs, blinding the three captives below. Rachel winced, but the stairwell protected her from the worst of it. The bolt slammed aside and the doorknob turned.

Her perception of time entered the adrenaline-fueled slow motion of a car wreck. As the door began to open, she reached blindly forward and grabbed handfuls of Korbus's baggy sweatpants and bathrobe. He cried, "Shit!" as he fell over her and tumbled the length of the steps, landing facefirst on the floor below. His skull made a sound like a thick melon smacking the concrete.

Faith found her voice and screamed.

Korbus rolled onto his back, wincing, and put a hand to his forehead. The impact had vertically split the skin between his eyebrows, and blood poured out. "You fuck-ing *bitch*," he said in disbelief.

Rachel sprang down onto him, driving both knees into his groin with all her weight. He tried to grab her, but his hands slipped on her sweaty skin. Then she took hold of thinning hair and smashed his head repeatedly against the floor until the solid *thunk* sound changed to something wetter.

She was speckled with his blood, and when she re-leased him he did not move. She rolled off him, breathing hard, and tried not to slip into shock at what she'd done. *I killed him,* she thought in numb awareness. *On purpose.* She looked at her red-smeared hands. Was the blood hers, from where the plastic tie had cut anew into her wrists, or Korbus's?

She forced herself back to the moment, glanced up the stairs, and froze. The door had swung shut behind him.

With all the speed she could manage, she crawled up and, balancing precariously on the top step, managed to reach the doorknob. It did not turn. She shoved against the door, but the wood merely creaked.

"No!" she screamed. "No no *NO!*" She pounded on the wood with her fists, and it sent her falling backward down the steps. Again she landed atop Korbus's body.

"What happened?" Patty asked. Her voice sounded tight and slurred.

"We're still locked in!" Rachel almost shrieked. She undid the belt of Korbus's robe and began going through the pockets of his sweatpants, searching for the keys. She glanced at the watch on his wrist: It was after twelve. Midnight or noon? she wondered, then realized he was dressed for bed. They were lucky, she thought, that he couldn't sleep.

She came up empty and turned her attention to the bathrobe. The only sound in the basement was Patty's labored breathing.

Finally, Rachel held up the key ring she'd retrieved: easily a dozen keys, all unmarked except for numbers scratched onto some of them, all possibly the key to the cellar door. This would take a while, especially since, with her ankles and wrists tied, balancing to reach the doorknob was tricky at best.

"Can I help?" Carrie asked shakily.

Rachel nodded toward Patty. "Stay with her." Faith stayed motionless, eyes wide. Her freshly tattooed legs and hips had scabbed over, but her sweat softened them in places and made tiny trickles of red.

Suddenly Patty moaned. Rachel turned in time to see her fall on her side. She breathed with a rattle in her throat, the raspy way people do when they can't get enough air.

Carrie looked up helplessly. "You'll never find the right key in time."

"The hell I won't," Rachel said, and began worming her way back up the stairs.

Again, the ascent took forever. She would slip and freeze, praying she wouldn't drop the key ring through one of the gaps in the steps. She was exhausted, and every movement took all her concentration. At last she reached the door and wriggled so that her legs were braced enough to hold her torso upright.

She began methodically trying the keys one after another. Her hands shook, and that made it harder. Time crept by, marked only by Patty's whimpering below.

"Hang on, baby," Rachel murmured. "Just hang on."

She had three keys to go.

Then, like a scene from some teen horror movie, a hand grabbed her ankle.

She had no time to react. The keys flew from her hand, and Korbus pulled her inexorably toward him. She shrieked and tried to wrench free. They slid down the steps to the concrete floor together.

Patty moaned again. Rachel flashed to the inscription on Patty's CD: *To Rachel, who stayed to the end.*

"I don't think she's breathing!" Carrie cried.

"You *bastard*!" Rachel cried, and suddenly she was again atop Korbus, again battering his head against the floor, lost in a red rage of fury that she'd failed to save

Patty. Nothing else mattered: not the pain from her own injuries, not the humiliation of her nakedness or the violation of her flesh. She'd tried to do one thing, and this *asshole* had stopped her. That beautiful, sweet voice, that soul that was a treasure, was gone.

Korbus had gone limp, but she didn't stop. Something cracked like a large walnut. The sound of his head hitting the concrete grew squishier.

"Rachel!" a new voice cried.

She turned and looked up the stairs. Marty Walker and a uniformed officer stood, guns drawn and pointed, it seemed, *at her.* She blinked, and suddenly she felt cold, and afraid, and tears swelled in her eyes.

"Call an ambulance, Marty," she said, her voice small and weak but utterly calm. "A black widow spider bit Patty.... Please, hurry." Her vision began to blur. "Please..." She looked at Patty, who lay as still as Korbus.

Then she passed out. She never saw Ethan push past the officers, his bulk making the stairs creak as he charged down them, calling her name.

CHAPTER THIRTY

I S THAT A BLINK, or are you just glad to see me?"
Helena said.

Rachel's eyelids rose like a rusted garage door. She
squinted into the light and for an instant thought she was
seeing the bulb dangling in Korbus's basement. It sent a
surge of adrenaline through her, and with a gasp she sat
upright.

"Shit!" cried Helena, jumping back into Marty. He
caught her, and she fluttered a hand at her chest. "Christ,
Rach, don't *do* that!"

Rachel looked around at the hospital room, then down
at herself. White gauze and tape encircled her wrists.
When she shifted her feet, she felt similar bandages on
her ankles. An IV needle was taped into the back of her
left hand. Her hair was pulled back from her face, and she
wore only a light hospital gown. The room was a double,
but the other bed stood empty.

She flopped back on the pillows and sighed with

relief. If this was a dream, she'd take it. "What hospital is this?" she croaked.

"University," Marty said.

"Do they take my insurance?"

"They do." He wore a neat suit, with his badge hanging from the front breast pocket. Only the dark circles under his eyes betrayed his weariness. "How do you feel?"

She managed a smile. "Like reused coffee grounds." Then, with a rush, everything came back to her, and she sat up again. "What about Patty? The girl with the spider bite? Is she okay? Can I see her?"

"She's fine," Marty said reassuringly. "They got to her in plenty of time. But if you hadn't told us what was wrong with her it might've been different, so you saved her life."

"You saved all of them," Helena said, her voice tinged with wonder. "You killed that guy bare-handed. You're a hero."

"Yes," Marty agreed. "It's . . . pretty amazing."

"I don't feel very amazing," Rachel said. "How long have I been here?"

"Not long. We brought you in at about one this morning."

She looked around again. Marty said, "He's not here."

When she turned to him he continued, "I sent Ethan home. He needed a shower and some sleep. He stayed here until the doctors assured him you were out of danger."

She sighed and closed her eyes. "I could use some coffee. What are the chances?"

"Christ, even here I'm a waitress," Helena teased, then leaned down and kissed Rachel's forehead. "I'll be right back."

When they were alone, Rachel asked Marty, "So I really *did* kill him?"

"Yes," Marty said.

She waited for the remorse, the disgust, the fear. She waited for any feeling at all. None came. "Will you arrest me if I say I don't feel bad about it?"

"No. Do you want to talk about it?"

She thought about it for a long moment. "Yes. But not right now."

He nodded.

"How did you find me?"

Now Marty was silent for a long moment. "Actually, Ethan figured it out. He suggested that your tattoos might be the thing that you and the other girls had in common."

"Wow," she said. Her stomach tingled a little. "So he..."

"He didn't eat, sleep, or stop until we found you. He was with me when we came into Korbus's house. He carried you to the ambulance. But..."

"But what?"

"Helena's right. You're the hero. Based on what the other women said, you would've gotten them out soon anyway. True, it would've been too late for the girl with the spider bite, but..." He shrugged and shook his head. "What can I say except, wow."

Before Rachel could reply, Helena returned with three

coffees, which she distributed. "I tasted it," she said with a wrinkled nose. "Don't expect much."

"I'll check back with you later," Marty said. "I'll need a statement describing what happened, but there's no rush. And there's a guard outside the door, to keep out the riffraff. You're going to be pretty popular for fifteen minutes once this story gets out."

"What was wrong with him?" she asked.

Marty shrugged. "Korbus? Who knows? Some men just have issues with women, I guess."

"No, I mean physically. He said he was terminally ill."

"Oh. Yes, he had pancreatic cancer. He had only a few weeks at the outside. Must've taken everything he had to do all that."

Rachel nodded. "That explains a lot."

"It explains some. We may never know it all." Then he left.

Helena said, "I have to go too. Lord only knows what Jimmy will get into."

It took a moment for that to sink in. "The diner's open?"

"I took the liberty of hiring another waitress yesterday. I warned her it was temporary, but you might want to consider keeping her, especially if you now have a social life." She kissed Rachel again, on the cheek. "They say you'll be out tomorrow or the next day. I'll be here to help you get home. Unless you have another ride lined up?"

"No, I want you," Rachel said.

"Ew, it would be like doing my sister," Helena joked.

After Helena had gone, Rachel got out of the bed and

walked stiffly into the bathroom. In the harsh light, she undid the hospital gown and stood in front of a mirror.

Little scabs and Band-Aids covered her hips and thighs where the most pronounced splinters had been removed. Purple finger marks encircled one leg above the white ankle bandage.

But they paled next to her new tattoo. The hospital had coated it with antibacterial lotion, so it gleamed and twinkled as she moved. She had to admit, it was intriguing and beautiful. But it was also, she thought bitterly, a form of rape.

AROUND MIDNIGHT, when she felt certain no more visitors would appear, Rachel begged the nurse to let her use a laptop, ostensibly to check her e-mail. When she was alone, she logged on to *The Lady of the Lakes* and began to write.

> Mystery solved. Some scrawny old guy was keeping pretty girls in his basement and drawing pictures on them. The girl who died was an accident, and now the bad guy's dead too. You can read all about it in the paper. So for a while, at least, the sidewalks and streetlights should be safe again.

She scowled. It was a pretty weak entry, all things considered. And she hated the thought of sending *her* readers to the *Cap Jo*. But she didn't feel up to writing in any more detail and then checking to make sure she'd said nothing to give her identity away. This would have to do. She posted it, erased the cache from the browser, and shut down the laptop. *The Lady of the Lakes* was back in business.

THE NEXT MORNING Rachel was watching the local news when the door opened and Julie Schutes entered.

The reporter closed the door and stood with her back to it. Neither spoke for a long moment. Finally Rachel said, "May I help you?"

"We've met before. Julie Schutes, *Wisconsin Capital Journal.*"

Rachel calmly pushed the button to summon the nurse. "Oh, I remember you. And I have no comment. On anything."

"I'm not here entirely as a reporter, Ms. Matre."

"How did you get past the guard?"

She shrugged. "I know most of the cops. They like me." She crossed the room and stood at the foot of Rachel's bed. "So before I get tossed out, you should know that I dated Ethan Walker for a little over two years. We were very serious."

Rachel kept her reaction to herself. "I'll add that to Wikipedia."

Julie spoke carefully, as if she'd practiced the speech. "He's too good for you, Ms. Matre. Seriously. He needs someone who can help him in his world, not drag him down into theirs."

"Like you?"

"I don't know. I realize how harsh and selfish this sounds. I appreciate that you're a business owner and local hero, but the first doesn't really count and the second will fade in about a week. You're from the proverbial different worlds. You run a diner for college kids and borderline transients; he's a war hero who puts up buildings worth millions of dollars."

"We only went out once," Rachel said.

"Yes, well, for his sake, just remember that. Don't hurt him, but don't try to hang on to him either."

The door opened, and a nurse entered. "Can I help you?" she asked Rachel.

Rachel nodded at Julie. "Toss this bitch out, will you?"

RACHEL AND ETHAN walked to the end of the pier that extended from the entrance to the Yahara River locks. The channel allowed boats to pass from one lake to the next along the straightened, deepened, and maintained stretch of river that cut across the isthmus. Birds danced in the wind, and waves cut through the water.

They stopped at the most isolated bench. Rachel sat gingerly, easing down around the bruises, splinters, and cuts. Her bandaged wrists made her look like a failed suicide. Ethan waited until she'd situated herself, then he joined her. They sat in silence.

"How long until you start the tattoo removal?" he said at last.

"About three weeks. They want everything else to heal up first. Less chance of infection that way."

He nodded.

She turned to face him. She'd avoided his phone calls and e-mails while in the hospital and cut short his visits with claims of pain-medication drowsiness. She knew he was confused by her response, and in some ways so was she. He'd gone through hell for her, risked reliving the awful experience in Iraq by accompanying the police to Korbus's house, and certainly deserved better than he'd gotten from her. Yet she felt essentially nothing. She was not angry or embarrassed, just ... numb. Until her feelings returned to normal, she knew she'd find his presence in her life as much an irritant as a blessing. And that was completely unfair.

She licked her lips and said, "Ethan, I need to tell you something."

Her tone made it obvious this wasn't good news, and she saw the fear and disappointment in his eyes. He kept his voice neutral, though, and said, "I figured."

"I owe you my life. And I like you a lot. But I don't think I'll be very good company for a while. I certainly won't be good company in ... *that way.*"

He nodded. "I can understand that."

"I'm afraid if you stay around right now, every time I see you it'll remind me of what happened. And I don't want that. Not for me, not for you. So ..."

He waited patiently.

She leaned over and kissed him on the cheek. "Good-bye, Ethan. At least for now."

He looked down, then out at the lake, then up at the sky. She swore she heard the crack when his heart broke.

"If you're sure that's what you need," he said, "then I'll honor it."

"I'm sure," she said, with a finality she didn't feel but that she knew she needed to fake for everyone's sake.

After another long moment he said, "I guess I should take you home, then."

"No, I'll walk. It's not that far." And she stood before she could change her mind.

He did as well. "Okay. If you ever need anything, you know where to find me."

"I do." She kissed him again, on the lips this time, but as chastely as the one on his cheek. Then she turned and walked away without saying another good-bye. The tears, born from the image of him in the arms of that leggy blond reporter, didn't start until she was well out of sight.

What do you know? she thought ironically. *I can still feel something after all.*

AMBIKA PEEKED into Ethan's office. He sat looking out the window at the state capitol building, hands behind his head. The bronze statue atop the dome glowed in the afternoon sun. "Can I get you something before I leave, Ethan?"

"Hmm? Oh. No, thanks."

"Did you see the bid on that community center?"

"I saw it, but I haven't looked at it. I will, though."

She nodded, turned, and left. He heard the outer door close, then lock. He glanced at the clock on his computer screen. It was four o'clock.

He took out his cell phone and scrolled through recent calls until he found Julie's number. He ran his thumb over the call button.

Then he closed his phone and put it back in his pocket. He could hold off. What had happened between Rachel and him was worth the effort, even if she never knew what the waiting cost him.

THREE WEEKS after Rachel left the hospital, Patty Patilia stood in the diner's doorway, waiting for her eyes to adjust. Clara, the new waitress, said, "You can sit anywhere. I'll be right with you."

Rachel looked out of the kitchen, saw Patty, and came around the end of the counter. The two women hugged very gingerly, careful of each other's wounds. They sported matching wrist scabs.

"How have you been?" Rachel asked, and took the stool beside Patty.

"Sore but productive," she said. "Apparently a near-death trauma does wonders for your creativity. I've been writing songs like a madman, and I've got gigs booked through December. *Paying* gigs, even."

"Some silver lining," Rachel said.

"Yes, but I'd just as soon have skipped the cloud."

Clara brought them coffee, trailed by a watchful Helena. The new waitress spilled a little on the counter, which made Helena cluck in disapproval. Rachel said, "Helena, Clara, this is Patty."

"Hi," Helena said.

"I saw you on the news," Clara added. "I'm glad you're feeling better."

Helena leaned close and whispered, "Don't banter, you have a counter full of people waiting for refills."

"I've been a waitress before," Clara snapped softly.

"Not here, you haven't."

The two women moved away. Rachel shook her head. She liked Clara a lot and would have to tell Helena to lay off pretty soon. To Patty she said, "I'm glad you're feeling better too."

Patty scowled. "Yes, except that everything itches. How about you?"

"I start the tattoo removal next Monday. Apparently blue and black are the easiest colors to remove, and those were mainly the ones he used on me."

"Your own silver lining?" Patty said.

Rachel shrugged. "It's still going to be no picnic."

"That's actually what I came in here to talk to you about. Carrie Kimmell doesn't have insurance, and she can't afford to get her tattoos removed. I'm doing a benefit for her this Saturday, and I wondered if I could post a flyer about it."

"Of course."

"And you'd be more than welcome to attend. I invited Faith, but she's trying to, ahem, *distance* herself from the events."

Rachel nodded. She'd seen Faith's parents on TV and doubted they'd let their daughter out of their sight again until she was forty.

"There's one more thing." Patty looked down at the

counter for a moment, then said softly, "That day in the basement, you...you promised to tell me why you did what you did. You know, when you...you know."

Rachel blushed. "Yeah." She looked up and said, "Helena? Patty and I are going for a walk. I'll be back in a few."

"Sure," Helena said. "Clara and I can handle it until the lunch rush."

"If she'll let me off the leash," Clara added.

"I think it's time for Clara to fly solo," Rachel said. Helena started to protest, then nodded. Clara beamed.

Rachel held the door for Patty. "It's one of those stories that's easier to believe if you're actually there."

Patty shrugged. "Okay." When they were outside, she asked, "Where are we going?"

"To the lake," Rachel said.

ABOUT THE AUTHOR

ALEX PRENTISS left the South and was delighted to find Madison, Wisconsin, waiting. One marriage and two kids later, Prentiss is still glad to be living, and writing, in Madison. *Night Tides* is Alex Prentiss's first novel.

A lake filled with memory . . .
A woman drawn to the spirits . . .
A murder that severs that connection . . .

When you're in over your head, all you see is

DARK WATERS

A new Lady of the Lakes novel
by Alex Prentiss

Usually when you help capture a serial killer, your job as
a good citizen is done. But Rachel Matre, a diner owner
by day, is also the Lady of the Lakes—which means
she's connected to the lake spirits of Madison . . . and
therefore to the city itself.

When a community-center development becomes
the source of controversy—and murder—Rachel
finds herself once again in the middle. For not only
is her sister the prime suspect, but the construction
company is owned by Ethan, the man she is
powerfully attracted to.

And when the spirits she has always counted on, for
both information and pleasure, go silent, Rachel is
forced to find answers on her own—answers about the
spirits, her sister, and, perhaps most important, Ethan.

DARK WATERS
The follow-up to Alex Prentiss's debut novel, Night Tides

A Bantam Book coming in Fall 2010